WHEN A PSYCHOPATH
FALLS IN LOVE

Also by Herbert Gold

NOVELS

Birth of a Hero

The Prospect Before Us

The Man Who Was Not With It

The Optimist

Therefore Be Bold

Salt

Fathers

The Great American Jackpot

Swiftie the Magician

Waiting for Cordelia

Slave Trade

He/She

Family

True Love

Mister White Eyes

A Girl of Forty

Dreaming

She Took my Arm as if She Loved Me

Daughter Mine

SHORT STORIES AND ESSAYS

Love & Like

The Age of Happy Problems

*The Magic Will: Stories
    and Essays of a Decade*

*Lovers and Cohorts:
    Twenty-Seven Stories*

NONFICTION

Biafra Goodbye

My Last Two Thousand Years

*A Walk on the West Side:
    California on the Brink*

Travels in San Francisco

*Best Nightmare on Earth: A Life in
    Haiti* (reissued as *Haiti:
    Best Nightmare on Earth*)

Still Alive: A Temporary Condition
    (reissued as *Not Dead Yet*)

*Bohemia: Where Art, Angst, Love,
    and Strong Coffee Meet*

Herbert Gold

WHEN A PSYCHOPATH
FALLS IN LOVE

A Novel

ISBN-10: 0988412276
ISBN-13: 978-0-9884122-7-9

Library of Congress Control Number: 2014940261

Cover: Keith Carlson

Jorvik Press
PMB 424, 5331 SW Macadam Ave., Ste 258,
Portland, Oregon 97239
JorvikPress.com

ABOUT THE AUTHOR

Herbert Gold was born in Cleveland, Ohio, in 1924 and raised in the suburb of Lakewood. After several of his poems were accepted by New York literary magazines, he moved to New York at age seventeen and studied philosophy at Columbia University. While there, he fell in with the burgeoning Beat Generation and befriended many writers, including Anaïs Nin and Allen Ginsberg.

Gold won a Fulbright fellowship in his early twenties and moved to Paris, where he did graduate studies at the Sorbonne and worked on his first novel, *Birth of a Hero*, published in 1951. Since then he has written more than thirty books and received several awards, including the Sherwood Anderson Award for Fiction, the Commonwealth Club Gold Medal and the PEN Oakland Josephine Miles Literary Award. He has also taught at the University of California at Berkeley and at Stanford, Cornell and Harvard.

Since 1960 he has lived in San Francisco. *When a Psychopath Falls in Love* is his twentieth novel.

For my daughters,
Ann, Judy and Nina,
and my sons, Ari and Ethan.
You are blessings for me

Prologue

In his life filled with distractions and occasional secret lusts and rages that seemed perfectly justified to him – they were *his*, after all – Dan Kasdan had never killed anyone; never shot, strangled, poisoned, or stabbed – not even once. As a rational person, he believed that the first time should be fully earned.

He considered his incentives and found them reasonable. It was for the young woman who called herself Petal, which was not what her parents had named her, and how Dan and Petal shuddered into each other. It was for Amanda, his daughter, and Sergei, Amanda's son. It was for D'Wayne, his daughter's husband. And might as well admit the truth, it was for Dan Kasdan himself, because it was his first murder.

Earned or not, it became his life's desire and his plan.

A clacking sound grew near. Overhead, gulls were fleeing, wheeling around, swooping, celebrating their wings, consecrating their dominion over the sky of San Francisco, darting onto morsels of urban street sushi, just as their mammal neighbors not far away, the scavenging seals of Pier 39, were snatching sea takeout into their snouts. These colleagues had developed an appetite for happenstance food. Ferd Conway grinned and waved skywards, accepting good fellowship with the gulls. He was fond of snacking, too. Pigeons or gulls, seals or sea lions, it didn't matter what folks called them. Like Ferd, they had found a congenial home in this corner of the universe.

He was a friendly attorney-at-law, Ferdinand Conway, Esq., only called Ferdie sarcastically (recently by an investor in a sure thing project that became the victim of circumstances beyond the general partner's control); but he was Ferd for almost everyone, a bite-sized name for a likeable dude, a live-and-let-live dude despite the formal "Esq." on his business cards. Silence didn't fit his lifestyle.

Due to the little problem between them, Ferd Conway had invited Dan Kasdan, his dearest friend and partner, to an air-clearing stroll among Mother Nature; that is, on the paths that followed the contours of the Bay between Aquatic Park, Fisherman's Wharf, and Pier 39. Other than a few hundred tourists, a tag team of bongo virtuosos gathered in the WPA-era cement Roman ruin bleachers, and competing antique ghetto blasters broadcasting rap calls to revolution, all was peace and harmony. Ferd, grateful for Dan's forbearance, kept the silence for a moment, in case Dan wanted to offer something in the way of reproach. Why should a bird migrate toward the open sea when it could supplement the avian food group pyramid with discarded soft McDonald's buns, garnished with mayonnaise, ketchup, and human saliva? The pterodactyls had gone extinct too soon. If they had only hung in there, Wendy's, Burger King and Big Whoppers could have set up a bulwark against the ice age. "You know what the stock ticker symbol for McDonald's is? Same as the first three letters."

Kasdan waited.

"MCD. Ray Croc was a submarine, sneaked by the terrorists into Indiana or Iowa, wherever the hell. MCD, man – Mad Cow Disease!"

Ferd hated silence. The murmur of nature lovers on their cell phones and the cries of tourist children, needing immediate snacks, only deepened the silence between Dan and Ferd. He ducked as the flock swirled overhead. Once his hair had been the victim of an earthbound splat, and it was just after a nice professional shampoo, and the memory haunted him. Still, Ferd clung to a mood of fondness. The gulls, the barking seals, even the tourists, and Dan Kasdan were all his fellow seekers.

He scanned the sky, examined his shoes, aimed his suspicions at the sky again. "I'm a loyal friend if you'll excuse a little shiftiness due to the times, amigo. This is America."

"Thanks for leveling."

"You'll have a beautiful goddess to worship, I don't care how old you get to be, plus the financials to keep her horny. Need I say more?" He read Kasdan's expression. "Okay, I'll say more. Security for your grandson the Crip, please excuse the expression, is what I really concentrate on. Your only daughter, plus the future healthy grand-kids, no more retards, who she might bless you with later on... Not that a goddess to worship is anything to sneeze at, either. You know where Cartier is? Tiffany, downtown? Every goddess I ever met is a normal female unit. Rubies are red, pearls are white, your goddess likes jewelry, she'll pump you all night?" He winced with appreciation of himself. "I'm a poet, who knew? But back then I figured to pass the Bar for the ample security. Some guys just settle into interpreting for the Speedy Gonzales chulos with low hourly rates..."

"Thanks for telling me where I went wrong," Kasdan said.

"... and less security. You're not even Civil Service. But with my help, thanks to me, I will never lie to you, amigo. Didn't a president say that, a primo example to all? I swear, I won't mislead you, neither." Was that a look of panic? Was he going too far? "Unless I do it for my own good, then of course it's understandable. I'm a normal male unit. Ferd Giveth, Ferd Taketh Away."

Ferd Conway grinneth, also. He believed teasing, right-on teasing, was one of his strong points, but sometimes, with the best intentions and all the good will in the City and County of San Francisco, it misfired. He knew how to deal with it. Looked nonchalant. Looked blithe. A minor embarrassment, more like acknowledging a burp than flatulence. He picked up the pace of their stroll along the beach at Aquatic Park with its babies and mothers, sturdy Dolphin Club swimmers out in the water, chattering schizophrenics, invigorating salt smells mixed with tidal urban wash. Now that the little problems about Amanda and Petal had been smoothed over, thanks to Ferd's grace under pressure, his *savoir* get-along, surely Dan could see these hiccups in their friendship in the right light, put them into perspective for his own benefit, as Ferd sincerely desired.

Good thing seals didn't fly like gulls. Nobody's fresh shampoo or clean shoes would be safe.

Later that morning, Kasdan was home on Eddy in the upstairs flat which was what the career of translating for the many Speedy Gonzales of the criminal justice system had earned him in the way of housing. Despite his efforts to simplify his passage on earth, his mission in life turned out to be to interpret and sort through too much personal data.

Amanda, the daughter who had found him, was beautiful; not her fault. To be the young mother of Sergei...

Love and trouble do happen. Ferd's appreciation of her wasn't really Ferd's fault, but perhaps it was. Many men might be tempted, and in Ferd's case, feeling so close to Dan, maybe it seemed logical for him to crave Amanda. It was only human. Green sprouts push through cracks in asphalt or cement; the alleys of San Francisco give fertile hospitality to seeds blown by the wind and dropped by birds; dusty shoots hang on during the dry seasons; Ferd Conway loved. He freely acknowledged himself as a normal male unit.

Amanda's dark-eyed beauty was her mother's fault (Kasdan remembered that Margaret had muttered in Spanish when they made love). And Amanda's lostness and need? Margaret's fault, who never told her three-night lover that they had a child. Or Dan's, who should have suspected something, who was only searched out and unearthed by his daughter when she was already a young woman. So now things were as they were.

Kasdan padded about in his socks, no shoes, picking up dust, opening and shutting the cupboard with his small stock of tomato soup, baked beans, corned beef hash, Dinty Moore fuel, tracking blame. He kept emergency rations in case of flu or debilitating gloom. He was practicing at home the craft of tranquil and preferably silent killing. He knew it was important to plan and anticipate. He turned it into a kitchen project. He pushed two cans of StarKist Chunk Light tuna fish into one of his socks and slapped it into his hand. Ouch. Swung hard against a skull, it would cause damage. He stared at the sock, dust balls still clinging to it. His left foot felt cold. Murder by tuna fish seemed undignified.

Then he tried a device one of his translation clients, a veteran of Soledad, had proudly described to him. Using a cigarette lighter – a Bic in an ashtray, left over from his smoking times – he melted one end of a toothbrush and embedded a razor blade in the plastic. The plastic cooled, the razor now barely visible. Pasqual Ramirez had explained about hiding it in his clothes... No. Unless he sliced an artery deeply and quickly, it would be slow, messy, and distressing. Out in the world there was no shortage of knives.

He stacked the tuna fish back on its shelf and pulled the sock back onto his foot. He finished off a Safeway orange juice carton and disposed of the toothbrush in the outgoing trash.

Poison was only an idea, a bad one, too complicated.

His personal strength might be sufficient for strangling, especially given the advantage of surprise, but probably not.

So it came down to a knife. Sometimes simple answers are the best.

Fred Conway's condo was spotless until just a moment ago.

"It's over now, Ferd." Kasdan gripped the knife, point up, in ungloved hands. Blood and something like mucous, maybe it was mucous, trickled down his arm. He could deal with the matter of fingerprints later.

The genuine surprise enacted on Ferd's face caused the same twitches, eyes-wide stare, and backing away gestures as the repertory of mock surprise during his normal business negotiations. He had no previous experience with being killed. Also, he was used to doing most of the talking.

"It's past time for you," Kasdan said.

Ferd extended his arms, palms forward. He was only human, like anyone else; and besides, he had no weapon. "Hey, you're not even giving me a chance to defend myself."

"Pick up something heavy."

"I don't want to do that. You're my buddy."

"Mi amigo, right?"

"My cowboy." He was smiling and moving toward Kasdan, who stepped backwards. Dan's lower back bumped against the wall. His shoulders must have been hunched; they didn't touch the wall.

"Hey, hey," said Ferd soothingly.

But Dan slipped sideways, not wanting to be touched, knocking over a lamp, glass shattering. It crunched under foot like snow.

"That's my favorite lamp," Ferd said. There was reproach in his tone. "It's Tiffany, from a yard sale in Fairfax. You should be more careful, please."

Kasdan stared at the kaleidoscope shards mixed with strips of plastic.

"You're not serious, are you? You're just testing, aren't you?"

The leaded separations between the colored glass weren't leaded at all. They were glue and plastic. Kasdan knew it was wrong to be distracted by the thought of a Cost Plus Imports lamp from Taiwan which had traveled into the bedroom of folks in Fairfax who later changed their minds and moved it into their yard on a Saturday afternoon. This was one of Kasdan's bad habits, his thoughts drifting, at the mercy of distraction, settling for a skimpy life... And finally the lamp had been carried into Ferd's condo, where Dan Kasdan was putting an end to things.

Ferd's lips were bunched in a pout. He opened his hands again. Still nothing to hide; stretched open his pink-palmed hands, pink with normal blood circulating normally, amigo, the blood of a fellow human being.

"You want to see how I'll, I don't know, beg or plead, one of them? Yo, amigo?"

He was moving closer. Kasdan held the knife handle down because he had heard it was how a knife should be held in combat, but the blade up, pointing toward what he believed, without formal training in anatomy, to be vital organs. Ferd stopped moving.

"How many times I got to ask if you're serious, Dan? Now I really need the answer, okay?"

No answer.

"See, Dan, I know how it looks, but I really like Amanda a lot. She's special. A mature guy like me could be a good friend to her over the long term. No need for D'Wayne to find out or even suspect, and why should he care if he doesn't know? A shower and you're clean again. Everybody's got a little history. But okay, I could just stop, back off... So you're not serious, am I right?"

Now he might say it takes two to tango and Dan shouldn't step in the way of nature, and this is San Francisco, after all – but he didn't. He said something else. With a knife near his peristaltic regions, in the dangerous ready position, twitching upwards, preparing to slide upwards, Ferd avoided the blah-blah-blah of poetry about the force of nature in a place of perpetual springtime. It was time for practicality, designer brass tacks out of the Ferd Conway Law Office.

"Okay, I know, I admit it, always knew, that's why I decided to be your buddy, even-steven, anything I make, half is yours, okay? Like part of your family – look at it that way. You can oversee the counting. *Halfies*, man. Do the accounting yourself if you like figures, okay? I admire you cause there's a lot of dog in you, even if you don't bark much. How's about that? So *bark*, will you?"

A space of silence to give Kasdan time for consideration. Space of silence ended.

"Why don't you, cat got your tongue? My opinion, why waste words, but I think I'm asking in a nice way."

Kasdan was trying to hold his extended hand steady. The knife was vibrating a little. It was an unfamiliar posture, right arm stretched out, hand gripping, fingers tight. He had prepared for the occasion by buying a switchblade with a good fit in the handle, but it was meant to be a slicing instrument, not a waiting one. He was standing in Ferd's condominium, fully equipped with a range of human emotions, only asking decent gratification, just as his clients did, the miscreants and the merely hot-tempered, who had trouble with both impulse control and the American language.

Kasdan's lips were moving as if he were counting. Ferd took this as a good sign. Kasdan was continuing the discussion with himself, counting Ferd's virtues, the plusses and minuses, sure that other qualities, both positive and negative, would reveal themselves in due course if he put his mind to it.

No gold chains. (Not since the Seventies.)

Showered every day. (Except when late for a hearing.)

Generous splashes of aftershave. (Not necessarily a virtue.)

Also helped the frail and distraught mother of a client, Enrique Gutierrez, a miscreant, a stupid schmuck who thought he could shoplift a stack of negligees at Victoria's Secret, cross dangerous Bryant, in front of the Hall of Justice, steadying with his arm the stupid madre of the stupid jackoff shoplifter. Kasdan, who translated for Enrique, was watching; he noticed; Ferd's eyes in their restless scanning had made sure of this. On the other side of Bryant, on the steps of the Hall of Justice, Ferd slapped his hands together to try to shed the madre's burrito aromas off his person, but smiled magnanimously, like a priest, over the pleasure of doing a nearly rewardless good deed.

Of course, if the stinking madre of the perp had died in traffic as an illegal pedestrian, too stupid to find the crosswalk, there would be zilch chance of getting any money for his services beyond the Legal Aid minimum. Señora Gutierrez made her way slowly up the ramp incline required by the Federal Aid to the Obese, Stoned, and Other Differently-Abled Act, but paid for by the taxes of patriotic citizens.

Another Ferd Conway virtue. Sometimes picked up small checks, like a true professional in the legal field. Kasdan was still counting and listing virtues, Ferd warily watching his lips.

Ferd deserved to see his time on earth ended. True, this was a negative conclusion, but it was Dan Kasdan's strong opinion.

In all fairness, list-making should not stop yet. Kasdan needed to balance matters with an account of his own flaws.

Tended to be critical. Persistently judging Ferd Conway. Neglected Ferd's sunniness, his default-setting glee, which came onto the screen especially when big-hootered Lady Justice tipped the legal scales in his favor. Rivals from the DA's office gloomily snapped their laptops shut when one of Ferd's malefactors got off because a witness failed to show up, due to Ferd's careful ministering through intermediaries and from an untraceable ethical distance...

Well, no point in Dan's berating himself. It was stipulated: Ferd treated life as a zero-sum game which didn't preclude his winning. Dan was now working the corners himself, in his own way, ready to take on his responsibilities as a father, a grandfather, and a person capable of vengeance... *By God, Ferd had it coming to him.*

Demonstrating his good-guyness, despite what some might claim, Ferd moved slowly, aiming not to startle, and reached for what he called a "muchas gracias" letter on the coffee table from a client who wasn't even Hispanic or Chicano "or whatever the chulos call themselves these days." Here, read it. I'll wait." This non-Hispanic chulo wrote:

> You tha man, bro. Lookin 4 kool-ass lawyerin,
>
> Tha 1 with tha attitude, fortitude, innertube.
>
> Respeck you all-ways!

"Got to say Yo to that, am I correct, Dan? Sincere question; over to you."

Kasdan held it between two fingers of his left, his other hand. "I think you wrote it yourself." He put it back exactly where it had been, leaning against a Ronson table lighter, an icon of generations-ago weddings, near an ashtray containing a juicy medicinal marijuana butt, the roach awaiting a call for further treatment. "Like you made your deal with Petal."

Ferd's hand waved away the thought. He could spray the air with denial – Petal Who? – but a rational man had other options. He emerged from wordlessness with words. "Now you're gonna say I made a deal with Amanda, too? Things happen, dude. You're gonna say I'm a bad person, like you made a big discovery, Cowboy?"

Kasdan wouldn't think of it.

Ferd shook his head. Gloom, pesky gloom. There was a switch-blade sprung and no trust around here. But he let it pass, Dan didn't even credit his expert forgery of a sincere thank you letter. He sent a glance, needing solace, toward the ashtray.

In Ferd's cozy apartment, his way-of-life condo, with all the furnishings needed for comfort (Eames chair from Busvan, ice machine, big-screen color teevee with VCR and DVD attachments, subscription to Cable, permission to smoke a joint when the occasion called for it), Dan Kasdan failed to appreciate how thoroughly Ferd had organized himself for an agreeable future. It should have been an example for losers like present company. There was a faint astringency in the air, sweat, hair product, cannabis. Today, tonight, however long it took, would be the last time Dan could enjoy Ferd's accoutrements. He stabbed, he pulled the blade up and it made a whispering sound as it separated fat and gristle.

That was how Kasdan might plan and imagine it. Sometimes things don't work out according to plan.

– 1 –

Fortunately for Ferd Conway, sin had been abolished in San Francisco, along with ethnic prejudice and old age. (Earthquakes were still under study.) When an alleged sinner was about to be hung by vigilantes a hundred and some years ago – a doctor whose crime and medical specialty have not come down in history – he was asked, "Any last words before you go?" He answered: "Not at this time."

Like the defunct doctor, who remained optimistic until the noose dropped, Ferd felt marked out to be happy and successful, and generous enough to enlist Dan Kasdan in his career plans. The matter wasn't too complicated for a man who spoke Spanish almost as well as he spoke depressed American. Carry a briefcase with hidden funds, talk to a lawyer on an easy-going Caribbean island, open the briefcase to buy a nice beachfront property, register the papers with a sleepy clerk in the easy-going nation's records-keeping office... "I speak Spanish, not French or Creole," Kasdan said. "That's a mere detail," Conway assured him.

A few other details to watch out for: long lunchtime siesta closures; carjackings and street murders, but only at night or during the day; lots of unspoiled seaside frontage in this fucked-up tropical paradise... "I count on you to pay attention, Cowboy. Why else would I share?"

"Got it. Registry closed between noon and four."

Ferd beamed. His killer smile expressed confidence, an aspect of his total faith in Dan. "One thing I like about you, always did, always will, is you don't look like a felon or any other perp." When there was no thank-you for the compliment, Ferd added, "Actually, that's only one thing. I like and respect, always did, always will, many things... just can't think of them offhand." Lips twitching a haha; urging of answering haha from Kasdan. Still no response. Ferd unswitched the killer smile, kilowatts wasted. "Hello? Hello? You there, Cowboy?"

"Listening."

"You should be a more easy-going male unit, like me."

Kasdan was distracted by the quartet of Hall of Justice lawyers at the next table, emitting their brags with raised voices, each demanding his turn for attention from colleagues and competitors, trading the effluvia of sweaty nights and uneasy dreams, their mingling morning breath now being mutated by coffee, later to be sweetened by breath strips if they happened upon someone cute. In San Francisco, an alert attorney can get lucky at the oddest moments, sometimes with the wife of a client who shouldn't mind because, depending on musculature and degree of concentrated attention, her husband also is likely to get lucky in prison.

Since Ferd Conway had the idea of bringing his favorite court translator, Dan Kasdan, into a junior partnership deal for a nice offshore payday – Ferd, of course, receiving his entrepreneurial portion – he needed to practice the arts of camaraderie, moving matters along. Mornings at the Caffe Roma across the street from the Hall of Justice, 850 Bryant, San Francisco, USA, were familiar to Dan and Ferd, therefore abetting the smooth moving of matters.

The little explosions of the Roma's espresso machine were like a crack of lightning close by, followed by spurts of steam. For Kasdan, cafe latte was a treat after merely boiling water for Nestle's Instant on the stove in his dusty flat on Ellis, although frequently, truth be told, he found the morning *San Francisco Chronicle* more fun than camaraderie at the Roma. It was Kasdan's habit to prefer the festival of local and world disasters to early morning chat. But since he frequently needed to work with Ferd, translating for Pasqual or Jesus or Mateo, he often joined him in the morning. This time it was more serious.

Harvey Johnson, checking out the sports section across the crowded room, made a face of big-lipped pout, deep-furrowed disapproval. The black homicide detective was Dan's closest friend, formerly a frequent easy laughter, still a deep-voiced laughter, but often sinking into gloom as he tried not to let on. His son had been shot in the neck in a drive-by in Newark, lingered in a coma until Harvey signed to take him off life support. He didn't need to let on to Dan. Later Kasdan planned to tell him that he had joined Ferd by prearrangement; he wasn't ducking the friend with a years-old grief he chose not to advertise. Under pressure, Kasdan planned to clear himself with Harvey as soon as he figured out how to do it right.

In a troubled world, given to unremitting felonies, Ferd's fellow advocates for the defense held up standards, with careful forensic haberdashery, shirt, tie and cufflink areas gleaming. Pinkie rings encircled middle-aged pinkies; undershirts or souvenir tee shirts hid chains from judicial review. According to California code, competition about dress was to be understated. San Francisco Casual had long supplanted the traditional dark suit except in major civil litigation. At the Roma, a few former radicals dressed like defendants, expressing solidarity with the afflicted. "All prisoners are political prisoners," E. Joe Langford liked to remind them over his morning half-caf, half-decaf soy cappuccino, careful not to get soy foam on his goatee. He wore a clip-on ponytail, but even E. Joe removed it for court appearances. Apart from a few traditional Bay Area ideologues, the Roma crowd was mostly into gain. No fedoras, no antique gold pince-nez reading glasses hanging from chains. On the other hand, several pairs of designer sunglasses pushed up into hair; the glasses would need wiping, due to scented hair gels.

Kasdan was still picking up the conversation at the next table. . . "Nice tan. Bottle or salon?"

"Maui."

"Better watch out for that global warming these days, what with the melanoma out there. Personally, I avoid ultraviolet like the plague."

His adversary glanced at the radical lawyer's beltline. "Obesity is out there, too, E. Joe. So tennis keeps my weight down."

"You get a deal for Maui, like all the other used-up places?"

"The Kapalua Bay Hotel, my man, where you gotta wear all-white on the courts."

Across the room, Harvey Johnson sulked, sending spite signals to his pal from a corner table too small for his bulk. The homicide dick never joined the lawyers; after a study of the Sports section, he tended to his notebook and laptop. He didn't see why the court translator failed to plop down with him, alone with nothing but an espresso and a note on his screen to remind him that the accused was carrying a Sig Sauer, not a Glock.

A scream like a car alarm stopped everything for a few seconds. Coffee cups and chewing were briefly suspended, but it was only a scream of laughter, only a defendant coked up for his imminent guilty verdict. All returned to what they were doing (espresso, bagels, muffins) or saying (words). The screamer pulled his fingers through long greasy hair, happy to have gained a moment of attention from really important assholes, something to savor in his pod in the county jail, eating mush ladled out by cooks lacking basic cuisine finesse.

Every table was taken; breakfasters were pushing away depleted cups and plates to make room for their own; a few good citizens cleared their tables. Having his own guests, a gentleman of the older school, Myron Ventorsky, put the previous guests' dishes on a chair. If they fell off and broke, well, they fell off and broke. Breakfast amid this din needed to be redeemed by a firm hand because work was work, fun was fun, and in the old days breakfast involved standards of service.

Ventorsky embraced the obvious, his late middle-aged skin and wispy baldness, reminiscing for his guests: "I started to prep this law student in my office, summer job – paid, not an intern – files and get me the coffee and I thought I should be nice. Blue eyes, an angel – *looked* like one – so I said, Hey, Heather, her name, great lunch on her" – outlined the air to make sure his point was taken – "treated her with kid gloves as the evening wore on, the dinner, no drinks first but then a nice wine, it was Saturday night, the drinks came later, and then this Heather looked at her watch, she yawned in my face, she said: Just fuck me, okay? Just fuck me and get it over with. I got an early date with my mom for church."

"No class these days," Gary Farr, a solo practitioner, observed. "Where's the romance?"

"Condoms in her purse!" Myron sighed. "I'll tell you, I miss the days when they put on the diaphragm ahead of time, the pill.

Gary shook his head. "Man, you forget, they didn't *wear* the pill..."

"... or," – Myron nostalgic, witty – "they just said no, but you can go to church with my mom and me. I can always use a little worship."

"... and *then* she'd sit on your face."

Everyone cackled. No one remembered the old days as quite that good.

Kasdan felt a longing to be elsewhere, even outside on Bryant, where in the forever-springtime of San Francisco, the miracle of green pushed its way through cracks in the sidewalk, shoots sprouting from windblown seeds or ready to start their new life after being airlifted in pigeon droppings.

It was time for Ferd Conway to further his business with Kasdan, but they were not alone. Kevin Nappy stood at their table, seeking mentorship from Ferd. "Apropos," he was saying, a fresh-faced University of San Francisco Law graduate who passed the Bar on only his second try, now just beginning his career as a gay activist. He was building a practice in the arcane specialty of defending purse snatchers who specialized in mom and grandmom figures; he hoped to work his way up to political blood splatterers and formerly Catholic disrupters of religious services.

"Apropos, my client said he bumped this biddy down because he needs a hall area rug. It wasn't personal about the lady even if she happened to be a pink-plastic shopping bag Chinese. His domestic partner said…"

"Apropos?" Ferd demanded.

"…they had the nice flat, the cozy vestibule, but all they had was this tatty old hunk of carpet in the hall. A new Laura Ashley hall area rug, providing she makes one, would complete their living situation. This granny's credit card…"

"Apropos? A hall area rug is a defense of need?"

Kevin strained to ignore the sarcastic critique from his pro tem of counsel. Putdowns were part of the breakfast networking experience at the Roma; a new lawyer could bond with a veteran while the veteran was offered space to speak his or her mind. "Ferd, all I'm saying is not necessarily only straight people are subject to spouse-equivalent nagging."

"I got no fabulous fuckin hall area rug, Kevin. All I got is a polished hardwood floor hall area and I'm satisfied with that. Am I wrong?"

Teasing worked off the excess roasted sugar and caffeine fumes. Here everyone was equal except for those who were not. Fun simmered, cell phones summoned, fellowship reached a boil. Only Harvey Johnson across the room disagreed in general with the proceedings. Although Kasdan sat silent, his chair tilted slightly away from the table, he was part of Ferd Conway's group. Kasdan would settle with Harvey later, or maybe not. A friend should find it in his heart to forgive a friend who was formerly without extensive plans but now was developing some and needed to act in accordance.

At ten o'clock, the Roma would turn quiet, but it was not yet the hour and the shout-outs were still accelerating. At another table, a happy-faced lawyer in a yellow tee shirt with the copyrighted smiley face stenciled on it – this lawyer not in court today, just hanging out with the gang – was delivering a current case summary to a less happy-faced audience. A senior practitioner, not Myron Ventorsky, listened gravely. (He was carrying a death penalty draft appeal in his briefcase.) Happy Face, given name unknown to Kasdan, was outlining his defense of a 49-year-old preschool teacher charged with sexual molestation of a child. "He says the kid, age four but looks older, came on to him, so who's the real victim? My client was just innocently inspecting him for pubic lice."

The guys were chuckling.

Happy Face shook his happy head. "Barely out of training pants and a hardened molester already."

The guys were interrupting with questions. If the kid grows up to play for the NBA, he doesn't want to have a record... Ferd leaned toward their table; maybe this was the group for him, more fun than somber Dan Kasdan.

"My client intends to sue the kid. We're going to go after mom and dad for harboring the little pervert."

"Take it on contingency," Ferd said. "Is the kid being scouted already? The Raiders need a center."

Happy Face, giddy with all the attention, yelled: "You're my boy, Ferd!"

Fun, sociability, and networking was a competitive sport as the morning got going. Harvey, big-eared, registered the noise and pleasure from his corner table, disapproving more of his friend Dan than of the breakfast assholes at the Caffe Roma across Bryant from the Hall of Revenge with its Elevators of Sighs and Holding Pens of Multi-Ethnic Correction. The counter women, sisters or look-alike cousins, plucked up bagels and muffins with tongs dripping crumbs and answered requests for "the usual" with rapid nods or witticisms ("Extra mayo on that poppy seed bagel?"), almost always correctly sliding "the usual" forward. Upholding a Roman tradition, living to the fullest the American dream in the golden west, the sisters or cousins hustled at top speed through the morning rush.

Myron Ventorsky, the senior counsel with recent hair plugs marching across the desert between his old hairline and his forehead, expressed hilarity by nodding sagely. Despite his rashness with the cute church-going intern, he was a man of methodical habits and hair plugs to match; they were planted in parallel rows, like saplings in a formal garden of hair wisps. Perhaps, without the new plugs, he would have laughed, but they itched this morning. He raked his fingernails over the doomed plants. "Funny," he muttered. Implants were not guaranteed; they looked pubic, parched; but interns, if carefully chosen, were supposed to require only a generous bar tab or perhaps a few lines of coke on Saturday night.

The distinguished horny advocate for the downtrodden wore a pink button-down shirt with a giant raised collar, wings engulfing his wattles, too tight for him now – what used to be called the Tony Curtis collar – giving Myron less a look of Tony Curtis, age thirty, than of choked sanctity. Not what he was aiming for, unless he was just trying to use up his veteran shirt products before his imminent unfortunate demise. The tight collar, the flush of his cheeks, the bulging lashless hyperthyroid eyes hinted that soon the Caffe Roma breakfast crew would be mourning a gracious and beloved colleague, a devoted Giants and Raiders fan, a man with a wide circle of admirers scrambling viciously to pick up his cases.

Kasdan rested his eyes on smaller tables where the guys with the tattoos and invisible cock rings conferred with significant others (tears) and lawyers (indignation). Generally speaking, the men with the metal and perma-inked decor were defendants. The older ones who needed bandanas looped around their necks to steady their hands for the first coffee of the day could be either defendants or lawyers now in AA after release from suspension by the California Bar Association. The pretty teeny-tinies on spike heels with the new briefcases were the fresh-hatched Asian lawyers you'd better not call "girls." The loner next to the unisex room, eating salty nuts and a dill pickle for breakfast – he'd brought his supplies in plasticine baggies – was a Russian immigrant planning to patent a cure for hangovers and AIDS. He had ordered his tea in a glass. San Francisco, once a destination for White Russians fleeing the Bolsheviks, was now a prime settlement for others seeking what their Chinese predecessors called the Golden Mountain (translation: The Land of Uncertain Promises).

One of the bandana guys, his hand steadied, was pouring something from a small bottle into his second or third cup of black coffee. It could be considered medication. The skin of his face was pitted and eroded with fresh pink marks where someone, perhaps himself, had scratched his itches. Eczema is major to the one who suffers it, even if it's caused by "issues." The Roma was a place of routines. Even Harvey Johnson over there, brooding about his only son; even Dan Kasdan, wondering how he could redeem the lost years for Amanda. Even Ferd Conway. The Roma was a place of routines and not yet resolved issues.

Harvey snapped his laptop shut with a clean, sharp, irritated click. Dan heard it all the way across the cafe because he was tuned to Harvey's critical judgment. He made the mistake of meeting his friend's eyes. Harvey was mouthing the word *stupid* and Dan wasn't sure whether he was saying his company this morning was stupid or he was stupid.

Probably both.

Dan's shoulder twitched in acknowledgement without going so far as the actual event of a shrug. This was the only answer that occurred to him.

Harvey, you're giving me your Responsible Negro Leader look.

But I gotta do, Harvey, what I gotta do.

What I want to do.

Fog-bound when the Roma opened before dawn, the sidewalk on Bryant haunted by night fauna, insomniacs and addicts and scurrying small animals breakfasting in the piles of short-order refuse, San Francisco turned bright, sunny, all-revealing – pretending to reveal all – by the time the defendants headed out into the day, along with their loved ones, their lawyers, the cops, and the staff workers at the Hall of Justice. The rats retreated into their rat holes with early morning snacks. Caffe Roma's population, inspired by bagels, muffins, caffeine, and the clatter of others, exited sturdily onto Bryant, as from Lourdes, having entered with rheumy eyes and slumped shoulders. Now they could hope for victory in the contests of the day. Some would win, their slates temporarily cleared. The lawyers expected to win, no matter what, although at times it came to pass that they couldn't collect more than their retainers.

Harvey Johnson left the Roma, moving fast for a hefty guy. Didn't want any friend to catch up with him.

Ferd Conway put his hand on Dan Kasdan's arm, asking him to stay awhile. Before they went ahead with the deal, he wanted to make sure they were on the same page.

− 2 −

When the rubber glove went snapping over his friend Doc Feldstein's fingers, good old tired Marvin's right hand, Dan Kasdan tried to think of anything else but the seasick procedure about to take place. *Oof.* Just another medical wiggle. Oof, oof again. Unfortunately, this internal wiggle was not a byproduct of rough water kayaking on San Francisco Bay with some young woman in need of impression by his fine prostate and general good health.

Gray of head and beard where once his hair was dark and glossy, a licensed Spanish court translator-interpreter for smalltime miscreants when once he might have been a Foreign Service officer or a CIA operative in Latin America, Kasdan had gone all these years without killing a single person. Occasionally in the past, a woman may have felt spiritually wounded by him, but this had never been due to intention on his part. Kasdan himself, of course, had suffered wounds in the normal course of events (distracted from the Foreign Service exams by sloth, not cleared by the CIA because of Vietnam era protest). He hadn't really wanted a bureaucratic career. Life, fairly long so far, showed signs of being shorter than he had expected. His dad had turned gray at age fifty, but thanks to Vitamin E, Kasdan had kept his genetic endowment of dark hair until age fifty-one.

"Try to relax," Doc Feldstein advised. "Think of something else."

"Easy for you to say," said Dan Kasdan, upper lip beaded with sweat.

Prostate examination was one of those occasions when even an agnostic said, Oh, God, which happened to be the words breathed by Kasdan after his wordless Oof. Then distracted himself with: Well, at least it's only one finger...

He was trying to be a good father to the daughter he had met (been tracked down by) when she was nineteen. Better late than never, so you can make up for lost time, Dan, was what Amanda kept telling him during the months of their first acquaintanceship, emphatically using his first name. ("Do you have to?" he asked. "Should I call you *Mister* Kasdan?" she answered. But then relented:

"Dad.") It was to her credit that she searched for him; and then that love for a daughter fell upon him with its flood of consoling endorphins. What the new life-adjustment came down to: It was now time to hurry with nurturing procedures. Amanda would have preferred to make his acquaintance during those dramatic days when layabouts like him met layabouts like her mother and listened to Bob Dylan on vinyl records; before herpes, before AIDS, before so many risks became really risky. And that should have been Amanda's right. But Margaret Torres and Dan Kasdan had just bumped together, then cheerily gone on their separate meandering ways.

"Just relax," repeated Doc Feldstein.

"Unh," said Kasdan.

"This'll take another minute. If you tighten up, it's no fun at all."

"My sphincter has a mind of its own."

"Dan, are you a man or an asshole?"

"Right now... oh, unh," said Kasdan, gasping a little, "the answer is obvious."

A victim of normal wear and tear was resting his chin on a medical table, his pants and his jockey shorts at his ankles. His yearly physical revealed that he was in pretty good shape, except. There seemed to be an accumulation of *excepts* as the metabolism burned along, occasionally glitching. A historical glitch had been the woman, Margaret Torres, who reappeared out of the mists of the several-years-long Summer of Love, informed him she was pregnant ("You were in such a hurry I forgot to tell you I'd gone off the pill"), and moved up north to Mendocino to raise the child with the two hundred dollars he'd given her for the abortion. Two hundred dollars wasn't enough for washable diapers, cereal purée, much less the other baby crap, even in a coven of mutually supportive witches and worshipers of Gaia, Mother of Earth and Sea. Amanda, the daughter of Margaret and Dan, presented herself to her father nineteen years later with a stock of grievances, a boyfriend soon to be a husband, and Kasdan's grandchild on the way.

All this came as a drastic interruption in the regular course of a becalmed bachelor's routines. "I hope it doesn't bug you if I'm pissed sometimes because you abandoned me, Dad," Amanda said. *No, not at all, spices up my life.*

The veteran Spanish court translator with his dusty apartment on Ellis in the Tenderloin had expected comfortable diminishment, not passionate increase. A meteor just fell from the sky – two of them, Amanda, followed by Sergei.

Is this pokery still going on? What's Marvin's finger looking for, an exit to the freeway?

"Easy, easy," said the good doctor. "I could do without the groans. Try to appreciate me, I'm an old friend."

"Finger's not my friend."

"Nearly done now, Dan. Just one little curve here, round the bend, okay?"

Marvin used to keep a miniature television on the table for the patient to focus on ("Zone in," he'd say, trying to be a California boy), but found that most of his prostate patients had no interest in the daytime soap opera zone. They preferred to rest their chins and grunt. The Age of Aquarius had come to this.

Its survivor, Dan Kasdan, in his unassisted living facility, a dusty (because rarely dusted), musty (but no asthma yet) apartment in the Tenderloin, found solace in a surrounding terrain of alcohol, speed and crack, transvestite hookers, non-transvestite hookers, massage parlors, soup kitchens, southeast Asian families busy with first-stage America experience, and more homeless Vietnam veterans, it seemed, than there had been combatants in Vietnam. Not that he really needed solace. What did he have to complain about? It was within walking distance of the Hall of Justice. His life was a sausage which he survived, even if the ingredients were unknown. Nobody knew the troubles he'd seen; even he didn't know them anymore.

Of course, he stayed away from actual sausage; it was neither a low-cholesterol meat nor a healthy vegetable; mind wandering, as Marvin had advised.

Occasionally, say once a week, Dan Kasdan and Harvey Johnson saved their pennies and poisoned their breath by eating (Harvey extended his pinkie and called it "dining") at the Good Karma India-Pakistan Bountiful Buffet, where the cook's cat wore booties which Mr. Krishna knitted himself. Past the lamb with curry, the chicken with curry, and the curry with curry, the cat went skidding after a panicky mouse like a speed skater, its bootie-clad paws fumbling at its catch. It decided to play awhile with the frantically peeping little creature; the cat boxed, leaped, and trapped the mouse between its bootied paws, having learned the trick of it. Supper could wait, mouse with curry sauce.

Harvey, a detective who read the world news daily, commented that someday there might-could be peace and good karma between India and Pakistan, but never between cat and mouse. Also a fount of inside civic dope, Harvey passed on to Dan the news that Mr. Krishna's real name was Mr. Patel.

The cat had miscalculated its one-sided match. Sudden knockout; mouse expired; the bootie-clad domestic relative of lions, tigers, leopards, jaguars and pumas stubbornly continued batting it around, hoping for further play. Mr. Krishna said "Shoo," and typical of a spoiled pet, his mouser ignored the command.

Dan and Harvey observed the action. Dan tried for philosophy. "We make some of the same mistakes again and again, everybody does. It's human nature. We're recidivists. We're animals."

"Speak for yourself," said the plainclothes dick. He liked to chase perps in his workout suit because he thought it made him look attractively overweight, in addition to fearsome, in case a fine lady passerby happened be observing the hot pursuit. "I keep fit."

"So do I," said Kasdan, his tone revealing him as a liar for an alert interrogator. "But age, getting older, it's inevitable."

"Maybe. But that's my story and I'm sticking to it."

You do that, Kasdan thought, and then said to his good buddy: "You do that."

Harvey was muttering disgustedly under his breath: "Recidivist, recidivist, try saying that three times fast."

Harvey was one of the bits of good luck in Kasdan's life – a friend to whom he could speak aloud what he thought. Add that one to the discovery of a daughter, who had almost immediately given him a son-in-law who was a security guard in a full-service whorehouse and a grandson who was whatever this grandson would eventually turn out to be. His retracted life had been turned inside out due to a for-gotten incident with a Margaret Torres during the trailing ends of the Summer of Love. Neither Dan nor Margaret had understood that the Summer of Love would not last forever.

All Dan's friends were growing older. Harvey, who varied his rou-tines by sometimes going undercover in a body builder's tight black

tee shirt and black jeans – his stiff strut made him the most conspic-
uous overage plainclothes dick in the San Francisco P.D. – had taken
to patting his new paunch, complaining about diminishing poker
skills, and now he announced, "When you get older, it's harder to tell
the difference between an oncoming fart and an outcoming shit. I
still get it right most of the time."

"Mind if I don't stand next to you, Harvey?"

"Now that you're a daddy," said his pal, "you're not really one of
the guys anymore."

"A grand-daddy," said Dan Kasdan.

Oof. Done. It helped to let the mind wander rather than stick with
the discomfort.

Doc Marvin's finger slid away. Doc Marvin was finished. Doc Marvin
Feldstein wasn't talking for awhile; he was disposing of his rubber
glove; he was deciding to be straight with his old patient. Here and
now, nothing else was called for. A matter of respect.

"The biopsy was pretty definite. It confirms the PSA count. You're
too stubborn about treatment, Dan. Today...."

"Today what?"

"I think it's growing. We didn't need confirmation, but in my
opinion it's confirmed."

"*We*," said Dan Kasdan. "In your opinion."

Marvin had pestered him, so he had consented to their little date
for the finger-equals-seasickness procedure. He wanted to keep his
doctor happy. No real surprises today.

Marvin was droning on about Kasdan's oncoming death without
actually using that word, so that it hung in the air like a cloud of dust
mites, while Kasdan gratefully took the offered bunch of Kleenex and
did what a man does to make sure he's reasonably tidy after doing his
doctor the favor of submitting to an unnecessary procedure. Pedaled
the medical waste can and disposed of the tissues. Always enjoyed
opening a can with a foot on the pedal; a sanitary procedure plus a
cause and effect mechanism, offering the consoling miracle of logic
working at a distance.

Now that he was on a roll, Marvin wanted to lay out the options.
Dan's condition could still be remedied. Statistics were invoked, but
because of the intersections of proba- and possi-bilities, nothing was

absolutely certain. Marvin tended to get formal at moments like this. "You'll never again feel as good as you do today," he added with a certain amount of sighing and hyperventilation that did nothing to lighten the occasion.

"Pardon? Lost you there."

Marvin repeated his words with a sigh almost like a yawn, his eyes filmy.

But Kasdan was pretty sure he could prove his friend wrong, or if not wrong, at least irrelevant. For sure he would feel as good as he did today. Harvey was right; resolute intentions matter. Harvey was frequently partly right. Kasdan understood that Marvin was making drastic predictions because his patient was a contrary son of a bitch who needed to be turned around by drasticity. Marvin appealed to the ornery side of his patient, his friend. Once more, wearily, naggingly, he explained about the prostate, the excess of it, popping out of the normal casing – slipped a kind of armor if you want to think of it that way – and growing; unfortunately, growing in a weed-like, messy, uncontrolled way (Marvin wheezed slightly in the effort to unpronounce the word 'malignant'); and so what was called for was surgery, radiation, radium implants, eventual chemo likely, hormone treatments – in the field there was a certain amount of discretion and clinical difference of view about treatments. With the hormones, okay, they might lead to a fat deposit here and there, a little fattiness, nothing very obvious, maybe breasts swelling, but no real change in the soul of a man unless you count loss of interest in sex, which Dan's dear devoted friend, the pompous doc, called 'libido.' But the alternative...

"It's inevitable anyway."

"Likely to come sooner."

Kasdan grinned.

Said his good friend: "This is no joking matter. What's so funny?"

"Maybe not for you," said Kasdan. "But *come sooner*? I like your choice of words."

Marvin ignored insults from the career linguist. "Invasive," he repeated, a nag, not letting go. "When I felt it with my finger..." Kasdan winced. Did he have to mention the finger again? "... plus the PSA count, the lab reports confirmed, reconfirmed... Dan! Are you paying attention?"

"Every time you did that, once a year after fifty, right? And I heard the snap of your rubber gloves, and I said this is the part of my physical I really don't like, and you said every time, every year."

"'If you liked it, I wouldn't do it.' I don't have that many jokes, so I use the ones I have."

"You see?" Kasdan asked. "You try to make jokes, too. It's not a sin."

Marvin looked glum. "Okay, okay, try to... Now you've got your daughter. Your grandson. You've got your retirement plan, don't you? You want to stay acquainted with them, Dan?"

Actually, despite what Marvin thought, Kasdan was measuring the situation, conditions, eventualities, even if his dear doctor and urology counselor had no idea of what he was thinking. It was not in the good doc's repertory. Previously these thoughts had not been in Kasdan's repertory. Previously, if he woke at night to pee, he went back to sleep without a care in the world except for an occasional twinge of conscience about something he might have done better. For example: he didn't really have a retirement plan.

The course of Kasdan's personal life had so far been empty of murders. Personally, he had not yet killed anyone. Sure, there had been dreams, wishes to avenge wrongs, irritations which led him to imagine pressing a button that could make the creep who stole his parking place, his wallet, or his lady friend just disappear. Wishes don't count. His own death was never the one he had in mind, but now his future had been washed in hot water and shrunk down to a tight fit. The lines of force, according to the good doc, called for a sense of urgency. Amanda might miss him if he were removed so soon after she had made his acquaintance.

"What are you thinking?" Marvin asked.

"It's too warm in here. Is that for the benefit of the geriatrics?"

"Pay attention. I have the right to ask that, Dan. What we think, and the second opinion you insisted on, confirm ..."

"Are you insulted about the second opinion?"

"It's your right. Professionally, I agree, even if personally I know what I'm doing. I agree with myself. We can go for hormones first, slow down any proliferation..." Marvin was avoiding the rude words, *tumor, growth, spread.* "... keep the extra cells out of circulation, then maybe we'll have surgery ..."

"Who's *we* around here?"

"... chemo, some people like the radium implants, Sweden, for some reason. Some go for radiation alone – there's a guy, Walsh, at Johns Hopkins ..."

"Quite a menu you're offering, pal. *We* is *me*."

Marvin toyed with a present from a drug company on his desk, a paperweight containing a happy senior citizen reaching toward the sunlight inside clear plastic. It was a vision of the blessings of cortisone in a superior formulation. He flipped it upside down when he caught Dan staring. Snow swirled around the happy senior citizen.

"After the hormones, sometimes the other options are more effective."

"Will I still be able to get it up?"

"After the hormones kick in? Problematic, but you may not even want to."

"I will. I've a good memory."

"Later, it depends. This is art, not science, Dan."

Marvin sighed. Dan wasn't making it easy for him, but this particular discussion was never easy. "Okay, there's that other choice. The Dutch, the Poles, some of those peripheral medical systems – the Hungarians ..."

"That's the choice I choose. Do nothing. Don't you call it 'watchful waiting'?"

Marvin still sighing. Office noises, medical hush. The clinical tiles and pipes, the nurse with soft white shoes, the door not quite shut, the filing cabinets. The framed family photographs on Marvin's desk, the diplomas on the walls, the beige sound of Muzak because the doctor needed to concentrate and needed his patient to focus. Marvin's do-not-disturb mutter to a folder- and chart-bearing technician who parted the door and peeked in with a look of urgency.

"Last I looked, we're not Poles, Dan."

Time was money in the era of HMOs. Marvin Feldstein would take all the time in the world for Dan. He leaned forward in a chair with a bulge constructed especially to support his spine. Marvin had lumbar region issues; even a doctor needed help with the problems brought on by anxiety, a few extra pounds (maybe forty), a weakness for the consolations of fondue and old-fashioned cooking with high-density butter. The fact was that from the get-go human beings were not designed to take stressful parade positions or spend years in classes, labs and examination rooms. Hunters and gatherers roaming the forest and fields weren't out trapping fondue or harvesting French sauces.

Although scoliosis involved soft tissue changes, the normal attrition of gravity, cartilage wear and tear, sheaths narrowing to impinge on nerves, Marvin Feldstein had noticed by the time he reached the age of fifty that this type of normal complaint was – here came a professional summary beyond mere diagnosis – the shits. It was a pain in the butt and related regions, such as the head. Sympathy for his patients was bad for the neural sheaths; so had been his marriage with its lack of sympathy from his wife; so were the host of non-cartilage-related hassles. Like this one: explaining to bull-headed Dan Kasdan that he would die if he didn't take the best medical advice while admitting he would also die if he did. Timing was the only issue. This justified avoiding the words 'death' and 'die.'

Dan was asking, "I've got time, don't I? Marvin? To do some things I want to do first?"

"Depends on how long you take. I can't guarantee any time frame."

Immortality was one of the enjoyments of youth, like deep and uninterrupted sleep, which both Dan and Marvin had gradually given up.

"Why that expression on your face, Marvin?"

"It's just my look."

"It's even worse than usual. I'd describe it as sour if you asked me."

"I didn't ask you. Okay, it's my back. This pot I carry isn't good for me, but I seem to like things that aren't good for me. Last night I had dinner at that new Swiss place out on Clement – you know it? Chez Somebody, but the chef, he's terrific, really gourmet, oh boy the fondue, is from Hong Kong.

"Chez Fong? Fang?"

"I should do leg lifts. Maybe I should try acupuncture."

Then they just sat there awhile amid the muffled technology creaks and grindings through office walls. Marvin was the kind of doctor who couldn't adjust to assembly-line stacking of patients prepped by nurses, ten-minute HMO-approved appointments, twenty minutes for serious cases. Kasdan let his eyes wander as if it were happenstance that he didn't meet Marvin's fixed stare. "Okay, so you've suddenly gone all Polish on me? Now you're in love with watchful waiting?"

"Been doing that all my life, Marvin," Kasdan said.

He re-admired the diplomas with their calligraphic notations on the wall. Kindly board-approved Marvin, making a living complaining only about his back

But his sighs were contagious. Kasdan decided not to sigh in return. He converted the impulse nimbly into a yawn; stood up; stretched. "Thanks for the interlude," he said, and shook his old buddy's hand.

Kasdan had saved a few bucks by parking on the street, not in the medical building parking lot (first twenty minutes validated, after that pay for each twenty minute segment.) A pleasant walk in the September sun down Geary would fix him up nicely, as usual, although generally it wasn't the offer of a death sentence which needed fixing. While basking, strolling, enjoying, just ambling, admiring the leafage of trees and the grassage of grass, he took the time to go through one of life's occasional periods of re-adjustment.

Elbow burn from sex in the missionary position used to be his worst ailment. This was no longer true. Maybe he could think of a hungry tumor with its network of greedy new baby blood vessels as a fashion accessory for late middle age. Murder was a relatively original consolation.

By the time he eased himself into his Honda, beat up by its time on the road in San Francisco, beat up by collateral parking damage in the street near his flat on Ellis, his spirits were repaired. Elbow burn used to respond to Jergen's Lotion; impending final silence required a stronger treatment

He called himself to order, as he sometimes had to do during his Spanish-English interpreting service for alleged perpetrators, so-called purse-snatchers, accused gang members, night strollers charged with burglary only because they happened to be found in some stranger's bedroom at three a.m. Occasionally he worked for a shooter or knifer, unjustly caught in the act, but this didn't offer the experience he needed for his own case. The logical choice for a first killing... Already he was ahead of most of his clients, who seldom pre-selected their victims. The Hall of Justice, 850 Bryant, the court-rooms, hallways and holding pens, was not a resort of considered arrangements. Under the circumstances, the logical choice was someone whose life he did not value but whose death could both profit and gratify him. Now, whoever could that be?

The question seemed a bit hard-hearted, but anyway: who could it be?

It's obvious, Signor Kasdan.

Ferd Conway, the expert plea-bargainer sliding along the corridors at 850 Bryant, just as smart as those shitfaces from Stanford Law, Boalt, or Yale, no matter what the shitfaces thought about him. Ferd Conway, eking his way to prosperity but not yet awakened to the regular use of dandruff-remover shampoo (flaking scalp and snowy shoulders), and this was far from his worst character flaw. Ferd was representing the Yerba Buena Foundation with its complex tax-free enterprises of massage parlors, escort outcalls and coke-dealing, when Amanda had checked in by telephone with the words:

"Mr. Kasdan? I'm your daughter."

"Who?"

"Margaret Torres is my mother."

"Who?"

"Nineteen years ago. I don't put you down for not remembering who you fucked, Dad."

So now, as a father with limited time on his hands, he could try to be useful to a daughter with needs. He could give his only child something to remember him by, such as money, in addition to warm wishes.

Ferd.

Ferd Conway, who persisted in calling him Cowboy, although Dan asked him not to. In due course, at the proper, most profitable, gratifying moment, he would live up to Ferd's rakish name for him.

You'll never feel as good as you do today?

Oh yes I will, Kasdan decided. It was a new life ahead. Cowboy Dan was planning on good days to come, profitable and gratifying, after exercising due diligence.

Stubborn Cowboy Dan.

– 3 –

So what that he was going to die; doesn't everybody? *When* was the more interesting question. No one here was offering a date. Since Marvin had predicted it, "absent radical decisions, absent miracles that don't happen except in the National Inquirer" – absent treatments that would make Dan Kasdan less of a Dan Kasdan – he needed to get busy with a few present obligations, Amanda, Sergei, and the husband and father, D'Wayne.

D'Wayne was now family, too, professionally the greeter and screener at the Yerba Buena Foundation, a clinic which was intermittently closed down by chickenshit cops who were impatient for promotions. The chickenshit cops claimed this therapy center was just a brothel that happened to keep computer records of its clients' individual preferences. "Them's patient histories," D'Wayne explained, "plus, I'm only there to run security."

Doorman at the Yerba Buena Foundation did not make easygoing D'Wayne a prolific earner. There was no family health plan. Although the Foundation provided compassionate support for clients with sexual problems, such as sudden horniness after the bars closed, and "issues," such as special needs not remedied by an uptight wife or girlfriend, it was subject to eruptions of civic interference. The job had been adequate for a bachelor; but now D'Wayne was married and his baby had issues of its own. When Kasdan remarked to Amanda that he didn't feel real overjoyed about his son-in-law's career, she dutifully mimicked him: "I didn't feel real overjoyed, Dad, about not meeting my father until I was a grownup trying to hustle up a life. So now why don't you say, 'I hear you, Amanda'?"

I hear you; pretty sarcastic. It was what the county mental health counselor told her to tell her father to say if he wanted to prove he was paying attention, cared, was digging the emissions. *I hear you.* (Also: I wish your mom had let me know our two-night run – maybe three nights – had resulted in this angry darling, standing with arms folded across her chest and one hip cocked, so I hear you.)

Kasdan believed his appetite might not follow him into the heaven he did not believe in, so he should take a big bite out of the world as it was before he left it. He wanted to leave Amanda and D'Wayne with occasional kind thoughts about him. Whether Sergei would have a kind thought about him was a matter up to the nervous system of Sergei.

Their apartment smelled of baby piss and Johnson's Baby Powder. It was a smell which brought a fond smile to D'Wayne's face when he returned home to Mose Sergei (not yet decided whether to call the child Mose or Sergei; in due course a decision would occur). The smell was one Kasdan might have known if he had been present during the early life of his daughter.

"Dad," said Amanda.

He said her name, he tried to hug her and her beauty, slick with sweat. She stiffened, pulled away, and then suddenly sank against him. She couldn't get used to her son's diagnosis. Sometimes Amanda seemed okay, but then she turned into a broadcaster of grief. Mose or Sergei was snoring in his crib – are babies supposed to snore? Kasdan had never learned about such things. The child was yellow, a pale yellow-green with a wet pink bubble at his lips, as if he had hepatitis or malaria, or perhaps these were the colors of "developmentally disabled," as the pediatrician put it.

Yellow-green may have been a trick of Kasdan's aging eyes or San Francisco morning light reflected across the alley from the next building. Perhaps it had nothing to do with muscular dystrophy but was an heirloom tint, thanks to a black father and a Hispanic-Jewish mother. The skin of Sergei Mose, like his name, should have seemed *interesting*, a genetic privilege, interestingly ethnic. Unless the scientists worked faster than they seemed to, the beloved son and grandson was born to trouble and disappearance before he could enjoy his interesting skin color.

He cried; all babies cried. He cried too much. It's wrong when a baby cries too much. Sergei bawled; the bawls diminished to whimpering; then he opened his mouth and howled until he was hoarse. It hurt Kasdan in the chest to hear it. He couldn't imagine what it did to Amanda and D'Wayne, day and night, their son suddenly waking for no good reason, convulsing, choking, screaming for breath. "An error of metabolism, nerve signals to the muscle cells," the pediatrician mumbled, trying for vagueness and succeeding – no comfort to a mother and father who loved their son. It was their right.

The child cried with cramps. He might not live long enough to learn the word "cramp." In his body and soul, he seemed to know this was a terrible injustice. The child twisted and screamed. A helpless grandfather could do what was necessary. He could get money from Ferd Conway. He could take pleasure in the getting. Sergei might be taught to extend his life with the help of doctors who did not mumble.

The child slept while his grandfather watched over him. In this respite, it was a joy to Kadsan that his life had a plan beyond getting out of his bed on Ellis in the morning. In his sleep Sergei twitched like any other person twitching in a dream, with visions of the future or the past, a life before his life or a life to come, dreams sparking in a tangle of ganglia and appetites which were genetic collages of parents and grandparents; including the grandfather now watching and partaking of this ordinary miracle. The grandfather leaned over the child with this strange new passion, love, in which he was enrolled for a late study. It felt something like hatred and something like adoration. Longing and hurt burrowed into the flesh of living creatures. Dogs twitched with dreams, too; dogs with their snarling wolf ancestors slept under the imprint of appetites to breed, nurture and kill.

A bubble of saliva grew at Sergei's mouth. Kasdan remembered that sometimes he woke from a dream of love-making with his face wet, tears of desire or a wetness from lips imagining love. A richness of drool gathered at the parting and down the soft, so soft skin. If Sergei lived long enough, later, if he survived his childhood, his lips would remain dry in sleep. And still later, at the age of his grandfather, the old guy, Sergei would again give up control over saliva flow and the dreams no one really controls. Kasdan tried to remember: did he need to wipe his mouth when he awakened to pee at three in the morning?

Sergei wouldn't live long enough to have a swollen prostate. Calamity had come for him in a rush before the oily placenta had been wiped away and before much else of life had come to him. A consultation like Kasdan's with Marvin Feldstein was not on the schedule for Sergei Mose.

Along with his gentle snore, a soft bubbling, the child shivered. He was wetting his diaper. The room smelled of baby talcum powder, the

Johnson's perforated can, just over there on the thrift shop changing table with its pink rubber sheet; the room smelled of baby powder and piss; an astringent, charming, sincere smell, it seemed to Kasdan. Sometimes he ate sour pickles out of the barrel at Tommy's Joynt on Van Ness, also an odd smell to treasure. He wondered if he should try changing the diaper. It was easier all around to let Sergei rest.

Kasdan watched. He never sat so still, marveling over a child's busy sleeping, dreaming, pissing; his grandson was a multitasker! Kasdan felt the nerve behind his left eye, the one that twitched when he was tired or distressed, begin its signaling. Who could take care of this child without a lot of money? How could this child find every possible remedy for an incurable affliction?

Kasdan's personal migraines, that throb of anxious nerves, had occasionally interrupted his routines even before he knew he had a daughter – an ache of things wearing out in the flat on Ellis where he was spending the nights of his life. It had always been a selfish head-ache, only concerning the harborer of the headache.

"Dad?" Amanda called from the kitchen. "What're you doing in there?"

"He stopped crying. He's sleeping."

"So what're you doing?"

He had pulled a chair up to the crib. When a child slept, even this damaged child, the mother's voice would not awaken it.

"You're just sitting there in the dark, Dad?"

"I know. It's restful."

Kasdan was going further to be useful and entertained than Ferd Conway could ever imagine for the sucker he called Cowboy.

"Sometimes I think, Dad...." Now she was going to start to cry. Ignorant though he was, an innocent in fatherhood, Kasdan recognized the cloudiness, swelling, reddening, the incipiency of tears. "Sometimes, Dad, I think it would be better...."

And her lip would bleed if she bit it any harder.

"Go ahead. Say it."

"I can't say it to D'Wayne. I can't tell D'Wayne."

"You can tell me."

There were flecks of blood on her lip. "It would be better if ..."

"No! You don't want to say that!"

"But I think it, Dad. I can't say it to D'Wayne, but that's what I think sometimes."

Surely D'Wayne thought it, too. Surely Kasdan thought it. Surely everyone around here sometimes thought Sergei might be better off not born. But here Sergei was, there in the next room, bubbling saliva in his sleep, and their voices were low as if he might be listening.

Kasdan put his arms around his daughter.

"I have to tell someone, Dad."

He pressed her hard. "I nominate me."

"I'm afraid of D'Wayne."

"What? What?" He had never suspected anything. He knew the stories about black men and white women, but not D'Wayne, no, not him.

"He's in pain, Dad. He loves me, he loves Sergei, he's in pain, we don't know what to do."

"He might hurt you?"

She pulled away, furious. "What! That was what you thought? Dad, what's wrong with you? I mean he feels helpless, he's trapped, he won't run away from me, from us, he doesn't do anything except, except be miserable ..."

"You should have said you're afraid *for* him."

She pulled away and glared across the immense distance of disdain and eighteen inches. "I stand corrected, okay. How about trying to know me a little, Dad?"

Kasdan might have been better at the squalls of family if Amanda had grown up with him instead of revealing herself only when she was already a citizen of a poverty and lost souls district. He may have seen her without knowing she was his daughter. Now she was saying he was too busy correcting her language to see her. "So what's your deal with the shyster, Dad?"

"Ferd Conway?"

"You know he comes around? When nobody's home but me and Sergei?"

"Ferd?"

"... when he thinks I'm alone, and he sits and sighs and runs his mouth and sighs, like he's got the hots or something – he's not just waiting for the bus, Dad – it's creepy. Keeps coming around, 'popping in,' he says, says he just wants to say hello, so hello? Says he's your best friend, he's just in the neighborhood anyway, so how am I doing, what's happening, don't I get lonely all day here or wish I had some fun ..."

Ferd does that? Ferd did that?

In a rush, she got out the rest of what was on her mind, some of it, because with a daughter there is always more: "He says he's very good, excellent, outstanding in bed, so I said sure, I'll bet, specially when you're there alone, and he acted like he liked that, haha, said you make jokes, too, like father like daughter, blood tells – he said that... He put his hand here, here..."

Along her knee, sliding; along her thigh, sliding.

"... and he asks if I'm still nursing, cause my boobs are nice and humongous, so that means I don't have to worry about having an all-white kid with him ..."

In court, Kasdan once had to translate something the prosecutor said to Kasdan's client, a Bolivian: "That just makes the cheese more binding." He had trouble with the translation and the Bolivian dish-washer said, "I don't get no constipation."

"*What*? He's talking to you about your breasts? He's talking to you about birth control?"

"Don't say anything, Dad. I know you wouldn't slap him around or anything because you're such good homies, probably high-fiving a lot. I guess D'Wayne'd slap him around – you know, *respeck* – big thing around D'Wayne – so I don't tell D'Wayne this stuff. Anyway, things are like they are, so what's the point, Dad?"

Ferd was just making the cheese more binding.

It seemed to Kasdan that there had been sufficient family sociability and confiding for one day, but then D'Wayne showed up, happy to find his father-in-law visiting. He flipped open two beers, didn't offer to pour Kasdan's into a glass – they were family, after all – checked on blessedly sleeping Mose Sergei, said he'd be insulted if Pop left as soon as his son-in-law arrived, threw himself into a chair, removed his shoes, invited Pop to do the same. Kasdan felt good about being called Pop for the first time, and twice in a rush of his son-in-law's hospitality.

It turned out to be an interesting day to visit his daughter, her husband and Sergei. He asked why Amanda and D'Wayne had given their son a name that sounded partly Russian to him. D'Wayne said, "Man, I don't do those African names no more, Katanga, Lumumba, Stokeley. H. Rap ain't even an African name, man. But D'Wayne, that's *bad*, I don't know where my mom got her input. *D'Wayne?* Shee, man, Wayne with a doohickey? So Russian looks kinda nice. They got a great history, you know what I'm sayin'? Sergei Pushkin was an African prince, least his grandaddy was."

"Pushkin's name was Alexander."

"It was? Middle name, man. Whatever, I don't want no kid of mine be call Aleck."

"I guess."

"Which is the natural thing in life, Pop" – third time! – "not to disrespeck you askin'."

Out of respect for his father-in-law, D'Wayne had taken to saying shee instead of shee-it. Also he no longer tucked a giant magenta plastic comb in his hair, but kept it in his back pocket for use as needed. Kasdan appreciated his sensitivity (street smart, D'Wayne had caught a judgmental glance some months back).

They were just hanging out, enjoying a brew, Amanda relaxing sleepily in the rocking chair Kasdan had bought for her after Margaret Torres informed him that this was what a new mother needed, when Sergei woke up. His eyes blinked open and he stared into the world. His fists with their tiny pink fingernails clenched, his mouth opened, and he began to howl his protest against the universe into which he was born. He had no choice. Amanda held him against her breast. He twisted and screamed, seized the nipple, and as she rocked, abruptly subsided into greedy suckling sounds.

When D'Wayne sampled the Muslim creed, he liked the idea about taking one step toward Allah, then Allah takes two steps toward him – like a dance, see – but it got crowded in the mosque in Oakland, it was a trip across the Bay Bridge, all those shoes off the dudes' feet raised a stink, especially during the hot nights of Ramadan. D'Wayne sampled it pretty good, but then moved on. Until he and Amanda got together, he didn't have no call to stick with things, not necessarily. But he still liked that Muslim black bread, whenever he happened to pass by the bakery, although he tended to eat it with pork chops, which was strictly against the Koran.

"We had this kid, what, thirteen months now," D'Wayne was saying, "We know the story."

"You can never tell," said Kasdan.

"You the optimist, Pop. We know the story and it ain't gonna improve much."

"Maybe not entirely, but in advance you can't ..."

Careful not to awaken the sleeping child nestled against her,
Amanda said softly, "Not, Dad." Not improve.

D'Wayne stared at Amanda, blinking at her, at Sergei, and then
turned back to Kasdan. "But he's still the main thing. You understand
that, Pop? If you do, explain it to me."

Kasdan couldn't explain it. But Amanda was the most important
person in the world to him, and before he found her (okay, she found
him), nobody had been what he lived for, not even himself. He didn't
understand it, but it was obvious. D'Wayne didn't need it explained,
either, but he wanted his father-in-law to try for both of them.

Sergei existed. He was born. Therefore, no deal. It just was.
D'Wayne was telling him what he felt, what almost everyone felt,
which just made it more mysterious. So then what? Get Amanda,
D'Wayne, and Kasdan's grandson the tax-free help which Kasdan
wasn't telling them about. Ferd Conway happened to exist, too. The
satisfaction that came alongside taking and giving was his right. This
was America, wasn't it?

Amanda was stirring in the rocking chair which was good for a
nursing mother, easing her stressed back, rocking the child to
peacefulness. She was holding Sergei and he was fussing. It would be
a hard time again, as it frequently was, day and night, if he began to
thrash and scream. Kasdan knew babies were supposed to fuss sometimes between wakefulness and sleep, despite the rhythm of rocking
along with a feed at the mother's breast.

He thought he smelled milk. He had been surprised that it was
bluish and watery, not at all like the milk at the Caffe Roma. When
Amanda met her father's eyes, watching her as she rocked Sergei,
tears came flowing silently, without sobs or a catch of her breath, just
flowing, familiar.

Kasdan knew not to ask why. His own feeling for the child was a
drawing pain in his chest, a peristalsis of hurt pulling at him, pity for
Sergei, Amanda, and D'Wayne, and enough left over for himself, the

man who was trying to pay his debt for the years lost by Amanda and her father. He had bought her a bentwood rocking chair with a cane seat. He planned to do more to make things between them more like right.

Sergei emitted a soft snore, a warning snort, signaling that he would wake unless someone pulled him snugly to her breast. "This one doctor said we should put him in a.... a home. This other doctor, second opinion, said it was up to me which way I want to ruin my life."

"Up to us," D'Wayne said. "Not ruined, Mandy." He took the child to his chest, standing, slowly swaying. He moved Sergei's thumb to his mouth and the child took it. Kasdan, knowing he was ignorant, knew he shouldn't ask if that would be bad for his teeth, helping him sleep that way.

"I'm not gonna send him away, Dad, like the first opinion said. Some people do that."

"I didn't send you away. I had no idea about you at all."

"Dad! It's not about you! But it felt like you sent me away. I'm gonna keep him. I'll take care of him. He'll be okay."

The face of Ferd Conway floated through the room, invisible to all but Kasdan. His needy crinkling eyes. His grin. D'Wayne swayed, touching the chair, rocking himself, Amanda and Sergei. Kasdan was still seeing Ferd, reading the print of scam on his face, while Amanda took the baby back, touched the thumb in his mouth, the baby snoring a little, not snorting now but making tiny soapy bubbles. D'Wayne was grinning because *he* had put Sergei more soundly to sleep. "Hey, blue is a good color for you, I like denim on you, Dad," Amanda said.

"Sidewalk sale. They left it in the sun too long and it got this color."

"Kind of like bleachy white you can call it? I should try that on D'Wayne."

D'Wayne laughed in his rumbling coughing caramel way, not a smoker's wheeze but a big man's style, like Harvey's indulgent roll of sociability. "Keep you in the dark, you be black like me, Mandy? So far it's only your heart is black."

Their eyes met, D'Wayne's and beautiful Amanda's, and Kasdan marveled again at the gifts his errors had brought him, this once-fatherless daughter now a young woman with freckles dusting her nose and hurts dusting her soul, quick to resentments and griefs but her edges softening. She had found, in rapid succession, a father, a husband and a son. There in beautiful Amanda's arms nestled Kasdan's grandson, while the grandfather thought: Maybe we can all be forgiven, maybe we can be redeemed.

Sergei was sleepy too much of the time, then awake and howling too much. Kasdan woke too much at night, needing to pee, having to stand patiently in the dark for the relief that used to occur with vigorous abruptness. And during the day... Now he was standing in the bathroom. "What're you doing in there?" Amanda called.

"Thinking."

"Thinking?"

He was supposed to be giving his attention to his family. So he came out of the bathroom. And for no reason that Kasdan could understand, like an avalanche without a storm or an explosion, Sergei's face suddenly turned purple, his eyes rolled up so that only the ghostly white was visible, his mouth gaped open and he began to scream. Amanda said, "Hush, hush baby, quiet," speaking very calmly although the piercing shrieks were like toothpick thrusts to the ears. She had achieved this calm by living through the explosions. There was a cost Kasdan couldn't calculate.

I can't calculate it, Kasdan thought, head down, making his way out. I have to do something else.

There was a rush of footsteps behind him. "Dad, you forgot to say goodbye!"

He stopped, confused. "Didn't I?" He didn't even recall saying he was leaving.

She threw her arms around him. "Are you thinking about something?"

He considered a proper answer to this complicated question. "Sometimes."

"You're worried?"

"Sometimes. No, I'm not."

She hugged him tightly. "I have to get used to how you are, Dad."

"Me too," he said.

"I never had one before. I don't know how dads are."

"Neither do I."

They stood in the hall. She dropped her arms. "So goodbye, Dad."

And he could feel her watching him, that laser penetration on his back, as he proceeded down the stairs, bouncing a little on his soles, not a care in the world, emitting backwards zaps of carefree, the mechanism of defense operating as it was intended to against laser penetration by a daughter. Sergei abruptly gurgled away his last shrieks, erratic even in his metabolic despair, again fallen asleep, just as if he too chose not to worry about the state of the world. It was a normal infant's right. Dan Kasdan decided an older person could also claim this right.

The outer door lurched before he could reach it and an energetic visitor propelled Kasdan back upstairs. "Surprise! I don't care what, you can't leave now."

"I was on my way..."

"I don't care what!" Ferd repeated, vibrant, encased in charm, accepting no answer but the one acceptable to him. With steamroller good cheer, a loudness that included not just the company but the walls of the apartment, he declared, "Hey, you guys! I'm popping over just to say hello and catch a look at the progeny. Look at this!" He had brought a blue plastic bathtub boat for Sergei. "Does he go sea-faring by himself yet, Cowboy? Proud gramps! Man, to run into you visiting like this..."

D'Wayne rolled his eyes, sank into his chair, head between massive shoulders. Ferd was bringing too much cheer for the occasion.

"... find you like this without an appointment, Cowboy, it does my lonely heart good, it's a bonus, because at least somebody got himself a nu-cular family. Is what I hear squawking in there the progeny waking up? Aw, isn't it cute? Does it like boats yet? Pink is for girls, am I right, Sergei – blue is for boys and you're a boy?"

Amanda held the child close again. Ferd's eyes darted from Kasdan to Amanda to D'Wayne. He set the blue boat down. He sniffed the air meaningfully. "Diaper time! Somebody around here now gonna show me if it's a boy or a girl. Little details like that, not so important at its age, but gets to be vital when it grows up, are we on the same page, Cowboy?"

– 4 –

Since two's company and four or five, counting the kid, were a crowd, Ferd made it a quick visit. He presented his enthusiasm, good wishes, and blue plastic boat, and then, once the diapering started, backed gladly out of there. No need for a non-father to share the smeared caca experience. Leaving along with Dan also gave him an unexpected opportunity to develop the friendship plus business combo while the proud grandfather hurried on his way. Ferd Conway, proud senior partner, could just trot along with his junior partner.

"You think," Ferd inquired, "hey, slow down, you think he'll ever learn to go potty? You know, like on his own?"

He gave Kasdan a sideways, pursed-lips look, even his nostrils twitching and pinched, as if Sergei Mose smells were pursuing them down the street. When Kasdan said nothing, possibly insulted on behalf of his family, Ferd quickly made peace. "Jeez, maybe he's just having fun. The nice mommy rubbing him, tickles his chubby ass, kinda like that? I don't blame him."

Again Kasdan's infuriating abstention from response, not even a kidding one, followed Ferd's friendly probe. Ferd pitied the fretful court translator with his withdrawals, distractions, his addictions to gloom and the loser's life. Ferd was trying to rescue him, pull him out of cocksucking doldrums. He inhaled noisily to illustrate the oncoming thought. "I could just breathe the love in there! The family feeling!" He nudged Kasdan with his elbow. "Excuse the wake up poke, Cowboy, but besides the whole family devotion, very moving... the baby piss? Not being able to afford help? Clean-up?"

"We all pitch in," Kasdan said, while admitting to himself and not to Ferd that so far he had pitched in less than needed.

"Right," Ferd said, conceding the point, "and okay, we've had the nice visit, we've bid hello to your loved ones, we stayed until it was time to bid goodbye because it was in my heart to analyze what your situation and dire need is. So now we have a little summit conference, Cowboy?"

Early on, before Ferd used Kasdan for anything but translation services, he tried to call him Ace; once or twice he tried Big Guy, although Kasdan was actually only a medium guy in size, although diligent in Spanish interpretation; sometimes Ferd still used Amigo or Chico as a tribute to the profession. But he had settled on Cowboy, probably because Kasdan seemed to dislike it most. Ferd only teased someone he really cared about; he hoped Cowboy understood.

Because life should be a festival, Ferd led Dan to a place on Folsom where few summit conferences but many festivals were celebrated. He called it a "venue." Matey's Down Under wasn't an Australian saloon, despite its name; it was the West Coast headquarters of NAMBLA, the National American Man-Boy Love Association, which was going through difficult times because of recent hostile publicity about friendship between consenting children and mentoring adults. Ferd had offered the volunteer staff his legal advice, free of charge. (Of course, any billed expenses had to be covered.)

Since boys like snacks, sweet things, pretty bite-sized goodies to tease the palate, and plain saloon olives and hard tack don't fill the bill, Matey's Down Under was a tavern with a small kitchen, microwave and fridge, and pleasant semi-secluded booths with wooden partitions to shield courting couples from jealous eyes, at least partially. The courting couples often enjoyed demonstrating their mentoring activities. The benches had been rubbed shiny by backsides and etched with spillage from lazy snackers. There were also sticky spots. Ferd sighed contentedly. "Cozy," he said. He rubbed his hands together and ordered a pitcher of a microbrew draft. He poured for both of them, like a mentor himself, against the side of their glasses. "Some guys like foam, we don't," he declared.

"Tell me more," Kasdan said.

Ferd opened his arms, still carrying the charm excess he had dispensed for Amanda, Sergei, and D'Wayne, but the gesture was blocked by wooden partitions constricting intimate booth gestures. Adjusting to circumstances, he brushed a lank lock of sandy hair across his forehead. The transplants were doing well; no scabs at the sites, though new ones might appear if he sprung for a boyish follicle which might, in due course, turn out to be an advisable extravagance. Ferd would have to do the cost-benefit analysis, depending on his resources.

They sipped. Ferd regarded Dan. "Perchance having second thoughts, amigo?"

"Problem is, I'm not sure I've had first thoughts yet."

"Haha. But the violins are singing and the night is young, so let me tell you more."

Kasdan waited for the more. The walls of Matey's Down Under were moving slowly around him; the partitions of their booth were moving in the opposite direction, a carousel within the carousel. Beer, at this hour, on an empty stomach. He occupied himself with breathing deeply to remedy the momentary dizziness. He raised his glass and downed another refreshing swallow.

"Okay, to review, you've got the swartzer son-in-law, the daughter you want to make up to for your neglect – don't get me wrong, no blame accrues, you just found her, she just found you, but still – you got the congenital-type grandkid, who knows where that happens from? You got, to sum up, the responsibilities. On a need-to-know basis, amigo, I can promise you an outcome." He raised his hand, worked his shoulder, reached over the pitcher and their glasses to touch Kasdan's arm. "Outcome favorable," he said. "No capital offense, that's for sure, and it would be hard to fuck up this profit center from a little transport of funds plus real estate purchase details. All of which is, when you come right down to it, a contribution to your welfare by a friend sympathetic to your problems."

"You," said Kasdan.

"Right on! We'll drink to that." He raised his glass until Kasdan did the same. They drank. Ferd said, "Ahhh," put his glass down, high-fived the air since Kasdan's answering high-five was not properly located in the space between them. Ferd chose not to interpret this lack of high-fivery as reluctance. Kasdan's dizziness, perhaps caused by the beer, subsided, perhaps thanks to the refreshment of the beer. The walls were still.

The swinging door to Matey's Down Under swung open, letting in a flash of purple neon, illuminating the fading hand-lettered sign at the entrance, "We Support Our President's No Child's Behind Left Alone Act." A muscled dude in Texas rancher dress, Stetson with wide brim pulled low, paused to check his watch, his cell phone, and the company: no one at this early hour, before school let out, except Kasdan and Conway, a pair of obvious adults. The rancher proceeded inside anyway. Ferd could address him as Cowboy and receive nothing but enthusiasm for recognition of his achievement, mirrored wraparound sunglasses, snap-button rayon shirt with orange piping, and a protective coating of lip gloss against the sirocco winds of the South of Market district.

Ferd observed the new patron with a critical stare. The rancher sensed that he was being evaluated, waited to see if an invitation to share their pitcher followed, ordered his own brew, a Dos Equis, being a man with Lone Star style. No invitation followed; those were the breaks. Ferd whispered to Dan, "What a guy. An ass as big as all outdoors."

A golden oldie by Johnny Ray, heavy bass reverb, piercing sob of poor dead Johnny, issued from the antique Wurlitzer. Lights throbbed along with the music. After a short period of reverence, although Ferd didn't know if Johnny Ray was really dead, he continued to process the friendship between Ferd and Dan. Truth to tell, he suspected a lingering reserve. He was not imperceptive. While Johnny Ray sang about the little white cloud that cried, the lawyer acknowledged that life is often unfair and the quality of love and friendship is often not symmetrical. Some care more than others. Business can increase a budding intimacy; it can also bring complications. Issues turn up during human interface. But since Ferd could use Dan, needed to use him, and Dan needed to be used for his own good, Ferd would not give up. "Love your sense a humor, Cowboy, "he said when Dan responded only with a sullen watchfulness, "but you didn't laugh at *my* joke. He does have a humungous butt, didn't you notice?" Ferd took revenge by calling him Cowboy because it annoyed, it increased the sullenness, it gave Ferd a leg up. Sometimes, for variety, he still tried Big Guy.

Further truth to tell, Ferd really didn't want to increase the sullenness. He felt Dan should appreciate these masculine tribute nicknames, but recognized that intimacy and trust were issues he needed to work at. Affection, Ferd had discovered, was, generally speaking, a catastrophe; this was also true speaking particularly. Yet he knew that Dan, new father and grandfather, imminent future senior citizen still stuck in a lifelong decline, had good reason to reverse his slide. In other words, for this non-cowboy with a bummer of prospects, Ferd could offer a leg up.

His voice tamped down as Johnny Ray finished the rendition. Ferd's eyes flicked from side to side, eventually landing straight onto Dan's stare. He moved toward shy avowal. "Hey, Dan, ever since I was born, got to level with you... I've been in the witness protection program."

"Nice way to put it," Kasdan said. "For what?"

"Advocacy of the downtrodden. My point is, I want to raise you to uptrodden. A bright, sincere, formerly young fella like you deserves a little lift in your, excuse me, sunset years. Tax-free capital for the daughter. A financial cushion for the not totally promising son-in-law, no racism intended. The best possible care for the grandkid with the problems. Maybe some valid medical innovators out there... pharmacologies ..." He took a breath. This had a dual purpose, also letting thoughts sink in. "Plus, I gotta level with you, you can help me, too. So you see why we're created here on earth to be more than buddies, now and then colleagues, only meet for the shitty little Speedy Gonzales cases? *Friends,* Dan? Our destiny?"

Sincerity filled the booth at Matey's Down Under (actual proprietor: Todd).

It would be wrong to say Kasdan didn't see the logic here.

"I don't see the logic here," Kasdan said.

"Wrong, wrong, *wrong,*" Ferd answered.

Kasdan said nothing.

Ferd had found his desired station. He focused the tuning, increased the volume. "So now you're looking at the logic because I'm showing it to you. You're wrong, I'm right, although I blush to say it. Any shrink I'd use, the one I call for the psychos, the semi-plausibles – Doc Blinder, you know him? – will testify you've been in denial, amigo."

Foreign static competed with Ferd. A radio from elsewhere, mambo sounds spilling off a rooftop, a guy pouring tar but keeping in touch with the world; an active tar machine bringing tar smells into Matey's (now Todd's) Down Under. "So here's our deal."

"All ears."

Ferd held off with the Cowboy or Big Guy, trying to be extra nice. He badly wanted Kasdan's assent.

"You're wondering, could it be pharma-cuticles? No, nein, negative, that's beyond tricky up to the point of risky. All it is is money in the form of cash. It's sanitary. And besides, why would we move pharma-cuticles abroad anyway? That's the wrong direction. Money, however, you can draw it out of an account, or even more better, buy property you can rent or bask in the adoration of the local girls. Haiti, man, the Free and Independent Republic of *Haiti*! The banks over there got computers from the stone age."

"Why me, Ferd?"

"And the bars in Port au Prince? You want some entertainment? That's where old Pong machines go to die. They got saloons! It's a nostalgia trip, amigo."

"Why me?"

"You have a daughter and her kid, Amanda in case you need a reminder. You know what I named my daughter with this colored honey of mine? Nocturia, that means night-time urination, because I woke up and this hot honey was right there next to me, breathing like they do, up and down, in and out, so nine months later, voy-la! Nocturia."

"You don't have a daughter," Kasdan said.

Ferd hated quibblers. "That's a mere detail, Cowboy. Anybody ever tell you you're picky-picky? Nocturia would be yay years old now..." He held out his hand, measuring her size at about five feet. "... if I had her, but that honey of mine was a witch flew around on a broomstick, no, a *mop*, and flew right out of my life. Lucky me."

"Nocturia," said Kasdan.

"You like it? Hey, so I'm a bullshitter, and you didn't know that? But tell me, your experience with Mom Torres, and her what, her coven, they don't fly around on broomsticks?"

There was so much to learn, so much prosperity to bring into Dan Kasdan's life with the support of Ferd Conway. "Okay, I'm not a really spiritual person," Ferd confessed, unwilling to profit from illusions. "I'm practical. Some folks think I'm just out for Numero Uno, F. Conway, Attorney-at-Law, and to an extent that may be true. But to clear things up, you could just ask Suki if I'm not considerate of the other person."

"Suki? That's news to me."

"Thought it might be. Never you mind, sometimes my life is a closed book. But for the purposes of partial full disclosure, I explained to her..."

"Suki?"

"... I'm spiritual, really full steam ahead spiritual when I want to, you know, fuck her in the ass and she said she just didn't feel like it that day – stubborn little goddess like that sometimes – so then I took the time to explain and I greased her up good, KY jelly, *considerate* – you got to be considerate, Cowboy, if your desire is for a tight-ass lady... That's reality."

Kasdan didn't interrupt while Ferd lingered in the memory, took a breath, winced, shrugged, busied his electric skinniness with impatient maneuvers; pulled his fingers, but the knuckles didn't crack – never mind, went on.

"... and now she'll stipulate, you can just ask her if I deign to introduce you, I'm a real spiritual individual sometimes, Sunday afternoon, say, and nothing else going on, plus super macho on occasion – with Suki it's *my* choice, amigo."

"Give me her phone number."

"Haha, you want to check? You're a sense a yumer guy, Dan." He fumbled in his pocket and brought out something green with a chemical menthol smell, adding another flavor to the roofing tar and draft beer aromas. "A cough drop? Yes?"

"No."

"Dry mouth. Due to ample full disclosure on your behalf, Dan." The cough drop had gathered pocket lint. He popped it into his mouth, took a pleased suck at it. "*No* is so often your answer, may I offer that adverse comment as a friend on your behalf? That's how you were spending all your no-fun, no-chances-taken, no zip in your life till I come along to hand you a future on a silver platter. Okay, so maybe you had a secret sex life, but who doesn't? So it doesn't count. Am I right or am I right on, fella?" Ferd's eyes shone with pride in another convincing pitch, a boyish gleam that would have looked like an honest man's gleam if it didn't look like a dishonest one's.

The day was fading. The tar machine had closed down. The purple glow of neon from Matey's Down Under deepened as late afternoon fell across Folsom and a few early drinkers pushed through the swinging doors. *We each of us owe God one death*, Kasdan remembered. And added: I'll pay in advance with this one.

– 5 –

A generous-lipped, lots of teeth, only partly fraudulent son-in-law's smile from D'Wayne welcomed him. The baby was already bundled and strapped for his expedition to Father Boedecher Park, nicely purged of its drug dealers every morning, so that the Vietnamese kids in the neighborhood could yell and play like true Americans with minimum true American risk from exposed needles, exposed psyches. D'Wayne didn't mind giving his wife an hour or two for another Summit Conference with her unearthed daddy. Sergei slept snugly in D'Wayne's arms. "Later, man," he said.

Kasdan decided the smile wasn't really fraudulent. Strained, maybe; responsive to last night's pillow talk with Amanda; acknowledging this situation, which required summit conferences between a new mother, new wife, and the old guy who would have been a total stranger except that he happened to be her father and she had dug him out of bygone times. D'Wayne's smile merely qualified things: *Whatever, man.*

"Later." Dan and Amanda listened to his footsteps thumping down the stairs while he murmured to the sleeping child. Kasdan could also hear a crisp premonition of his own footfalls fleeing down those stairs of this walkup not far from his own, although in fact he wasn't fleeing, he was alert here in a chair, he was offering himself up to what was happening between Dan Kasdan and the daughter who had decided to find him.

Amanda sighed, shrugged, made her gloom clear in the dramatic way of a daughter. Her expression reminded Kasdan of his own when he caught sight of it in the bathroom mirror in the morning, despite his best effort not to do so. An idea came to him: She might be depressed by their resemblance. But in fact, she was lovely, as far as he was concerned, and surely he was not. Her body bloomed with a new mother's opulence, no afterbirth withering, life's other distractions redeemed by the distractions of a baby, her stalwart soul rallying to the troubles of a very difficult child – so it seemed to Dan Kasdan, who had not yet redeemed himself as a parent, and so what did he know? He knew D'Wayne didn't need to worry about redeeming himself. He knew something without precedent was flooding through him just as his life seemed to be merely winding down.

Because of Amanda, he now managed to piece together flashbacks of Margaret, her mother, and that long ago bounce in the dark, an ironing board set up in her room in the Ruby Tuesday Commune on Page Street, his clothes strewn on the floor, hers neatly on the ironing board, because she was a flower rebel with standards, avoiding the stain of mouse droppings, and she was also a liberated spirit with a certain plan she hadn't shared with this careless floater in the Haight, Danny... He touched Amanda's arm and she glanced sharply at it, wondering what the hell he was doing, and then relaxed into the touch as he left his hand there; he was her father, after all, so okay, okay. "Hi," she said.

In the streets outside, veterans of internal and foreign wars were dying from drugs, exposure, spasms of violence; there were hookers not yet dead from AIDS or at the hands of these crazed veterans. Men with corrugated signs and Styrofoam cups may only have been veterans of shock treatment or genetic curses, but give them some change anyway, they were telling the truth – everyone is a veteran of something. Boys from the Projects in diarrhea-crotch jeans were running what a funny one called "farma-cuticles, wanna taste?" On the streets of the Tenderloin there was mayhem and chaos, kids tripping on their pants, and watchful East Asian children sticking close around their mothers as they headed to school.

In this family's flat, D'Wayne's and Amanda's, there were also varieties of mayhem, plus actual hopefulness. Kasdan took it on faith; he intended to help it be true. In his long years until recently, Kasdan had been a man who merely persisted like a street weed from day to day, with the expectation to be occasionally cut down or trampled but, with luck, taking root again in an alley. And then Amanda happened to him. He lived now with open compartments in his heart. New matters created new mayhem.

By this time, D'Wayne, doing his own father duty, was on a bench in an island of Father Boedecher Park. Kasdan and D'Wayne's wife had their private business. It was up to the father to start things. The daughter let him take his time, letting her ample, muscled, country-girl body relax. She knew how sleek and prepared she was; she didn't care if her jeans were a little loose in the butt; D'Wayne liked her that way, and although Kasdan didn't know the rules of fatherhood, he knew enough not to tell her to pick jeans a size tighter.

Beneath the Latina, forever-tan skin she inherited from Margaret, there was a paleness now, something withdrawn, shy, almost Irish, not really skin like Dan's when he was a child, before time weathered it. Why did this strike him as wondrously lovely? It did. It just did because they were deeply, finally, totally related, no matter how difficult it seemed to be so.

Shit, this is complicated, he thought.

"What I want to say," he began. "I mean what I want..."

God-damn complicated.

"... I didn't have a daughter."

"I didn't have a dad."

"Now you do." He needed her to answer, Yes, I have a father. He was sure she was figuring out how to say it.

She said: "Maybe you wanted a boy."

That wasn't what he needed from her.

"Maybe a son would've...?" she asked.

"No, no, no!"

She had it wrong, he hadn't thought about having a son, he hadn't thought at that moment, at her conception, about anything except that his clothes were on the floor and Margaret's were on the ironing board and he should avoid kicking its flimsy legs, and maybe he had also been thinking but not thinking that Margaret was snug and warm... Beneath his careful confused old guy act, that of a loser whose time had passed, Kasdan hid the soul of a confused old guy. This new stranger to himself suspected that the remainder of his time would surely pass quickly and then he'd really and forever be a loser unless he finally, really, and forever found this daughter, this grandson, these someones who might carry his memory into the future. He said: "It's time to be, how about that? – start out at least, first of all – friends? Okay?" He tried again, startling her. "I already have enemies, only he doesn't know it."

"Who?"

"You'll find out someday, play my cards right."

She refused to play puzzles with him. "Hey, maybe you're being funny, that what you're trying?" She extended her hand. "Okay, shake." He took her hand. They simultaneously, both of them, cleared throats, then laughed, pretended to.

Kasdan released her hand. "You yawn, then I'll yawn, that's how it works."

Then there was silence for a moment until he coughed, and before he quite finished, she coughed, a small sarcastic tribute to let him know she was paying attention, although it was not a yawn to answer a yawn. They were both nervous; a normal procedure during fraught situations in life, permissible for young and old alike. They shared a rustle of coughs with no phlegm.

"All due respect, Dan, *Dad*, maybe you could have done something sooner to find me."

"How could I even know?" Unnecessarily, he cleared his throat, as if he might cough again. "With all due respect..." Stopped. No echoing sarcasm allowed. "But you were the one who knew you must have a father, you were the one, you could have – okay, you were a kid, your mother didn't..."

And now he did cough, phlegm included.

"Margaret," she said.

No more explanation, though no explanation had been offered. Margaret in Mendocino didn't believe in father hunts. That history was unalterable, despite Amanda's anger about the ancient story of her childhood. Dan was sad for the same reason.

"I know I asked the first time we met, I asked this already, but I guess I was thinking about other things, remembering your mother, trying to... You know how it is, you meet someone, you register a look, they say their name, you're still registering the look, so you have no idea what name they just said... When's your birthday?"

"I already told you." *Tole you*, Projects talk, D'Wayne's wife.

"I know. You did. When?"

"January Nine."

"Okay, thanks."

She wrinkled her nose in a grin that involved nostrils, not lips. "Funny thing, I remember yours and you never told me." *Tole* again. "March Three. Mom wouldn't tell me your name, but she thought birthdays were like a big-time mystic thing, *shared* that much with me. She believed in *sharing*. What the fuck's so mystic, she said, trinity about the number three? Especially when she was a Wicca? March the Third and Month the Third of the Christian year...?"

"January Nine. I'll remember."

Kasdan wasn't sure she believed this promise. He hoped she might learn to feel it in her body like a kind of love, a kind of love-making. Flesh of his flesh, blood of his blood, feel it like an offer and a plea for forgiveness.

At present, she had other nourishment on her mind. Through a mouthful of yesterday's BLT from the refrigerator, heavy on the mayonnaise, she made her own offer. "That piece of shit you drive? I don't want you to buy me a car, but you ever decide to upgrade, you really should, man your age, it ain't safe – whyn't you pass it down to me? Shopping sometimes, and D'Wayne gotta go to work, what if the kid has like an emergency?"

Although it worked okay for him, the Fiat wouldn't be any good as a trade-in. But why should he answer this at all? Kasdan may not have been the most insightful new dad of this daughter munching at her sandwich, but he recognized nagging manipulation when it hit him in the face. Okay, maybe in due course, he could pass the Fiat down, yeah, sure...

"Just kidding, Dad. Hey, kidding! You love your piece of junk, sorry I called it shit, many apologies, it's your blankie, like you're committed. Everybody gotta love something." A germ of mercy stopped her. She pulled at her front teeth. A sliver of bacon was stuck there.

"At least you were kidding without opening your mouth too much," he said. "Your mom – mother– *Margaret*, she taught you to chew with your mouth shut."

"Learned that all by myself. Figured it out, man, 'cause I hate spitters. So thanks a bunch." She stared at her hand with its smear of mayonnaise. "Dad. But D'Wayne, something else, what you never asked? I'm gonna tell you anyway. He ain't that much older'n me, just built big, works out, born like that – *big*. It's only eleven years, not like a father complex. Even in the Projects, he ain't old enough most times be my daddy. Was y'all here thinking that was my thang?"

"No." When D'Wayne came to mind, she slid into her fake ghetto act. Dan Kasdan's daughter had not grown up to be perfect. The veteran court translator knew that D'Wayne wouldn't say 'y'all' if it signified one person, singular; a man of pompous grammatical experience understood about such things. Amanda was laying on the collard greens with chitlins, the fake ghetto, to make a point. "No," he repeated, to be on the safe side, with all due respect for his only daughter.

"I ain't no D'Wayne's baby-mama neither, I'm his certify wife, Dad – only one he got." She blinked challengingly straight into her father's face. "Plus, only one he gets."

"Great. As long as he's good to you and Sergei."

"Which he is. We gonna keep it that way, bro."

She was being bilingual, like her father, and arrogant, as he didn't think he was, not usually. Since he had had his fill, he said, "Enough of that, okay? And I ain't your *bro*."

"Badda-bing," she added thoughtfully, but seemed to agree that her point was made and she could come off it.

Dan Kasdan and Amanda were wrestling together like children, like an inaccurate father and a daughter inaccurate in her own way; a daughter who graduated from high school, got good grades, pretty good ones, could have gone on from there but didn't. It was all not having a father's fault, wasn't it?

She had already told him that D'Wayne aced his G.E.D., not like the other Project boys. Nobody had any call to feel sorry for Amanda and D'Wayne. They were husband and wife with their beloved son, forever and ever, no matter what trouble came their way, one for all and all for one. They were even legal according to the paperwork of the stupid State of California and the fucked-up U. S. of A. They were different from the fatasses who give the world babies, what daddy? And tote them around on MUNI, stinking up the bus. Did you know, Dad, there are even white cunts – excuse it, *chicks* – get stuck by some dummy on a magic night of romance and then hitch a ride to Mendocino to join a coven, screw around with growers, and don't have the sense or the consideration for their daughter to hook up with a rich one? A grower like the one Amanda knew with ponies, an Italian espresso machine, and kids he took care of until they put him in Vacaville? And then due to megavitamin therapy, he convinced the shrinks he was cured? And they let him out? And he let his kids all ride around the corral on his ponies? Margaret had this trick she learned from some Tantric witch, you squeeze the muscles down there where it counts, maybe could have used them to grab a future daddy for more'n one enchanted evening, weekend max, before he...

"Let's get back to the subject. How long were you looking for me?"

"Never did," she said. "Don't flatter yourself. Never did."

He knew she was lying, she knew she was lying, and she knew he knew. Therefore she decided to amend the lie: "Not for a long time, but then one fine day I did." Decided on further amendments: "Pestered my mom, you recall the lady – Margaret? She wouldn't say. But a kid" – scrunched her face into a knot: "we hoff our ways."

The context was all off. She must have heard a television comic doing movie Nazi torturer; even her ghetto act was better. She was nervous; things come out wrong in nervous times; Kasdan was used to his translation clients blurting in court while Ferd Conway shouted, "Objection, Your Honor, objection!"

"Tell you what, Pops. If I find you... if I find you... you'll be the first to know."

His very own daughter making up for lost years by making a joke. That meant progress, right?

"When we was younger..."

Were, he thought, and had the good sense not to say aloud.

"... you wasn't looking for me and I wasn't looking for you."

"Were," he said.

"No, I weren't."

The pedantic court translator and newfound father had noticed at 850 Bryant, and in deposition or mediation with interracial and inter-ethnic couples – "mixed" was the preferred term – that either the white one learned from the black or brown one or the other way around. Sometimes it got mutually mixed up, which may have been the case with D'Wayne and this daughter of Dan Kasdan, his grammar and final g's not being passed along with his genes. Amanda was rhythmically socking her fist into her palm, probably a pastime which she had picked up from D'Wayne, signifying boredom, need-ing to do something other than having this conversation; signifying that she was not really bored, but uneasy and needing to pretend boredom.

There were further comments which she hadn't yet learned how to make, but she tried a further comment: "Oh Dad, I wish..."

He waited for something more.

Nothing more came.

There had to be more.

"So?" he asked, and she answered, "So." So it wasn't yet enough if it ever would be, although he had asked the question and she had given the answer, both uttering the same word, so. Not my fault was an explanation which excused nothing, even if sung together like a duet.

Her eyes were wet. This didn't seem right to Kasdan. He couldn't tell if it was anger or something different. It should have been his eyes and he should have been able to know what her wet eyes meant. Maybe it meant she had allergies, like her father.

Her eyes, he decided, were wet with emotion, anger or tears.

Now she swiped her arm across her eyes and puffed out her cheeks. Kasdan didn't know what his daughter was doing, except that she had a plan in mind. She said, "I ain't need to be white chick rich, Dad, or Dan? Should I call you that? But I wouldn't mind gettin' negro rich, you dig?"

He dug. It wasn't exactly a new plan. He thought of suggesting she could stick a feather in her hair, channel her inner Native American, and declare war over wampum. Sarcasm was not a productive way to unscramble their history, put together their future. He said, "You can call me Dad." He said it as mildly as he could, but he was flatlining on her sudden swerves. His beloved daughter, the pain in the ass. He seemed to recall that Margaret also had sharp teeth and a way of biting, but driven by horniness, he must have decided she was just funny. Those were the days, weren't they? He was younger then, wasn't he? He said: "Amanda, you can come off the rap now, please."

Amanda's father Dan, also a pain in the ass.

She sneezed. "The baby powder," she said.

And yet he didn't long for the days with his buddy Harvey, with Ferd Conway, with his clients, with the Indian and Pakistani all-you-can dinners. He knew where he stood with them. Knowing where he stood wasn't enough. Amanda might be too much.

Things used to be easier. What was going on in him was like a chemical imbalance and a chemical rebalancing. When things used to be clearer, things were still murky, nights were lonely; Harvey's companionship only lasted through a couple of beers and maybe dinner;

late afternoons in the fading winter light admitted sharp glints of despair; spite toward Ferd Conway hadn't yet led toward a drastic decision that, yes, an incident of fatality and profit might be nice. Nothing but love was supposed to be clear. Even love wasn't.

It may have been something chemical in him, but Kasdan decided the wetness of Amanda's eyes was tears, tears of anger or tears of love, or – his chemistry still speaking in him – or maybe not, only his own acute searching of her eyes. He was confused about himself when he should only be confused about Amanda and his grandson. Cows just stand there in the herd, chewing their cud; but shouldn't a man, even a court translator with his job of sitting, receiving, and monotone delivering, pursue what he desires until he gets it? Wasn't that the plan about Ferd and the payday result?

"You know what's a bad thing?" he asked. "The worst of it might be, and we should probably make the best of it, is I'm the only dad you'll ever have."

"I don't think about that."

"Okay, listen, plus, you're the only child – you're grown up now, you're not a child, I know that – you're the only kid I'll ever have."

She pinched a smile in his direction. Her lips crinkled and fluttered, and fell into a fleshy pout, and then pinched out the smile again. "Unless some overage punk springs another surprise on you, like I did, you think?"

It could happen, he thought. No, it couldn't. Yes, it could.

"I doubt it," he said. "Okay, but you're smarter'n you let on. You got me there. But I doubt it."

It seemed as if they were agreeing about something. Maybe this was progress, even if he wasn't sure what they were agreeing about. He wondered if the pink blotching at her cheeks was a rash, an allergy. He might have had a remedy for that if he had seen her grow up. "Dear," he said softly, which didn't mean all he meant.

"Okay, hi," she said.

The city was creaking behind them, traffic, subterranean rumbles in pipes and walls, San Francisco bent by premonitions of earthquake. In his state of anxious attention, he thought he could make out the hiss of electricity flashing through wires, water throbbing in hollowed concrete underground, the earth turning, getting ready for upheavals predicted by both geologists, astrologers, and witches in their covens. Buildings would sway, maybe fall. Kasdan believed he would never rest again unless he could discover his daughter for real, not merely confronting this resentful young woman with sturdy arms, no longer those of a girl, and breasts, ample ones like the breasts of her mother when an incident had taken place in the nearly forgotten past. One night it happened, must have happened, or maybe in a late afternoon, that the spark of Amanda was created through no will or intention of either the careless insistent person or the somewhat willing other person. But maybe Margaret had planned an outcome.

"So Dad, I was wondering, excuse the question... was she hot? Did you think she was really hot?"

He had thought so, probably, as best he could recall. He let the question pass.

"Something fierce was she? One of those *chicks* they had in those days? On Haight Street? So you couldn't help yourself? It was meant to be, haha? Destiny? Really cool?"

"Please," he said.

"Your karma was it?"

Let her get it out, Kasdan thought, she has a right. But when it's out, shouldn't that be enough? "In those days," he began, and then thought better of it. Excuses didn't work in Municipal Court, either. So shut up, he advised himself.

Shutting up didn't much improve the ventilation. The air was filled with abiding anger, with floating motes of regret, and with the smells of baby powder and crackles of bacon. It remained necessary for Dan Kasdan, as the more responsible or at least the older person around here, to say or do something helpful. Something helpful did not consist of self-justification, excuses, nor even apologies; heartfelt apologies might go partway if there were a responding heart. He reached for a move historically tested during times of stress: "Are you hungry? Want a bite? That half a sandwich, all it was – you in the mood for a slice? There's a..." He knew he was yapping. "There's a Soup Box down past the corner. Hey, we both know the neighborhood..." Yap, yap, yap; Kasdan disliked himself. And then, as if checking out menu options was their business: "Pizza, or that falafel place – the Saigon fish sit-down...?" *Yap! Shut up!* "A baby that time, it could happen, the way a lot of us were, the way I was then, those days, Margaret probably told you, your mom, I guess we didn't think at all..."

A dog barking in the street outside seemed to have a better idea of what he was going through than he did, and expressed it better. That mutt with its exasperated yapping communicated less confusion than Dan Kasdan, court translator, did.

He needed air. He needed a walk on Ellis, Eddy, Taylor, or O'Farrell. He hoped he wouldn't scare off his buddy, the dog.

Amanda stood, saying nothing. Had she finished?

"Now, here we are, so can't we just do the best we can?" he asked. "Can't we try that? Isn't that fair?"

"Try that," she said. He didn't know if this meant she agreed. He believed they should find each other when they could, and they should keep trying, and right now they should find a place for a decent hamburger, nice fries, a side of tomatoes for the benefit of life eternal or fully vitamined health while they waited for life eternal. Or whatever Amanda wanted.

D'Wayne wouldn't worry if he found them gone when he returned with Sergei. After all, Amanda was safe in her father's company.

Limbered with strolling along, life a little easier out here on Ellis, they found the strength to review a few details. Dan to Amanda: "I want to love you. Let's practice for that."

Staring at a slowly cruising Cadillac, a confiscated vehicle containing two alert plainclothes guys, just for something to stare at, she muttered, "Okay, I'll try, too." And then: "Maybe." And then: "I don't know."

They were both ignorant of a certain state of being, the entity of father and daughter, and of what such might be. At this moment in the Tenderloin, on the street, life seemed a little easier, but not what Kasdan would call actually easy. He touched Amanda's arm. She didn't pull away. He let it rest a moment and then removed it. She didn't bring up the subject of the Fiat or money. Maybe they were making progress. Even the dog he had heard yapping was silent. He had touched her arm for a moment and she didn't pull away.

The next time they saw each other, it might be as if this moment had never happened, but it had happened anyway. Amanda intended to defy good sense, her father's good sense, because it was necessary in the obeying of her own good sense. Even if it was not. It was still complicated, wasn't it?

"Hey, see that asshole over there? Here every day?" Amanda asked. "Ain't even got enough brain left to unzip before he pees."

"This neighborhood," Kasdan said, "it's been okay for me, but you'll want to move when the kid gets a little older."

"D'Wayne doesn't mind. I don't either, it's *homey*, Dad. I'm like you, especially when cash flow's kind of tight."

– 6 –

Absolutely, absolutely, Dan Kasdan deserved a break, or if he didn't deserve it, at least he needed it, absolutely. Feeling not very bright, he knew there were many questions he should be asking himself, the present one being why the break he chose was to accept an invitation for what Ferd Conway advertised as "the boys' weekend of fun and frolic." Of course, there were those pleasant prospects on offer, a drive down Route One to Big Sur, tucked among mountains, sea and forested canyons; they might find bears, deer, whales, sea lions; they would surely see waves cresting on stony beaches, redwood cabins hidden in narrow niches, back-packers hiking and bearing buttons and stickers devoted to causes ecological, political and astrological.

The Sixties and the Summer of Love survived on steep slopes just off the highway. He could justify a few days of retreat as a test of his deliberations. His struggles with Amanda exhausted him. Other people lived with many confusions; he had made a life that eliminated confusions. Now he was paying the price – many confusions flooding over him. It was time and past time to get clear about matters; someday, somehow, he surely would. Absolutely.

"Yeah, okay, why not?" he replied to Ferd's offer.

"Hey buddy, is that enthusiasm I hear?"

What Kasdan already planned about Ferd was the first drastic action he had ever taken. He said, "I was surprised, that's all. I guess I always need things to sink in."

"You'll be comfortable! I'll drive in my fine sports vehicle, personally make all the arrangements. *And* talk hardly no business. What's not to be comfortable?"

"Thanks," Kasdan said.

"And what if you learn things, you really get to liking me, the way I feel about us, how do you feel about that? What if?"

Kasdan didn't have an answer to this question. He would face the problem if he came to it.

Silence was always difficult for Ferd Conway. He repeated, "What if, Cowboy?"

Kasdan was preparing himself. When the time came, he hoped to be ready. For now, he said, "Sure, thanks, I haven't been to Big Sur in years."

Dan used to pass his life without making things happen. Ferd made things happen every day. Dan found a daughter he hadn't known – that was a thing that happened – but he wasn't geared for surprises. Ferd seemed to be geared for anything, even an annoying traffic stop on the road out of Carmel. The highway patrolman wanted to know why Ferd wasn't wearing his seatbelt. Ferd said he had been reaching for a "hankie." The patrolman looked startled at the word. He fixed his gaze sternly on the culprit. Ferd met his eyes briefly, then dropped them toward the electronic book, poised ready to emit the summons, until he said, "Your nails, Officer. I love your nails. How could I get nails like that?"

The highway patrolman had a manicure with neatly trimmed crescents of cuticle, his fingernails shining under clear polish. He beamed and leaned into the Mercedes. "Gelatin capsules, plus a high-pro diet'll do the trick. Your nails look pretty healthy yourself."

"Not like yours, Officer. When I make a left turn, I use the turn indicator, but if I had nails like yours, I'd be proud, I'd extend my arm into traffic. A legal left-hand turn, it goes without saying."

The patrolman rose into an elevated mood. "Go and sin no more, Champ," he said, strolling tight-assed, aware of being watched, back to the patrol car. Ferd turned to Dan. "Learn, my friend, always learn to be nice when it's appropriate."

He waited until the patrol car sped ahead. He waved to the officer, who lifted his hand in a salute. "Sometimes charm helps," Ferd said. "It's a cost-free asset, which you can't always count on, but sometimes. How about an omelet for brunch? Eggs Benedictus? On this special occasion, break your diet of no-fun eating?"

This weekend started out to be nonstop hour charm.

"You know that song?" Ferd was asking. "'You Can Take My Wife, But Please Don't Take My Boyfriend?' That cop sure had clean pink nails, didn't he?"

Charm all the way south.

Kasdan aimed to avoid discordant elements, although his aim didn't always succeed. He felt his eyebrows knitted together in a frown. Here on California Route One, on a weekend of fellowship, he was taking the air amid the low music of a fine German motor and the nourishing sights of redwood and pine, green mountains, the Pacific Ocean below the road. He tried for Zen or yogic or some other valid go-with-the-flow unknitting of eyebrows. To be at one with the universe, that was the ticket. Since he had agreed to just hang out with Ferd for a weekend, he had better hang out with a willing heart – at ease, goddammit. And his eyebrows obeyed the command. The frown came unknitted.

Ferd seemed to respect an effort Dan was making, himself breathing the air, also respecting the sea and shadowed mountains, driving silently at peace.

"Hey! That's a deer!"

Not silently at peace for long, however.

Dan intended to test the boundaries of friendship, something beyond his hours with Harvey and the guys at the Caffé Roma, now that he was learning about something else with Amanda and Sergei, his only grandson. Something else? The difficult practice of love. So he could also practice, try to, friendship with Ferd, who was no stranger, who wanted to be his pal, who needed him. Dan wanted to take charge of himself and make things happen. Other people did that.

It was a day of clouds, sunlight, breezes, salt air; hum of tires, hikers along the road, Ferd startled by a deer. Although Dan had reached the time in his life when he scanned a menu and thought of cholesterol, he decided that a nice three-egg Denver omelet, or maybe a Spanish one, cooked soft with a dash of cream, might be a good choice when they stopped for lunch. Or maybe huevos rancheros with a fat glop of guacamole. It was only right to celebrate life's surprise sudden turns.

Lulled, Dan wondered if he could learn to value Ferd's friendship. He would face the problem if it arose. Ferd had a powerful way of insisting on their bond and it was Dan's obligation to take it under due consideration.

After a life in the city, Kasdan knew about the weed tree ailanthus, the scavenger gulls, pigeons, and an occasional circling hawk, the stubborn green stems pushing through sidewalks, the moss extruded on breaks between cement steps; but here on the winding coastal highway, he came close to speaking aloud to Ferd about wildflowers and lichen, ferns and squawking bird heads in their nests. He resisted making appreciative remarks to his companion, who glanced at Kasdan's head turning this way and that, peering toward the hills, peering toward the sea, blinking as the road turned and sunlight sparkled on the windshield. Ferd recognized what Dan was observing. "Nature," Ferd said.

Kasdan agreed. There was nature out there.

Ferd elaborated: "Different. A change."

He was expressing mellow solidarity; Dan was his guest; decency was required. Dan made an effort. "I had a friend, we were kids, he didn't know the names of trees, called everything he didn't know 'dogwood.'"

"Plants, too?"

"Yeah. He even called dogwood 'dogwood,' but he didn't know that's what it was."

"He still your buddy?"

"That was when we were kids. Lost track of him."

Ferd was delighted by this news and the sudden burst of conversation. He pointed out the window as they negotiated a switchback. "Hey, there's a dogwood out there." Kasdan remembered reading that before the white people came to California, when this part of the coast was the domain of a band of Indians, a person could step no place without stepping on flowers. He said to Ferd, "Let's pull over a few minutes."

"You need to pee?"

"No, just get out and move around."

"We're almost there."

Kasdan could wait to bend for a wildflower descended from times before the Russian trappers, the Spanish explorers, the gold miners, and tourists like Ferd and Dan. What he was planning was bad enough. He would try not to step on a carpet of wildflowers.

Kasdan closed his eyes. The low drone of the motor was like consoling music. He thought of Amanda and his grandson. He saw a buck deer with tangled antlers leaping across the road, then mashed against the hood of the Mercedes and howling with death grief; he saw himself ending his confusion with his head on a deer's body; he jerked awake and saw that he was not drunk but hungry, low sugar, a symptom of needing that omelet.

"Dreaming, Cowboy?" Ferd asked. "I thought I lost you there."

"Started to doze..."

"Hey, you can do that, sleep sitting up? I can't do that. You got talents I don't even know about."

"I don't know about that."

"But it makes you wonder, doesn't it? Nature, raw nature plus human nature..." And he added after a moment: "What a combination."

Kasdan thought of snow; he missed it sometimes, that shift from white to gray in cities, and the melting, the gray flow pumping into underground pipes. He didn't ski. In San Francisco, you only saw a light dusting of snow on hilltops, erased by the morning sun. People with money went to Squaw Valley to ski among white blankets of snow, hills draped in snow. If he had money, he might try that, if it wasn't too late for him.

"Nature's a kick," Ferd was saying. Probably he had been making other ecological remarks while Dan was busy spacing out. "To me, sometimes I'd like to be a farmer, a nice red barn, or a guitar player with a little organic garden, if I had my druthers about things." Ferd was swaying to the music playing in his head. Upon further thought he amended his agricultural and guitar career interlude. "Sometimes, anyway."

Dan respected a man with a sense of rhythm, music in his soul. Even if the music was inaudible to Dan, it could still be a comfort for another, such as Ferd. But then, fully emerging from a car-induced, swerve-induced doze, he heard the radio softly playing a song about love and eternal loyalty, a classic rock station in Carmel.

Around a sharp bend in the road, their first destination announced itself. "Here we are. They got the beverages, postcards, redwood souvenirs, all the stuff, plus a full-service view, Pacific Ocean down there. Man, they got it all organized. A grampa can probably order up whales on the menu, kids want to see them spout. Those citations – that the word? – they burp up a storm."

"Cetacea," said pedantic Dan Kasdan, court translator.

Ferd pulled into the parking lot and snapped open his seat belt. "It's Nepenthe, man. Paradise on earth since maybe 1952."

Here in this narrow coastal strip, perched above the eager appetite of the sea against rocks, stood a dressed-up survival of the days when Henry Miller took refuge in a nearby canyon. The house first built by Orson Welles for Rita Hayworth later became a café where Joan Baez sometimes sang around an outdoor fireplace for gatherings of rapt flower children, lovers of folk music and barbecue. This was still America, so Nepenthe grew, now with a parking lot big enough for tour buses, long-haul trucks, and families pursuing cheeseburgers and other essential road trip amenities.

"Well, when you gotta go, you gotta go," Ferd was saying.

"I didn't mind waiting."

"What a prostate you must still have, man!"

They were thinking of different goings. Dan was shaking his head and Ferd asked, "What's that about?"

"Talking to myself. Sorry."

"Well, say it to me. You think too much and you don't decide enough."

"Sorry."

"I'm here to remedy that. Try to help a little, okay?"

"Sorry," Dan repeated.

Ferd waited a moment. "Okay, whatever. It's beverage time for me."

On Route One, the road from Carmel into Big Sur and then south, the ancient Sixties survived. Hitchhikers put out their thumbs and expected rides. Kasdan jerked forward against his seatbelt as, rounding the curve out of Nepenthe, Ferd braked for a young woman holding a cardboard sign: a smiley face in yellow marker with a red balloon within which she had inscribed the word 'PLEASE!!!' Ferd mouthed the word and squealed to a stop as the girl, probably no more than nineteen, ran nimbly toward the Mercedes convertible and jumped into the backseat, twisting her backpack but not objecting to her cramped place behind two traveling gentlemen. Wisps of straw-colored hair poked under a woven yarn hat. "Hey, guys," she said, "can you guess how long I had to wait for you two?"

Neither guessed. She pulled off the hat, shook her hair free, raked it with her fingers.

"Love your wheels," she said. "So where we going?"

We? There was a sudden sharp animal stink, far gone in decay, a skunk or a fox, wheels skidding over the oily residue. Neither Ferd nor the girl seemed to notice. *We*? Kasdan thought. Ferd was suggesting to the hitchhiker that they stop someplace, maybe turn back to the River Inn, maybe just down the road to Dietgen's – which, he explained, is now called the Big Sur Inn, where he and his buddy had reservations – or maybe someplace else that looks nice; enjoy something; get to know each other a little... *We*, the girl had said.

The straw-haired girl had a happy giggle. She had said her name, but Kasdan asked, "Your name again? I think I wasn't paying attention."

"You should. Lulu," she said. "Hey it's not my name back home, but I call myself that, 'cause I'm an inspiration to people, specially men." She didn't explain why the name, how the inspiration, all the external or internal workings of it, but added merrily, "So you can call me that."

"Lulu," Ferd said appreciatively. "Wanna be my boyfriend?"

Even looking straight ahead, Kasdan could feel her start upright (no seatbelt, of course). "You mean girlfriend?"

Ferd was in the swing of adventure. "Whatever! Just kidding, Lulu. Cowboy here's my girlfriend."

Kasdan felt previous San Francisco judgments returning. Alone together on the highway, Ferd Conway had seemed like a different person. Now he was Ferd again, but a Ferd who glanced sideways at him, worried that he might be a disappointment. "Hey, I don't know what gets into me when I'm together with a great lady and an old – he's not that old – best buddy. Apologies all around, okay?"

"So let's cut to the chase," said Lulu. "I'm working this road. A threesome suit you nice boys okay?"

"Pardon?" murmured Kasdan, but no one felt it necessary to take account of his question. Ferd took account, instead, of Lulu's question. "Inneresting," he drawled.

"Here's the deal, but only if you nice boys wanna. You spring for a room, one of these places, motels, campgrounds, Dietgen's, whatever, or if you're in a hurry, we can go for the Vacation Special, Road-Trip,

Bargain Package, which we manage with our natural-born equipment here in this cramped nice luxury sports car."

Ferd laughed. "I got a strong back, but I'm not so sure about my friend here's spine. What do you think, Cowboy? You got an opinion?"

Lulu was waiting. Ferd was waiting. Dan said, "Please pull over to the gas station." He turned to look at Lulu, sitting on the edge of her seat, no seatbelt, smelling nice, leaning over between Ferd and him.

Kasdan undid his seatbelt, Lulu noticing, taking it as an agreeable sign of things to come, but Kasdan was reaching into his pocket. He pulled out a crumpled twenty dollar bill. He regretted it wasn't a ten because there was frugality in his nature, unlike Ferd's nature. "Please take this," he said, handing her the crumple. "I'm going back to the Men's." And to Ferd: "Please, I'd like her to be gone when I come back."

She looked startled at the word *please*. Ferd looked startled in general. Kasdan did what he announced he would do, scrubbed his hands with abrasive powdered gas station soap, dried his hands on his pants because the towel was oily, studied his face in the mirror not because he was interested in his face but because he wanted Ferd and Lulu to finish whatever transaction they had in mind before he emerged. He wondered if he had been rude, decided he had been, and added this incident to the debits in his conscience. Now his hands were desiccated claws, thanks to gas station soap and bad karma. He waited. He opened the door when another motorist rattled it. He had compassion for the need to pee; his conscience didn't need any additional burdens.

Lulu was already in a corner of the lot, her face shining, discussing matters at a diesel semi's high door. Ferd turned the ignition key with no comment. Then he commented anyway, "A twenty was that? Hey, big spender! She had a repartee with us, all she had, and you slipped her a *twenty*? Well, in the future, no need to worry about frugal, because you'll be the proud shopper for wheels like this one, plus whatever else... And you know, don't you? I was just putting her on. Just gassing for the companionship of it, you knew that, didn't you? I was on your side the whole time."

When Dan just nodded, Ferd nodded also. He had to get used to Dan's sometimes not participating in repartee.

"Lulu Clapped-Up is what I'd call her, but hey, you have to agree she was cute bad news, wouldn't you? Don't you?"

They didn't have far to go now.

At the inn, Ferd's selection, little Hansel and Gretel cottages, caves, nests, low-roofed nooks of reclaimed lumber and harvested rocks, had been tucked helter-skelter into a rising slope. Pride and gaiety filled Ferd's face. "Loving hands made this, you dig?" He was channeling the time warp, getting into the time warp spirit of their adventure. "Listen up, not for economy or anything, but just because, we could ask for a pad with twin beds, because the serenity can get pretty heavy sometimes. You know, talk to each other? Converse?"

"You only reserved one room?"

"I left it open with a maybe, this time of the year."

"I think I snore," Kasdan said. "I like to read in bed. We better..."

"Okay, okay, it was just an idea. Sometimes people get lonesome, Dan."

Kasdan was trying to remember if it was a witch or the big bad wolf that interrupted the serenity of Hansel and Gretel. It was the witch. Kasdan's cottage had a fireplace with a musty smell of ashes lingering in the air. Logs and kindling lay in a metal basket nearby, a nice comforter on the single bed. Ferd gave him no argument, just a little repartee, on the matter of separate rooms. Whatever Dan desired this weekend was perfectly fine with him.

The inn's manager, a young man in carefully ironed Levis – already an unusual amenity – invited them into "The Commons" for a bed-time hot chocolate, "home-made in our kitchen, not that instant shit. You can scamper off to your room and brush your teeth right away, so don't worry your pretty heads the least about dental decay or gingivitis." He raised his eyebrows, poured from a pitcher with the Serenity Prayer baked into it, and filled their mugs. When Kasdan finished his home-made product, the young man floated back, saying, "Another splash? A nip of our complimentary brandy for nighty-night?" Ferd winked at Dan. He was a co-conspirator, sharing a secret. He accepted the brandy in his splash, as did Dan. Even without the wink, Dan understood what Ferd was trying to tell him. It was a solidarity wink.

"Anything you need, just pick up the phone," the young man, Todd, said. "There's a complimentary toothpaste at your sink – the little dohicky shelf up there – but you look like a pair of dudes who travel with everything that comes in handy. But if there's... don't hesitate!"

An acrid smell of wood smoke as Kasdan drifted into sleep, not worrying about placing the metal screen against stray flying sparks. He had come to the time in life when, what the hell, he could try living dangerously, although not yet to the point of sharing a room with Ferd Conway. But why was he even here, letting Ferd create confusions of sympathy, putting him at the risk of moving toward comradeship? Kasdan was discovering new dangers in the late changes of his life.

The next morning, closing day of their "Boys' Weekend," Ferd and Dan met for breakfast in the Commons, where a long table covered in a tie-dyed sheet was spread with granola and, for allergic guests, a hand-lettered warning about possible peanuts; bananas (with hand-lettered notice, ORGANIC WHEN AVAILABLE), oat bran muffins ("Home-Baked In Our Kitchen"), orange juice ("Fresh-Frozen"), and Certified Fair Trade Shade-Grown Coffee. The afternoon manager, Todd, with the ironed and starched blue jeans, seemed also to be doing morning duty, his face unlined and starched, like his jeans. In the light of the rising sun, Kasdan noticed a glint of stud in his left ear. He rubbed his hands together and said, "Brisk! But the sun will shine today, just for us! May I invite you to make the most of it?"

After breakfast, alert after their fair-trade coffee, Dan suggested, and Ferd eagerly agreed ("Sure thing!") that they climb down the rocks across the road and see how close they could get to the water margin. There was Pacific Ocean nature out there, including a freighter bound for someplace with a cargo of something. Dan enjoyed the scramble down the rocks; enjoyed that he could still scramble. So could Ferd, who was here for exactly this sort of thing, even if it wasn't what he had on his mind. When Dan remarked about whales, sea lions, long-beaked pelicans swiftly diving, the rhythm of waves breaking against the lip of rock on which they perched, Ferd was with him all the way. "Birds, too," he said, although he also intended to discuss business concerns. Patience was a quality Dan was obliging him to develop.

Their knees were touching, just above the white churn of waves, the salt spray. Dan took deep breaths. He could hear thin eddies of brine gurgling and brawling between the rocks beneath them. Ferd sighed deeply. "Sometimes I'd like to be like you," he confessed, "stay home nights, no teevee – but I've got cable, and there are so many options – just stay home and read one or two fiction novels."

"Make yourself an egg omelet?"

"Why'd you have to say that?" Ferd squinted, moved his knees away, scrunched up his face, flashed a reproach at Dan. Sarcasm was a violation out here in nature. "I get it," he said, "went to college plus, don't forget, law school. Stay home, my buddy, like I said, only with some folding cash in the cookie jar and the phone number of a short-order sweetie, and I can say, Come on over, take a cab, I'll pay... Tell me that sounds good to you?"

It did. But right now Dan was busy with the smell of ocean, wafting its cleansing brine toward them. Ferd pulled up his pants to catch a little sun above the ankles.

"But then of course, if you had a righteous teevee, you'd know. I saw on this science channel, you know why blood is salty?" Dan must have commented on the air. Ferd answered his own question. "It's like the ocean! We used to be fishes in the sea, many eons ago!"

"I guess," Dan said.

"I *know*," Ferd answered triumphantly "thanks to the miracle of educational stuff you don't get on your teevee. I'm not saying you're a deadbeat. Even today, you could probably afford one, plus cable."

Dan heard himself mumbling. Probably he was making a comment or at least a remark. The rhythm of waves against the lip of rock made it unnecessary to do more than emit comradely, nature-appreciating murmurs.

All good things must come to an end, a rule which also applies to a two-day jaunt by future collaborators in an interesting deal which might turn out to be a great thing or not to be a good thing. But as long as they were still on the coastal highway, California Route One, leaving the outpost of Big Sur, heading back north to San Francisco, the mood of comradely warmth could be preserved. Driving intently, eyes fixed on the winding road – a life-saving intentness and fixedness – Ferd continued expounding on his subject for the weekend. And because he was imbued with total sincerity, this time no bullshit from a person qualified in the bullshit area: "You probably know I'm sort of, feel like sort of, a brother to you, even if you're the depressed personality that you happen to be. You should recognize things about yourself."

"Okay, right, thanks."

"So what I personally do is I get out of being a depressed personality. I keep moving, keep moving, all the time keep moving up and ahead. You stay there, stuck in the mud. I do it different, onward and upward. It doesn't look like the same thing..."

Dan mumbled, remarked, commented, "No, it doesn't."

"...but bottom line, long story short, we start from the same place, normal hopes and dreams. Basically I'm your brother, Dan, almost like blood – you know that?"

" 'Preciate," Dan said.

The memory of a clean and stony smell of salt waves, of mountains meeting sea, made them both stop talking. A darkness below the railing of the road, a moving shadow in the ocean, looked to Dan like a seal family or even a baby whale undulating, practicing its moves. Then the world as it interrupted his gaze westward. Behind them on the road came the winding sound of a siren – check, they were not speeding; check, they were wearing seat belts. A highway patrolman, red beam on high, swerved into the right lane, pursuing a culprit up ahead of them. It was a good omen. Together, Dan and Ferd sighed with relief. But the shadow image of seals, sea lions, or a baby whale had vanished.

Ferd paid attention to the steering wheel. He didn't want to go too far, too fast, but it wasn't about the driving. "I'm laying all this out, Dan, as a true friend. We spent a nice couple days, just so's I can open up, reveal myself, help you by revealing me, things men can share." He stole a quick sideways glance at his passenger. "Okay, okay, I'll say it. I'm not all I want to be. I know that. In your own special way, you can help me be better, and in nature back there in Big Sur" – retrospective sniffs of air – "I felt it, I know I can get closer to where I want to be. Not just a very well-off person, much more important than mere net worth. If we're friends, business plus friends, partners, I'll be..." He left the matter open to Dan's intelligent listening. "Can you see that?"

Kasdan tried. He was embarrassed. If he held Ferd's fate in his hands, assent was called for. But he had recently discovered other responsibilities, a daughter, a grandson. It seemed that acknowledging the pleasures of a drive, a change of scenes, a cozy inn on the Pacific coast, a clamber on rocks to the edge of the ocean, was as far as he could go. "I've always loved Route One out here," he admitted.

There were disturbances in Dan's chest, a flutter of anxiety. It was hard for a stubborn man, set in his ways, to give up a serious plan. But soon he would be back on Ellis Street.

Coastal California Route One and Big Sur now belonged in the realm of nostalgia, time gone by, which happened to be two hours ago. Here came the sprawl of San Jose and then San Francisco's arterial roadnets, feeding the city with traffic.

"That was a fun adventure, wasn't it? We did have fun, didn't we? Don't we, Dan?" Relaxed, one arm embracing the wheel, Ferd hummed a tune out of tune, trusting that Dan shared an abiding love for the Beatles. *All we need is love, love is all we need...*

Ferd's heart yearned, throbbed, like any other living person's, and also could be gladdened. Dan's closest thing to a brother might have been Harvey Washington, but the black detective was too sad, too pissed off by what life had dealt him, to be much fun during, say, a couple days in Big Sur.

Despite himself, and needing not to be, and with a bit of complicating panic, Dan Kasdan was moved by Ferd Conway. That way lay confusion. Kasdan hoped that, with events to come, he could surmount his warm feelings.

− 7 −

Kasdan disapproved of men who stalled, such as himself. He needed to stop. Consequences made him uneasy. Ferd was right; he had grown comfortable saying *no*. Dealing with *yes* required the acquisition of authority and Ferd was providing it, but uneasy lay the head that didn't wear a crown.

Kasdan presented himself to Ferd with blank stares, aggressive abstention. He asked if Ferd was laying a game on him. (Politely, he didn't say scam.) Ferd answered that it wasn't a game, but of course, life is a festival, so let's enjoy the run-up. All would come clear when the time came. "Finance is a practical matter, I tell you that sincerely, Dan, not to negate festival. I've got to be hunnert percent sure you're my guy."

"Up to the job, you mean."

"Passing the test of friendship, trust, and since you will undergo a bitty bit of stress.... call it ambition to get you through."

"You mean you're counting on my greed."

"Whatever. Your bravery, my friend, so try not to be hostile. This is still test time. Lunchtime, too, by the way, but no beer or brandy Alexanders, no Matey's Down Under."

"Todd's."

"How about a dining experience on me? Is that a go?"

Sociability resembled friendship, friendship was like marriage although less likely to end in divorce, and connection was part of how Ferd got the work done. Following the Boys Weekend in Big Sur, passing the time together in fog-swept, fun-filled San Francisco was the graceful way to go about it.

"Make yourself comfortable," Ferd urged in a sharing tone, striking the right note for strolling lunchwards. "Make yourself even more comfortable than usual, even if, in your opinion, you're okay. Go for à la carte, my friend. Since you don't like to be called Cowboy..."

"Or Gaucho."

"... or anything not your correct name, Danny, today I want you to make yourself absolutely table d'hôte. Speak your mind, your doubts and trepidations, and I promise I'll not accuse you of coldfeetism. Not out loud, anyway."

He threw his arm around Kasdan's shoulders. Gulls came shrieking overhead. Not to be nervous. Nobody could interpret Ferd's brief manly hug as anything but camaraderie, even in San Francisco. Still, reaching out in a snatch of male bonding, Ferd took the risk. Living boldly offered an example to Dan, although they were both startled by the sudden swoop and swift departure of the flock of predatory birds. "So much garbage in the streets," Ferd said. "More flying rats than there used to be, you notice?"

As they proceeded from south of Market toward an informal burrito and a sincere exchange of views, Ferd glanced fondly down Clementina – the alleys here were named after Gold Rush era washer girls, imported to do the laundry and provide good times. The wooden lean-tos were gone, replaced by senior housing cement blocks. The two buddies stepped around a cluster of hypodermic needles, passed a suspicious wet spot and a pile of cardboard where recent sleepers had paused overnight, passed the alleys between medium-rises where dust swirled and settled, swirled and settled, and sometimes lay undisturbed, eventually sprouting green shoots. "Nice," Ferd said.

They shared a fondness for ailanthus, the trees of heaven, which grow like weeds in San Francisco alleys. Reading Dan's mind, Ferd stopped to sniff at the licorice-like yerba buena in a crevice; broke off a stem and put it near Dan's nose. "Very nice," he repeated, "how God gives us green stuff."

"Sucks up the pollution," Kasdan said.

"Naw, naw. Where's your aesthetics? I mean it's pretty. It's very pretty, Cow... Dan." And in this mood of cajoling ease, he didn't add his observations about breaking up the monotony of worn-out architecture or opportunities for real estate turnover or how the fucking gulls and pigeons, whatever, carried seeds in their shit, the rats, the rat shit, but he did say: "Wind off the ocean, man, it swirls around," meaning that God's greenness could try to take over, as it does, even here, God making a best effort to provide vegetation. He slipped a sideways glance toward Dan, hoping to be recognized for the poetry in his soul. In the place where soul is found in a person.

Where that space could be found in Ferd Conway if a friend looked for it.

The moment gave Kasdan a moment of pause.

"Sometime why don't we have a walk in the country?" Ferd asked. "Golden Gate Park. I know this retired hooker grows her own vegetables out near the beach, where the cops don't circulate. She's white, all the other farmers are Cambodes, Viet Cong, squirrel-eaters. Sometimes I think it's, you know, majestic, that's the only word for it. The gooks catch the wild cats and cook 'em. You like cat chop suey? And the raccoons? Immigration policy, let the folks in, and that's what you get – a park with natural animal population control."

"Majestic."

"You got a better way to describe it? How people make out? Survive? My retired hooker friend, she was a client – shoplifting – they took away her food stamps, so now she's a what you call urban farmer..."

Lost in thought for a moment, actually just enacting Lost In Thought, he drew the moral for today's ecological stroll and burrito: "What I'm saying, I survive better than average and you deserve to share in above-average return on your commitment to life." No Cowboy here; super-nice sometimes worked better than one-upness. "Your only daughter, Dan. Your one and only grandkid so far. Knock on wood."

He rapped his forehead with his knuckles. Today's niceness required not rapping Kasdan's forehead.

"I usually avoid anything illegal," Kasdan said.

"Non es problema! Up front, you have plausible deniability!"

"To me that suggests – "

"Hey, a term of art. Listen up, why would I go to law school, take the bar, pass the ethics quiz with flying collars – haha – and then risk it all just for a secure future for you and me, plus your newfound family? To which you owe a lot of catch-up?"

If Kasdan wasn't taking the hook, Ferd would have stopped by now. Kasdan murmured: "Plausible deniability..."

"You got it! I'm so excited I can count on you, pard. You're on board! You get it!"

"Not unless you fill in the details."

"Until," said Ferd, this correction an explanation, "not unless. Hey, I'm an attorney, I know niggles when I hear one. So far, full well, we're just beginning the be-geen, Cowboy, even though me and you, we're been through a good legal relationship all along. We've done business, we've done amigo on the side. Remember that first time when you translated for Pablo or Pascal, whatever the fuck his name was, and I said you're terrific? I was only the court-appointed defender, so what was I supposed to know? But that was the beginning of when I knew someday we would have even more of a deep partnership."

Dealing with product – human beings from whom he could draw something useful, such as capital and income – Ferd was like the Safeway checkout machine. He scanned for the bar code. Each product wore its own very individual code. It was Ferd's job to decipher. Kasdan needed money, a lot of it. He also needed stirring up. This happened also to be Kasdan's opinion concerning himself.

So here might be where Ferd Conway could go wrong. Kasdan's code might not register correctly. He was eccentric, a Tenderloin bachelor, depressed so long he mistook depression for contentment. Ferd, with his experience at the Hall of Justice, took account of contingencies, such as an individual personality. It made life more interesting, like a festival. It made life more difficult. Sometimes it made Ferd Conway irritable.

So be it. He was checking off his favorite moral imperative: no fucking someone over without a warm compassionate smile. The ironic notch at one corner of the Ferd Conway mouth was optional equipment, adding to festival.

Also engaged in a thinking process, Kasdan questioned Ferd's genuine affection for him. Friends don't let friends go out into the world with smiles flicking about the mouth in that dissonant combo of compassion plus notches of disdain.

So what, at this lunchtime on a sunny dry San Francisco day near the Hall of Justice and its satellite bail bond shops and burrito resorts, was the program?

Explanations offered by Ferd Conway belonged to a different geography of explanation from those of other explanatory persons. They circled and ducked and basked in the sunlight; they doubled back and feinted and dodged in the general neighborhood of apparent clarification. They wandered restlessly through the legal and less legal universe, always expressing heartfelt sincerity. They really meant to please. They provided ample hints, suggestions, and promises of profit. They confused.

In the lock-up world of 850 Bryant, Ferd's miscreants usually came to know that their trouble was about to continue. As Ferd turned toward Market Street and the Tenderloin, touching Dan's elbow to guide him, his explanations clicked into place without actually making things clear. Frequently in court and in settlement conferences, he practiced the same skill. His summations caused judges to bang gavels. Sometimes they elicited threats of a tour in jail for contempt. ("Not *intentional* contempt, Your Honor. But if so, I apologize. I meant no harm to this distinguished jurisdiction...")

Dan Kasdan was not alone in his sense of the difficulty in finding access to what Ferd had in mind.

On the sidewalk outside 850 Bryant, among its geologic layers of litter and grief, they watched the once and future perps conferring with loved ones and crack connections. Bereft significant others of men moving along on the great chain of perpetration crunched their takeout tacos, licked guacamole from their fingers, dreaded the afternoon sessions in court, where smoking was not allowed. Hustlers hustled in winsome microminis, seeking those who could use an open-air spasm during the lunch break – females with short fat legs, trannies with long skinny ones and shadowy mustaches. Carts wheeled paper products up a ramp into the courthouse, bringing photocopy packs and toilet rolls and forms to be filled out, filed, and shredded. Jerry Barrish, the bail bondsman and metalwork assemblage artist, strolled by, treating himself to a sit down and be served lunch destination.

"That's Jerry," said Ferd. "Hey, Jerry!" – a hello transmitted by waves and delighted mouth-openings.

Jerry had better things to do than to wave back at Mex-eaters. He was aimed toward souvlaki or moussaka at the Six Brothers from Piraeus in the alley.

"That was Jerry," Ferd said with satisfaction.

Kasdan jiggled an invisible weight in his open hand, up and down and up and down. "So, Ferd. So. What are we doing?"

Ferd sighed. So hard, so delicate. Well, he had this money and the IRS seemed to think he might have it. They could go after the big corporations, the piggy LA partnerships which only hired kids out of Yale, but no, not the fuckin feds. In terms of legal art – he hoped his pal, the court translator, could understand this – it was a single-bind situation. Normally the f.f.'s would be too stupid to audit him, but in this case they were going for some kind of civil service quota deal. They were sniffing around what they considered hints or evidence or maybe just hints of evidence. Assholes. Probably someone told them something, someone who had something to gain by blackening the reputation of a well-respected San Francisco attorney, which was not the worst thing that could occur in a devil-may-care life filled with festival, but these jerkoffs were darkening his financial independence, his freedom of investment and quote-unquote joy-de-veever. These assholes, these jailhouse informers, these convicted criminals.

"What's the job, Ferd?"

Ferd had a good friend, mention no names, who as a courtesy accepted a Lexus plus a watch instead of a fee from a coke dealer who was going to prison anyway; you can't take the bling with you to San Quentin; drove the vehicle awhile, showed up with it on dates; wore the watch; sold it for cash in South City – the wheels not the watch – no taxes to declare – but did the IRS bother this close personal friend, no names, of Ferd? Not. Instead, they were looking to bother Ferd Conway, probably some Asian auditor in a cubicle in the Federal Building, doesn't even understand that an attorney is a person who represents the guilty and the not provably guilty alike, because that's the American way. Some jealous Asian auditor who lives his life at the YMCA without a festival attitude and sends his pay to a wife with a bunch of kids in South Korea...

"Ferd! What's the job?" Besides English, Kasdan spoke Spanish. That was his professional expertise. So Ferd, please stop the charm and the info about other people's tax scams and, instead, tell: How did Kasdan qualify?

Ambling buddies together; yet Kasdan still didn't have a grasp on the proposal. Pardon, but would Ferd excuse his incomprehension?

Ferd sighed. This was okay with him, to sigh, because in any case a man had to breathe and he might as well do it by sighing. People in general were pretty lacking in mental swiftness. Ferd did a lot of breathing by means of sighing. He was glad to review the deal for his dear friend and junior associate. "I thought you'd see that on a need-to-know basis, it would be better not to ask too many questions."

"I'm nosy," Kasdan said.

"Your kind, no offense, your people, they get ahead that way. Even if you personally never did, get ahead I mean, probably because gelt, no offense, money was not your object until your daughter is in abject need of some. The kid, what's his name again? The grandkid?"

Kasdan thought he replied 'Sergei', but distracted, didn't actually speak. Ferd thought better of repeating the question. On a need-to-know basis, he didn't need to keep on the tip of his tongue Kasdan's autistic or dystrophy or cerebral palsy gargoylism or whatever kind of shit syndrome grandbrat's name. The rug rat. Sergei Mose.

The reason Kasdan didn't reply aloud was not that he wasn't attentive. He was concentrating on the question about where some kind of money came from and why Ferd particularly needed Kasdan's help with it and whether, without being informed, he could afford to continue along with Ferd's offer.

Dot com... treasury... loans with interest... backers... stockholders... "But the fucking feds!" Ferd was still happily emitting static.

Kasdan was thinking: Asian massage parlors? Uncut cocaine? Skimmed payments to cops? Judges? Vigorish? After-hours protection for Matey's Down Under, plus regular hours payment to facilitate hospitality for chicken queens dating fresh-faced kids playing hooky from middle school?

"Fuckin feds are nosier 'n your people, excuse it again, I'm on a roll. It's just an expression. 'Jesus saves, Moses invests!' Excuse the kidding! Mean no harm! Nosier 'n Armenians or Hungarians. They're grabby, too."

"You don't want to tell me," Kasdan said.

"I just did."

"No you didn't."

Ferd's repertory of sighs included a new tune. It was a contented and respectful one. "That's why I like you, that's why I pick you to collect your commission, let's say a good per cent on the deal, off the top, and not someone else. Because what if people say you're sort of a nothing guy except you speak Spanish and translate okay, but actually you're one hell of a lot smarter'n anyone but me thinks – one fuck of a lot. I take off my hat to you."

Kasdan watched while Ferd lifted an invisible derby or perhaps a fedora into the air above his head. South of Market motes, dust stirred by feet and traffic, flickered like fireflies in the sunlight. The hat was not visible.

"Only I'm not wearing a hat, but you get the idea."

"Cause I'm basically smart," said Kasdan.

"Any smarter, you could wear a roadie tee shirt, take up a retirement career in bike messaging, deliver meth, make good tips. Steal muffins off the food carts..."

In one of the alleys named for Gold Rush era washer girls, Jessie, Minna, Tehama, or Clara, between a parking lot and a whorehouse said to have been used most recently as a rehearsal space by a Grateful Dead cover band, the tribe of mighty-calved Frisco bike messengers had homesteaded a space for lunch, comradeship, and an occasional restorative jolt of methamphetamine. They understood each other about pumping up hills in low gear, muscle cramps, dehydration, and taxi pigs suddenly opening a door as a crippling or concussive joke when a dude was just trying to earn his tip by quick use of a shared lane. The bike messengers didn't know enough to harvest the wild urban fruits nearby, ignored the blackberries that had somehow appeared among the vines, weeds, and bushes in the broken pavement next to the fence. Maybe they worried about thorns. The pigeons knew better, avoided scurvy through Vitamin C nutrition, eagerly darted among the berry clusters, stained the sidewalks with creamy droppings. Tobacco chaws added brown bike messenger droppings. Rugged individualists, some of them liked to tuck Skoal into their cheeks, while others preferred Copenhagen. Pedestrians tended to avoid this corner, but as a friend to the working man, Ferd waved cheerily: "Hey, Bilge! Chillin' out? Marvie! Your band got a gig at the Chameleon?"

And still with his friend of the working man cheeriness, murmured under his breath to Dan: "Fucking losers. Speed kills, plus it gives pimples. Don't you love how this town takes care of the losers?"

When Ferd began to skip grammatical sequence, subordination of clauses, pauses for logic or breath, it was a sign that he was in passionate convincing mode. Kasdan appreciated passion in a person, especially one who sought to protect him from a late life career as a bike messenger, one who was busy remedying his own return to the dust from whence we came. But having shown Dan a gathering of losers, Exhibit A, Ferd proceeded to a phase of sober brooding.

"It's in my condo. I keep it in, you may not believe this, a shoebox, and you can guess the consequences. No interest on the principal, just that polish smell. Tied up with a shoelace on a temporary basis. Someone needs to carry it, invest it, pay the charges, have a nice tropical vacation, but that's in addition to the per cent handling fee, which is only right. No taxes from you and me for the Feds to steal. My thought: foreign real estate in a place with rotten computers and the law of the forest!"

"Me," Kasdan said.

Ferd nodded. "You're the guy, Cowboy."

"Don't call me Cowboy."

"Sorry, I forget. You the man, Gaucho."

He waved away a fruit fly traveling incognito among the inorganic motes in the atmosphere surrounding this negotiation. They were entering Panchita's Numero Tres. Ferd was hungry and hoped Dan was the same. Appetite was always a good sign. "Let's order first, okay?"

Due to the stress of business, Ferd had forgotten his plan about a sit-down and wait for the waitperson lunch. At the counter, while they watched undocumented servers doing their jobs, hands encased by regulation in clear plastic, Ferd plucked a blackened strip of emery board from the pocket where he kept pens, cards, scraps of reminder paper. The pocket was his all-natural-fibers portable office. He buffed his pinkie. He shrugged and apologized to Dan for his manners; it would be different when they took a table. "Snaggle-nails. Maybe I got to eat more protein. Do you have any thoughts on gelatin, Dan? What I hate is I really hate a snaggle-nails problem, how about you?"

There was also a smell of shoe polish when he held up for inspection the results of his buffing. Ferd Conway was improving his look for Dan Kasdan, sincerely telling the truth about his shoebox full of money, while also asking for extra guacamole on that pork burrito, "Chica," because avocado and sour cream might be just the ticket to save a fellow from the embarrassment of fragile fingernails. "Feefty cents for extra," said Chica.

He splurged on a side dish of Mexican garnishes. He dipped a finger into the guacamole and sour cream, soft and oily food elements which can be the best part of an okay day. He licked his finger. He sucked at the soft stuff, preparing to deal with the sinewy

stuff in due course. "Veggies," he commented. "Very beneficial."
When Ferd's precedents about Mexican garnishes became habitual,
they graduated into a tradition.

He held up a warning hand, when Dan reached into his pocket.
Don't grab! "One check, Chica." He paid. They carried their com-
partmentalized Styrofoam plates toward the patio picnic tables and
benches which served for casual indoor dining at Panchita's Numero
Tres. They scored a corner under a SKI CANCUN poster. Ferd
preferred privacy for today's indoctrination activities. The poster
depicted an Indian-faced, serape-draped peasant, under a sombrero,
slaloming down a sand dune.

They ate in silence for thirty or forty seconds.

Fortified by nourishment, Ferd shifted into philosophic gear. He
explained to his best friend why it was more expensive to be poor
than rich, "not that you're really dirt poor, Cowboy, I'd never say that,
you're rich in precious family and that's priceless. But if you're without depth in financial resources, you have a moral obligation to
spend money to show you're on top of things, like a real man. If
you've got it, you get to not give a fuck."

"I see."

"Not yet you don't. I'll continue. Consider this a lesson from the
other side of the mountain. If you're poor, you think about money all
the time. You worry. You spend more than you got – credit cards – to
prove you're in good shape when, actually, you're dying. Sound
familiar? Me, I'm mezzo-mezzo, which means I could be better. But
you're not even single mezzo, Dan..."

"I'm okay."

"... so that's what I'm here to remedy."

He touched Kasdan's elbow. He offered another compassionate
moment of talk-lessness so that the import could sink in. He wiped a
tortilla across his garnish dish, but all but a green smear of the fifty
cents supplemental guacamole and sour cream had already been
gleaned.

"If you carry cash offshore, to Grenada, say, or Switzerland, that's
so yesterday, so twentieth century. The feds plant their agents everywhere who should be protecting us against terrorists, but no, what do
they care? So depending on the regime we put in due to corruption
and payoffs by the big boys, the Trilaterals, they can go after it. Off-

shore banking isn't the safety thing it used to be. It's tacky." He glanced at the SKI CANCUN poster, shrugged, made a what-can-you-do grin. He leaned close. He was moving in. Okay, *now*: "That's why I'm sending you to buy this beachfront property in Jacmel."

"What? Jacmel? What Jacmel?"

Ferd beamed. He was winning Dan over. They were already quibbling about details. He asked *What*? And *What Jacmel*? Ferd had worried that Dan might just say no, walk away from the deal, which was why he had softened, sweetened, greased, treated for the Super Burrito Extra with corn tortilla, done the job he was so good at – making friends, bringing trust into a suspicious world.

He pulled his tan lock across his forehead. "Jacmel, Haiti," he explained. "Hardly even offshore, if you think about it. Puerto Rico a stone's throw? Could be the Havana of our time, jalopies and faggoty little French cars, and the real estate is depressed these days, but when things straighten up, the chaos and killings and shit, and all that foreign aid and tourism starts back to a real picturesque-type black negro island in our midst..." He kissed his bunched fingertips. "Soars. Retirees who dig tropical weather, beachfronts, cheap servants during their sunset years! Girls of fourteen, fifteen, whatever their heart's desire! Twelve! Nice clean boys, if such be the delight! So voy-la, the real estate soars, and who do you think soars with it?"

They both knew the answer, but the question demanded a response – the uplifted eyebrows, the recent hair transplant, the sparkling eyes, the hand on the shoulder pressing for a query.

"Who?" Kasdan said.

"Cowboy. My man in Port O' Prince."

Once more an interlude of pensiveness so that imagination could flourish. Because he wanted to give Dan the leisure to meditate and he didn't trust himself not to indulge in over-persuasion, Ferd headed off for the Caballeros room. Because he knew Dan would be watching, he strode briskly, giving from behind an impression of lean agility and devil-may-care determination. Truth to tell, he also really needed to pee.

Upon his return, he would change the subject awhile, having piqued Dan's curiosity, let him feel the concern and affection. Dan could be recalling all the fruitful smalltime legal business they had already done together. Soon they would engage in serious business.

Ferd's most recent contribution to Dan's career had presented him with a Cholo client who complained in good-enough English on the witness stand, "What the fuck you mean, driving with a suspended license? I don't *have* a license."

The basic matter at issue was how much time Juan would serve for running over that pedestrian, a seventy-four-year-old Asian woman on the sidewalk, up to the point where she had to be considered dead. Juan, in a red neckerchief, had been doing wheelies and got distracted by rival colors, blue scarves, hanging out against the video store window. As mitigating factors, Ferd Conway would tell the court that the Cholo sometimes visited the mothers of his children when he felt like it.

Ferd explained about license suspension; Dan translated; Juan broke into a brilliant smile of total comprehension. He made it clear Kasdan's services were not required, merely a Ferd Conway shuck, by speaking in perfect English: "This blah-blah-blah is all caca, dude, but okay, you the man, Counselor."

Ferd hoped Dan recalled what he had already done for him, such as getting him hired at the city's expense, including paperwork, depositions, and standing by in court. The meditative silence for Dan under the SKI CANCUN poster during the interlude of Ferd's restorative peeing was now concluded.

Serendipitously, just as he returned to the table, something advantageous came into their lives. Ferd took a pause in his convincing, although his karma had been going great guns; the universe paused in its normal catabolic breakdown efforts; the miracle of Nature, mankind's friend, reasserted itself. Always a pleasure. A young somebody's receptionist, carrying takeout in a carton with a knotted plastic handle, leaned back through the open door of Panchita's Numero Tres to say Hi to a friend, and she stretched a leg to keep the door from closing, and the carton pulled at her extended arm, and the Vanessa or Stacy was a person who filled her tee shirt like a healthy girl who had just broken into triumphant adolescence, and the tee shirt was one which provided her boobs with pride of place – a SKI CANCUN tee shirt from Panchita's Numero Tres. Oh, that lean forward; oh, that blessed offering. They jiggled. Vanessa or Stacy (or Samantha) concluded her Hi. It was more refreshing than guacamole with sour cream.

Ferd nodded swiftly; nothing needed to be stated; *res ipsa loquitur*.

Nothing needed to be said, but Ferd said it anyway. "What we both like, am I right? Lunch all day and breakfast in bed in the morning, hey Cowboy?"

Dan said nothing.

Ferd continued. He took a deep breath, preparing for a major speech, the most important he had made during the past ten or twelve minutes. It was time; no shit. His lips emphatically compressed, he lay his hand on his heart. "When you're yay many years old and you really really really need the cushion for your poor sad daughter who's really pretty, I grant you that, but she made a few bad choices through no fault of her own because of her non-father rearing, no paternal guidance, due to... okay, and then, additional rotten luck, your poor sick grandkid is... okay, so something's got to, no, scratch that, *everything* has got to give. You can't just go along like you were an on-the-scene dad who always did his best, carpool, personal attention, birthdays, and the kid was a healthy mix-breed, was gonna grow up to be a running back or something useful, shop for a lot of bling-bling in the off season. Listen, my friend, like the fella said, I want to be perfectly clear, even if it hurts a tad, wounds maybe out of a deep longstanding affection – don't we?"

"Who?"

"Who what?"

"Who said that?"

Ferd sighed. This was a day of many sighs. Expressing inner feeling is tiring. "I did, I confess, I just did say that, your buddy who takes care of things and now he's giving you a chance, not that it doesn't take care of me, too. Think of it this way: You're a lucky Cowboy." Ferd now went out on a limb. Slyly averting his eyes, he brought up a touchy subject. "Sometimes your people chooses the easy way in, doesn't it? Isn't that one way they survive through all the holocausts and then they eat that matzah ball soup? To celebrate?"

Why, Kasdan wondered, did Ferd's eyelids sometimes seem to have a silky fringe when they fluttered, and then sometimes, as now, they were bald, red, and shiny? A trick of light, surely; a trick of perception; the universe, like San Francisco, was full of tricks.

"You know who some a my clients are?"

"Si. They're my clients, too."

Ferd ignored the interruption. "Not those." Ferd hadn't ignored the sarcasm. "Normal American, boys who stray, but you don't get them. More like straight hair. Your perps work in body shops when they get out of jail, or they're roofers. Think God lives in an electric guitar. Roofers trying to be hoods or rock stars. Tattoo their name above their cunts' nipples, give them the hepatitis."

"Right, the Hispanics need me."

"So when he goes back to jail and she finds herself a new boyfriend, what can a chica do, chica all by herself? Does she make room above her nipple for another name? End up with a big above-the-nipple roster? Like a rap sheet? Check that out sometime. Punks. Punks." Ferd shook off the thought. Musing was a distraction from his main business. "I have to go through the motions for them, Cowboy, till I arrange things otherwise, as you're gonna help me do. It's time."

"You're telling me."

"Help you break free of the punks, the Pasquals and Ho-zays and all those shitty green cards. You want to, you really do. I know it and so do you." Ferd lifted his arm as an invitation to high-five across the Panchita's picnic table, stretching, but Kasdan kept his hands dead at his side. It was ungainly. "Okay, but your secret is safe with me," Ferd continued, riding over his annoyance. After all, he wanted something from Dan, that was the central point here. He wasn't the receiver of supplication, as a criminal defense lawyer usually is. High-fiving is nice, but wasn't critical. Ferd reached for control with one of his strong suits: "And you got that birth-damaged grandkid to consider. Or was it genetic, the mix, Semitic – you prefer Mosaic? – and Margaret Torres? Sad anyway. I feel for you, Dan. Now you got to think of others. Try doing that, okay?"

Stubborn was Dan Kasdan's version of steadfast. His silence could drive a communicative guy off his rocker. But what blocked Ferd's path and drove him off his rocker only increased his desire to get right back on the rocker. Swaying with impatience, Ferd said urgently: "Take your time."

Kasdan didn't even admit he would. He just did.

Ferd helped the process along by fond reminiscence of some of their mutual clients. "That pickpocket, remember? He wasn't a

Colombian, wasn't even a gypsy – oh yeah, not your client, just mine, but I knew you needed work, so I threw it your way – he was a loyal white-ass Americano, so he didn't need to keep the trade secrets, like those Colombian gangs. Offered to teach me, like a true patriot. He could empty a pocket without putting his hand in. Just two fingers, making accordion pleats so it, like, shortened the pocket..." Ferd extended two fingers, thumb and index, plucking with them at the air. Kasdan moved away. Ferd grinned. "These accordion pleats, one two three, the pocket shrinks, your wallet jumps out. Danny, you don't even have to reach in! Your wallet jumps into my hand!"

"Dexterous," said Kasdan.

"Dex-terious, Danny. A flying fuckin wallet, then you fade into the crowd. But as an attorney, what do I need it for?"

"As a fallback position?"

Ferd gave him a reproachful grin. "Not even," he said. "Sometimes I think you forget what I tell you.

"What was that?"

"So then I have to tell you again."

"What?"

"See what I mean? I don't forget you prefer not to be called Cowboy, but if I know what I'm doing – alpha male unit, Cowboy – then I know what I'm doing. See, I said that twice, too."

"You did," Kasdan said as sullenly as he knew how.

"So does your breath still smell like curry? You tell me. It's just an opinion, but you do save your pennies at that el-cheapo Indian all-ya-can with the shrieking on the tape? I tell my Pakistani boys at the Xerox joint, go use the atom bomb already. Somebody's got to stop that Indian pop music."

"Last night." The Krishna Buffet was nearby; Kasdan liked Mr. Patel. "After I dropped off some shopping at Amanda's..."

"Why don't you just telephone out for shopping, massage, whatever – a guy your age? Take it a little easier."

Kasdan had no answer. He still felt capable of shopping and occasional courtship.

"When I make love... fuck," Ferd explained, "I like a woman who... I move gentle, gently, just so." He was having trouble being perfectly clear about a matter that required exactness, tenderness, the whole spectrum of cementing a sense of partnership. "I like it gentle, gently, but then I like her to thrash a little, jump around, till I say 'Slow down, cunt,' only I usually say it nicer, 'Wait for me, baby, don't get ahead of things.'"

He sighed.

Kasdan said nothing.

"Or if I'm tired after a long day dealing with the miscreants, a blow job'll do fine."

Kasdan said nothing.

"People don't listen, that's the problem with people. Especially dumb cunts."

Elbow pressed to his waist, he gave Kasdan a high school girl's cute wave and trilled the word "Hi-i!" It was a wakeup call in a lagging dialogue. It also served as apology for what some folks might call crudeness. Ferd was an expert at his line of work, probably the greatest expert; the work of being Ferd Conway.

"Let's get serious," he suggested. "We only live once, and then we die."

"Well, okay."

Ferd wagged his index finger roguishly. "Got you on cross that time, Philosopher. It's a fact. We only live once, but when we got a daughter we never raised to live after us, a grandkid wouldn't come into being without you, too bad about his handicap, handicaps, but what can you do – that gives you several lives to be responsible for."

Kasdan felt as if he were poking through a basement with his eyes covered and his arms extended, in danger of cracking his head.

"Responsibility, Cowboy!" Ferd was ready to rest his case and dismiss the witness. He was fully in charge.

Kasdan had no answer because there was no question. A silent moment passed.

Still expressing compassion about Dan's neediness, guiltiness, his grandson, whatever, Ferd fumbled for a cigarette, didn't have any, couldn't smoke here anyway, pretended to light up and crinkled his nose over the nonexistent cigarette, saying, "It's a terrible situation, Dan, terrible, terrible, but it can't be helped. So do what you have to do."

"What is it? How much can I expect?"

Ferd was delighted. Now Dan was talking. Ferd adored eventual directness in a colleague. Oh, brother. Everything was going copasetic and great guns. So about the cash-in, available shortly, near-future-wise, Kasdan deserved a complete explanation, along with careful instructions. Ferd conceded these points, although on a need-to-know basis, he didn't need to know everything. Okay. Okay. Okay.

This wasn't some internet scam. It was more in the service sector, more like courier service, but higher up, involving transfers and pur-chase. "Drugs?"

Kasdan asked.

"Oh, don't be like that. Oh, you're nasty. So Cowboy – pardon, Gaucho – pardon, *Dan* – these were hard-working youngsters, just nice deprived kids. Maybe no G.E.D., or they come out of technical training, their life coping skills are nil at maximum. They can cope, but they prefer to cop, haha. They can use a pick-them-up Monday mornings after a hard weekend trying to get it up when they're twenty-six like they did when they were seventeen. I helped."

"Drugs," Kasdan repeated.

"I *helped*. To keep the wheels of industry grinding. Which makes America the great nation we all know and appreciate. I did my part in the pharma-cuticle field."

"You don't anymore?"

"Withdrew. Silicon Valley kind of retrenched. I started to get that feeling like luck running out, you know the feeling? Except, *probablemente,* you had it all your life till you got the daughter, the grandkid, plus the good friend – that's me – to pull it all together for you..."

"I thought maybe it was massage parlors."

"Those Asians that don't know shit about taking the money out of the paper bags? I keep my hand in, Papa-san. But I was saying, you do me the favor, for your commission of course, your percent to be negotiated between buddies, invest in a property, that sunny real estate sitting on the ground there, offshore on a lovely beachfront, and..." His mouth opened; his mouth shut. Even an enthusiastic soul sometimes needs to take a breath. "I'm a lawyer, but I guess I should try to explain it for you without words of art. Simple language you'll understand. Mainly, I don't want the IRS doing any more sniffing and poking than they already started. I dumped my papers on a desk at the Federal Robbery Building and now they claim they want *details*. I was nice as pie to this equal opportunity hire trying to prove he's up to normal standards. Supporting documents! Equal opportunity chickenshit artist! I really need you, Dan."

"Thanks."

"And you really need me, Cowboy."

That was the point. Other people might howl in the wind through the crackling noise of downtown San Francisco, their intentions not clear. Ferd's tenor was sharp and high; it penetrated; anxiety guaranteed reception. Full comprehension could be reserved for due course later because of the aforementioned need-to-know basis. When Ferd lowered his voice to a confiding whisper, a near-whisper, the sincerity in his blue eyes, the touch of his warm hand on Kasdan's arm, the light emotional huskiness made his devotion to the cause under discussion (albeit under undefinition so far), the most important element in the lives of Ferd Conway, Dan Kasdan, Dan's family, and in fact, plus, go for it – the entire world! Therefore it was time to elevate the discussion; Ferd had learned about closers from his experience with juries.

"Being raised in another tradition, not that it's any less valid than the Christian great leap forward, I don't suppose you read much scripture growing up, did you?" Kasdan waited without answering. "Okay," Ferd said, "to each his own, that's the American way. But..." He raised his finger. "'The statutes of the Lord are trustworthy, making wise the simple.' Sometimes I ask for mercy for the client, Dan, but in this case, I'm only striving to wisen you up."

Kasdan knew it would be wrong to take Ferd's joy from him, so much need for love and to run matters. Ferd didn't mind if others made up lies about him, even true ones. His own story was incomplete, but he was in control. How it would work out was just a collection of mere details, like the busy San Francisco days and nights where he went about his business – true of the hookers and transvestites in the Tenderloin, true of the purse-grabbers and muggers, the dealers and the massage parlor operators, and true of their advocate, Ferd Conway, loyally sorting out their details. People need people when they get in trouble, don't they? In the Anglo-American legal defense system, one of the glories of democracy, every stupid fuckup deserves an advocate who can work the system.

Kasdan didn't forget his own needs. He intended to provide for the daughter he had neglected and the grandson who needed more than a court translator could offer.

"To answer your question," Ferd was saying, "which because I'm attuned to your feelings I notice you've iterated several times, your take-home, it's in the five figures."

"Does that answer my question?"

"Partner, compadre. Far be it from me to put down a totally normal curiosity. I wouldn't even call it nosiness. After all, it is your life."

He nodded with appreciation of his business-like clarification, even though friendship between partners should include trust and faith in each other's goodwill.

"So?"

Ferd's smile. A tolerant sigh. "With more TK, depending,partner."

So all in all, it was a pretty good South of the Border lunch conference, chopped pork, guacamole, sour cream, little traces of pepper, all in a wrap of tortillas home-baked in Oakland by loving Mexican machines. For health reasons, Dan had asked for the spinach tortilla. Just like Ferd, he needed time to move through his routines until his own special intention was ripe.

– 8 –

Not being a DA, a judge, or some highly bonused downtown partner out of Yale or Stanford, Ferd Conway wasn't toasty-tan from skiing Cancun or tennis in Vail; his pride required other nourishment. He uttered words like 'rectitude' with a crease of irony at the corners of his mouth, the notch more telling at one corner than at two (sometimes less is more). He made do without the tan, the diploma, the snotty vocabulary.

A graduate of one of the best night law schools in the Bay Area, he had dated the Extension Homecoming Queen. He aimed to make himself as comfortable as one of those Yale phonies, celebrating the festival of life more than they did. Just now, he had a, call it, hetero date. He was adjusting into position his best friend and colleague, easing the way with another of their famous summit lunches. Events were moving well, moving Dan along. He could feel the forward motion in his heart, its thrilling rapid flutter as Kasdan paid attention to Ferd's step-by-step introduction into a better future. This was a pleasure in itself. One of Ferd's favorite proverbs was: Strike while the iron is warm.

But he needed to be absolutely confident about commitment from the exasperatingly dreamy court translator. Serious funds were involved; offshore travel; passing through customs. It required another sharing of a table, a partaking together, a follow-up to their productive session with extra guacamole and tangy suggestions about the better life to come. He needed to outline the path for his junior partner with clear dotted lines. "How about some cuisinely dining?" he asked.

They strolled, bumping familiarly. Ferd considered Pakistani or Indian, that curry stink, but familiar Mex was still the safe way to go. Between friends, tradition bonds, just as in life in general. Also, en route, near the Hall of Justice at the noontime hour, they would surf the waves of secretaries and young female lawyers who were eligible for admiration; little Korean Miss Lee Assistant DAs trotting along on their teeny-tiny high heels, long-striding Wasp girls out of eastern law schools with their lambskin briefcases and hawing laughter; and not to neglect the flirty chicklets who run the spectrum nowadays from security guard to lower court judge.

Surely tax-free capital gain should clear up most ambiguities. Friendship and personal improvement aside, he had points to emphasize: help for Amanda and what's-his-name, the damaged mixbreed; an open path into a better future. Ferd was doing careful preparation for both security and affectional reasons. Further burritos (spinach tortillas for Kasdan) were called for. Eyes narrowed with concern, Ferd asked Kasdan, another subject but part of the whole enchilada, if he made out okay these days.

"Sometimes. When I was younger."

Ferd inclined his head gravely. "I saw that one giving you the eye."

Kasdan noticed her, too, a young woman proud of her power and testing, just testing. Across the burrito joint, gesturing in the air with talons glowing, she was giving her all to her girlfriend and also giving her all to the post sell-by-date gentlemen across the room; one of those San Francisco miracles – two alls to give. The gentlemen could hear her tale, part of it, because she had raised her voice in order to share with everyone, like someone new to cell phones. She was crossing her eyes and shaking her tresses (crowning glories, blond, with magenta streaks) and working the communication system in California croaks: "I said No Way!" And then, "Totally!" And then fluffing the hair with the talons: "Whatever!"

Someone had tried to do her wrong. No damage, of course.

"Love that," Ferd confided.

So Ferd and Dan had things in common. Kasdan also appreciated the hoarse California croak, the smells, vibrancy, and optimism of creatures who had conquered anorexia as a stage on their way to conquering the world.

"Me and you," Ferd said, "we go way back. Remember when Jefferson Airplane was high on the charts..."

"The Starship..."

"... sex was safe and Russians were dangerous? When did it turn around backwards? But even if you get HIV, okay, you'll probably die of something else first."

Prostate, Kasdan was thinking.

"But that herpes, though, that'd get you itching right off the mark, Herpes Simplex, Duplex, damn, they got the whole condominium out there. But say suddenly you're well-fixed, don't count your pennies, you're an upstanding male unit, no stupid curry breath – you get to pick them from top of the line, Cowboy."

For variety today, Kasdan ordered the taco salad and no burrito. He wasn't a slave to tradition. He was trying to remember that singer with the Airplane, her piercing yelp that sent shivers... Grace Slick, who was probably over sixty by now, 'Go ask Alice, when you're ten feet tall'... It was time for everybody to move on. Even Ferd was doing so: "You know I'm trying to be a good – well, make that a *true* friend – a worthwhile contact who will be remembered for the deeds he did in the hereafter." His voice trailed off. Deep thoughts saddened him. This went way beyond mere contact; it was old-time emotion.

"But?" Kasdan asked.

"Problem is, who's to say there's a hereafter? There's mucho question about that, Señor – not proven, you know? I'm not even sure there's a here and now, so let's deal with it, okay?"

Kasdan believed his daughter and grandson guaranteed his own hereafter on earth. Unless, and these were the normal risks, they didn't.

Ferd's lips shone pink and damp. He overcame an interlude of melancholy. He had shared what was hard to share – depth. But now that the deed was accomplished, he dried his lips with the back of his hand. They could proceed. Nearby, diners were slipping leftovers into Styrofoam with the furtive half-smiles of folks slightly ashamed. In a real *cuisine* restaurant, the waiter would do it for them. Ferd Conway, himself, never asked for a people bag. "Cowboy..."

"How many times do I have to ask you?"

Contrite, Ferd shook his head, shedding droplets of apology. "Cowboy, cowboy, cowboy, I always forget you don't like that, but I mean it in the best possible way – narrow hips, not too much butt, lean face, stringy old guy like you, don't even look too much like a Mosaic person. Probably twenty years ago, back then, Margaret Torres thought you were really a primo stud unit."

"You had something on your mind?" Kasdan asked.

"Always, buddy. Due course. Bear with me."

As usual, Ferd reached for a handful of sugar packets. The busboy, who noticed, grinned. Kasdan ventured to ask, "You munch on sugar to keep up your energy?"

"Oh, these?" Ferd pulled out the packets he had just tucked down with his handkerchief. "No, in case I meet a horse I like... Wanna couple? Quick pick-you-up? Hey, it's important to get a little something back when you give as much as I do."

Then the salt shaker disappeared into Ferd's pocket. "Don't have to buy salt, neither. Sometimes I brush my teeth with this stuff when I get to hating that minty Crest." Humorously he replaced the salt on the table. It had just been an audio-visual demonstration. "Cowboy, *you're* the expert on living cheap and saving up for your... now that you have that responsibility."

After lunch, they walked in silence through the alley alongside. They were digesting; Ferd was contemplating; his silence stretched for seconds longer than usual. Its cause was greenery, the persistence of nature as soon as the city gave it a chance. A fresh slim trunk of alley weed claimed Ferd's attention. He frowned with recognition; he smiled upon it. He broke his language fast. "So you know all about this dogwood?"

"Ailanthus," Kasdan said.

"The Tree of Heaven, Doctor Botany. Love it! You told me once, tell me twice, it came over from Asia, grows in any muck, just sticks in and grows... I listen to you! Only the females are good for a body – for tea, am I right? – and the male flowers stink. Girl flowers, yummy – how about that?"

"Thanks for listening."

Ferd bowed his head reverently. "Makes us both preciate nature, doesn't it? Pushes out of the dirt, cleans up the toxics, and it comes from across the mighty ocean."

"China."

"I just told you. Immigrants take over, they're non-native. We both love nature and that's a whole nother thing we both have in common together."

Heaven provides toxics, Kasdan was thinking, so that nature has something to purify. He asked Ferd: "You're making a face."

"If I was a tree of heaven, amigo, I'd be a male one with stinky flowers." He brushed against Kasdan, his pocket stuffed with sugar packets. Down this alley there were no horses to befriend, but elsewhere on the hills of San Francisco, where the wild herbs used to grow and sometimes still did, Indian and Mexican hunters used to chase game and rest their beasts near streams coursing down to the bay.

"Like if you cop a bunch of big bills in the form of money for you and yours, plus you don't owe any taxes anybody knows about? And only me and you are in on the secret? Let me ask you something: How does that sound?"

"Smells..."

"Not kosher, haha, say it like your daddy. You called him Papushka? But if nobody has any inkle but Danny Kasdan?"

"And Ferd Conway, Esquire."

"Goes without saying, but like the old saying, Follow your bliss."

Ferd was not only troubled by Kasdan's failure to express enthusiasm; he was also pleased. It gave him a mountain to climb. It was like courtship. It was a challenge.

"Dan, Dan, listen up, there's traveling involved. Fun and frequent flier miles, right? You got to have your wits. You're carrying cash. You're dressing nicely. You'll look middle-aged – that shouldn't be too hard. Just an ordinary guy, maybe a little depressed after a tragedy. Capishe? His wife died, his kid perished, Customs won't know it's just the normal way you are. No es problema."

He winked. His stride was firm. He had scored essential points.

Kasdan said: "I'm not sure of this."

"You'll end up secure for life."

"If I don't live too long."

Ferd shot a grin directly at his colleague. "Goes without saying. We know the statistics, the actuarial tables. I tried a wrongful pedestrian death just a few months ago, my first." The grin was withdrawn. "You'll be in profit, Dan. You want to end up happy? You'll do so."

"Still not sure."

"So get sure. This is America. All you need is a few details I'm gladly in the process of imparting, plus withholding on a need not to know. You'll end up next door to affluent."

Silence. No answer. No trees of heaven or yerba buena or moss in the sidewalk cracks or screaming gulls to distract them. Kasdan wondered why it was taking Ferd so long. He met Ferd's stare. Their eyes were meeting, facing each other down, or maybe they were just staring at the bridges of noses.

"Dan. I've got to make something clear, Dan. *Please*. You're the man for me."

All through history, from the dawn of the species, men had kept busy hunting other men, those who had women they wanted, or goods, or land, food, or drink, or sometimes just to keep in practice by killing someone. Why should it be difficult for Kasdan? He tried to imagine this Pacific coast, swept by salt winds and covered with clinging green, and a lonely meeting at night in the emptiness of nature, the amplitude of nature, by dim moon glow, when it would be safe to do whatever a man wanted to do.

Ferd Conway, like everyone, owed a debt to nature. Just this once, Kasdan promised himself, I'll pick the time of someone's going, the place, and the means. He wouldn't be able to pick his own time.

– 9 –

It was resolved, maybe. It was possibly determined. Kasdan was on the verge of being almost convinced.

All yet to be decided was what he might do to carry through the action he planned. Inexorably Dan Kasdan moved in directions he wasn't sure of. As an exercise in perspective, he tried not blaming himself for matters beyond his control, such as the weather of San Francisco, such as not knowing he had a daughter until she revealed herself, fully grown and lacking a father. Did not succeed in self-exculpation. Due to the willful habits of the San Francisco Bay, tidal currents, tule and ocean fogs, the rising of the sun and the turning of the earth, did not always perform for his convenience. The people of San Francisco and the world presented similar problems.

Margaret Torres, who had smilingly received him one, two, or three nights during the Summer of Love hangover, believed a child needed nothing more than the seed from a seed provider. She liked Dan okay for this brief role. A little money would have been helpful, too, but money always came with patriarchal hassles. She managed. Raising a daughter cost more trouble and more money than she had anticipated, but she managed. She had her principles. She even let herself keep most of the weight she gained during her pregnancy – her principles remained firm.

She stenciled a painting of Frida Kahlo on the driver's side door of her rusted-out VW bug. She colored the image with authentic Mexican acrylics. Later, despite her solidarity with the other women in her commune, she forgave Amanda for searching out and finding the seed-provider, a Spanish translator operating in the misogynist oppression system.

How, Kasdan wondered, had he survived so long without Amanda? He had felt the void. Though he didn't believe in karmic deficits (Margaret Torres did), the void had been a presence in his life. While he was busying himself with street hoods, carjackers, purse-snatchers, and cornerboy crack dealers grabbed by the law at 16th and Mission, his very own little girl had been busy needing someone to be her dad. But things were just as they had been and he was just as he was; that too is fate. It's called history. During his farewell to middle-age, Dan Kasdan had entered upon commotion.

Early in the new acquaintanceship of Kasdan and his daughter, he had wanted her to understand how he spent his life. He asked her to meet him for breakfast at the Caffe Roma. "So early? I don't usually keep those hours." But she roused herself in time so that he could introduce her to Harvey Johnson, who said, "The offspring! I see the resemblance, man. The best of health and long life to you both!" And, standing, he raised his tomato juice in their honor. His belt clanked against the clasp of his bullet-proof vest.

Ferd Conway trotted up as they moved chairs to join Harvey. "You never told me, you rascal, you got one. A sweetie of a daughter!"

Harvey stared. He judged a person coming, no trial necessary. The table for two could accommodate three but not four when the fourth was Ferd Conway. Ferd nodded and left.

"Friend of yours?" Amanda asked.

"Uses me with his clients. It's the job. Mostly it's translation between him and the defendant, or the prosecution, or there's a document in Spanish... I guess we're associates, sort of."

"Friends," Harvey muttered, tomato juice on his breath.

Amanda made a little shrug. Maybe her father was afraid of the plainclothes dick's judgment. It was obvious that cool Harvey Johnson, who looked like her boyfriend, now her husband, D'Wayne – muscled weight, belly laugh – wasn't a buddy of that Mr. Conway. But – what surprises there are in life! – it happened that Amanda had found a father, found he had associates and friends.

Even in San Francisco with its foreboding gusts of fog followed by California-like episodes of sunlight, daily life most often took the weather as just another given. Thanks to immersion in the rhythms of crime followed by punishment, Kasdan had learned that the full-moon connection with miscreancy was just another theory for the comfort of the police and witches dancing in the hills. Fallacious, no matter what these experts thought, *"Post hoc ergo propter hoc,"* said Harvey Johnson, going for Latin whimsy, pronouncing it like an expert. Still, weather stimulated novel desires for coziness in Kasdan. It was a mild later afternoon, no fog rolling in, no chill winds off the Pacific, when he decided to exercise a grandfather's privilege, a father's right, to visit his beloved only family. *Drop in*, was his plan; *just passing by, thought I would – hope you don't mind –*

Then how come you brought this paper tiger for Sergei? Amanda would ask.

Well, it's been in my car, actually it's a leopard, I've been meaning to –

What's it, a souvenir from a Happy Meal? He'll just mash it up, spit on it, wet on it, you ought to know that, Dad.

He was learning about family negotiations. Sometimes it helped to change the subject. "You smell good. Is it okay to say that to a daughter?" (*My daughter.*)

"I've been bathing for nineteen years, cept when I shower."

(Not that you were ever around, Dad.)

Sometimes the subject wouldn't get changed.

After he finished playing the conversation in advance, rehearsing it for himself, his Honda Civic was parked and he found himself walking up the steps with the paper leopard – maybe it was a tiger with spots – in a plastic bag from McDonald's, wondering why D'Wayne and Amanda couldn't have rented a flat on a street with a few trees and no buildings painted Cantonese Pink. Not that he had any problems with upward mobile Chinese folks investing their savings in the Golden Empire or Mountain or whatever they called California. Just because he had been downward stagnant...

The conversation with his daughter which he had rehearsed was not, as usually is the case with rehearsed conversations, the experience which followed.

"What're you doing here!" (Dan Kasdan erupting.)

"That's a funny way to talk, *whatchudoin here*. That's what you said, am I right? Questioned? Interrogated? Well, what I'm doing here is visiting a friend, that's the answer, okay? Visiting just like you, Cowboy."

Amanda turned to the sleeping child and spoke toward him as if Sergei were the line for getting through. "Dad, I'm in this here downer, this depressive, and Ferd kind of knows about these things" – sure he does – "and it helps me, talking, you know, Ferd talking to me, letting me express myself" – *so why didn't you let me do that so many years, Dad?*

Why were all the buttons on her blouse – okay, all but one – unbuttoned?

"You look like you want to say something, Dad."

"Hey, Cowboy, your lips are moving. You mumbling to your own self? There something here we don't quite catch? We're all ears, aren't we, Amanda?"

The baby was a problem. Generally Sergei gurgled funny, spit and shit funny, except it wasn't funny. Amanda and D'Wayne wanted their child. Amanda wanted to correct the laws of the universe which had failed to give her a father until one turned up, no thanks to him, after Margaret Torres sloppily dropped clues and Amanda picked them up. Then she worked her own progress through, gave birth to the boy, and it turned out that Sergei Mose would need care all his life. No one to blame. Not D'Wayne's fault. Laws of the universe.

So why shouldn't Ferd just want to help? He could provide. D'Wayne was an okay guy, no education and all, in a lazy big way and all, but clever white Ferd Conway could be useful. Because he had feelings for Dan and Dan's family.

Deep feelings are often helpful. "Truth be told," Ferd was saying, presenting depths for consideration, "I never had a kid, you know, not even like you did, Dan – a kid I never knew about till she was a terrific funky grownup girl. Never had one, far as I suspect. Let me be sincere just a sec."

In the light of all this sincerity, how come Amanda had to button her blouse back up when her father appeared without warning?

"... the kind of good luck you had, never had to raise her, but then voy-la! You get this precious treasure, the Surprise Girl I call her, quote-unquote, a stunner with a Latin tinge! Wow. And then lickety-split she gives you a grandson."

A room-inclusive congratulatory swivel of body with extended arms.

"... okay, a grandson with problems, issues, okay, grant that, I'm sorry."

"Thanks," Kasdan said.

"For what?"

"I was a little late thanking you for your congratulations about my family."

"You're welcome, Cowboy. Did I probably not give you an opening? It's all karma or some shit."

"Ferd?" Amanda said. "How about enough of this?"

He pressed his mouth together. "Lips sealed."

The winds of discourse subsided.

"Dad doesn't like puppies," Amanda said. "Stop peeing on his leg."

Through pressed lips, Ferd repeated: "Sealed."

Amanda was trying not to channel her mother and express too much impatience with her life's big males, hanging around this afternoon, all except D'Wayne. The sleeping, gurgling, yellowish-hued Sergei with his tangled arteries and irregularly sparking nerves was the essential one, but there was also Ferd Conway and Dan Kasdan, her found dad. She thought a normal person in her situation would do something in the hospitality line at this point, maybe make instant coffee and open a box of cookies. In her case, she opened her mouth: "And Dad, don't get sarcastic in my house. Only Amanda gets to be sarcastic around here."

Ferd took a release from his vow of silence in order to speak up for Amanda's father. He put his hand gently on her shoulder, but he was talking to Dan. Ferd's weather could change in an instant, now pensive, worn, concerned, bordering on haggard. "Do you remember when you thought you could be a rodeo rider...?" (Never Kasdan's ambition.) "... or anything your little heart desired, actor, finance champion – maybe you don't remember this – and then there was the minute it came to you that all you would ever get to be is *you*? Right? Well, I'm a person remembers. That's my sadness. I'm not going to get over it, but we can get over it together."

"Huh?" said Amanda.

"Maybe all I'll ever be is me, and you too, the exact same."

"Huh?" She bent, looking for something which seemed to have disappeared.

"Okay," Kasdan said, "what's up here?"

Ferd recovered swiftly from his tragic moment. "This is society. We're just talking. We're all gathered on a sociable visit, course Amanda lives here, she's our hostess, am I right, Amanda? Didn't you tell me drop by sometimes? Tell your father, dear."

Oh, surely now was the time. But not in front of Amanda and sleeping Sergei; that would make a mess; also profitless. Besides,

Kasdan had no weapon in his jacket or pants. Instead, his foot shot out on a death mission against what looked like a shiny brown date fallen to the floor. It suddenly grew legs and scurried, rustling, away. The cockroach escaped Kasdan's shoe. Both Ferd and Amanda, without comment, unobtrusively took note.

Ferd waited for him to recover from an inaccurate lunge, a failure of passionate impulse. Cockroaches were rare in San Francisco; even a man living in the Tenderloin didn't get much practice. Ferd was concerned with his own moment of revelation – the soul confession before Kasdan, Amanda, sleeping Sergei, and the cockroach, that all he was was what he was. Confession was good for his soul. "What you think of me in your heart of hearts," he said, "is none of my business."

Amanda was squinting and squirming. She was either concerned about her child or seeming to be or bored with her afternoon visitors. In his line of court translation, Kasdan had learned to interpret for himself the squirms and squints of the accused, not always correctly. But now his daughter was telling him aloud, "You know, Dad, before I met you, I learned from, oh, you don't know them, my friends..." *What kind of friends?* "... since I didn't have a father role model, you know how it is, I had to study other older guys..." She waved toward him and some kind of acrid perfume blew his way. Probably she was sweating into it. "... and Ferd's nice to me."

"What about your husband?"

She smiled, blinked rapidly through the smile. One of those friends must have told her it was a cute gesture. "What does that...?"

"What does that," Ferd said for her, "have to do with the price of guacamole, quote-unquote? Hey, listen, you don't think sometimes in the dark of the night maybe she's throwing herself away on this dude – no offense meant? I mean, no offence, but now there's the little birth disability, chromosomes maybe, uh, a development problem or two or three..."

"I don't want to hear this."

"Not behind your back would I say such a thing. Cause love plus doin' the dirty knows no color line, I understand that, and all credit to her and you – whoops, I keep forgetting, you didn't actually raise her, but in your heart of hearts, you care, always did, am I right?"

Silence from Kasdan. Silence from Amanda. Sergei breathing noisily in his sleep.

Ferd objected to leaving everything up to him in the way of decision-making and frank social procedures. He waited for Kasdan to speak. Kasdan did not speak despite the opportunity. Ferd turned to Amanda; Amanda did not speak. Two older men were concentrating their attention on her. For a moment this was very interesting.

After giving them all the chance in the world to contribute, Ferd took a couple of quick hiccupping breaths, priming the carburetor, getting the motor fed. Now was the time to try being extra nice. "Hey, not that you don't have a whole lot of exciting lifestyle going on," observed helpful Ferd.

"Thanks." This time Kasdan ignored the two glossy brown dates shining on the floor. If there's one cucaracha, there are always more. Next time he might bring boric acid and ask Amanda if he could put it into the cracks under the sink in the kitchen, using a spoon, which he would then wash carefully. He assumed Sergei would not be crawling under the sink, but he might lick the spoon.

Ferd absorbed the gratuitous insincere thanks which had recently been sent his way. "So, Cowboy" – unwilling to give people more time for thinking than they deserved – "since I really like the girl, okay, now she's a woman in her own mind, but she's still your daughter to me, very lovely, but I wonder if she's sort of, you know, because she didn't grow up with an actual father in her life... okay, Wayno's probably a good stud the way they are, right, right, a hunk. I'll grant that, smooth moves, that liquid action, ethnic – but when he gets a little older? What then? You and me, Cowboy, we got our maturity, but Dee Wayne? Think he'll have that?"

Amanda overcame her trance, two men discussing her. "That's out of line. You're out of line."

"Sorry, dear." He gave her a comforting smile. "Right, the father of your babe and all. Just like Chevy Chase – you don't remember, he used to be well-known – just like the Lord Almighty, he used to be well-known, too – a husband gets to say, I'm God and you're not."

"He's my husband. Doesn't have to be God."

"I'm not speaking ill."

"Really bullshit, Ferd." She looked alert more than angry. No need to be angry – it was all about her.

Kasdan asked, "You don't speak ill of anyone, do you?"

"Not in front of them, anyways. Not the Muni Court judge nor God Almighty. Cept you, Cowboy, but that's because we both got the same sens-a-yumor. Who knows, we could even be brothers." He considered the chances. "Well, cousins at least. You look more like Semitic. I don't think I have any Mosaic persuasion in my blood."

He believed his pulled-down forelock, the daredevil stretch of transplanted sandy hair, gave the impression that he had just flown down Pine Street in an open-cockpit World War I Spad, Captain Ferd Conway of the U.S. Air Corps. Rakishness required care, also faith that his forelock would fall right when the follicles taken from the back of his neck adapted to their new home. He kept a brush in his glove compartment and a comb tucked into his jacket pocket. Ferd had nothing but contempt for those long-handled combs that stick out of back pockets; those were for twerps and perps and D'Wayne, the hip-hop hubby with no finesse. Ferd personally, himself, would never wear aviator sunglasses at night, no matter how bright the neon and fluorescence; pimps did that, thinking they were cool; D'Wayne did that, too. Personally, himself, Ferd needed no cool other than his own internally generated supply.

Amanda's nose was again twitching in a way that a lover might find cute except that it meant to say, without actually saying it, I've had enough of this. But she spoke it aloud anyway, with a small addition. "I've had enough of this shit." At last. Kasdan was happy that she was about to dismiss Ferd. Which wasn't what she did. "Ferd and me got some business together, Dad, and since you managed to keep your mouth shut for eighteen-nineteen years till I dug you up..."

"You know the answer to that."

"Whatever." Nose twitching. "I was out there and it took your kid to find you. Maybe you weren't looking. Whatever, now just lose me again for today so Ferd and me..."

"Amanda," he said.

She peered at him. "That kind of hurt daddy face is so over, Dad."

"*Over* is over. You're a grownup..."

"So now we're starting to act like regular family? Fighting?" In her forced grin he recognized his own face when, just for practice, he tried out a smile in the mirror. Photo-face image registered, she sighed and delivered the universal daughter to father signal of bored impatience. She glanced at Ferd, just a glance, no wink; just a little twitch of the eyelid in just one eye – no wink. Okay, she winked, but only once. "Day growing late, Dad. Sergei gonna wake up, need more gruel, Dad. Whyncha come by for, I don't know, let's be polite, I'll make you a sandwich tomorrow, say?"

She opened the door and stood there. In the turmoil of what he saw, smelled, and heard here, Kasdan's chest hurt. Ferd was murmuring, "Hey, Mandy, your nose is real cute when it switches around like that, like a rabbit. You need a carrot?"

Kasdan heard heavy footsteps on the stairs in the hall. Sergei stirred and coughed, waking. Then, seeming to respond to the footsteps, Sergei began to kick. He recognized the sound. He was welcoming his father home. He knew in his damaged infant self that this was his father.

D'Wayne stepped through the open door. "Yo, whoa, we got a party here?" He was carrying a KFC bag with a drawing of the defunct founder beaming like Santa Claus.

"How you doing? I was just leaving," Ferd said.

"Folks not treatin' you right?" D'Wayne hugged Amanda, then breaking to his son, bending, crooning softly, "Baby, baby, baby."

Sergei was drooling. Even normal infants do that until they grow a little older and then the lips are just wet, just glisten.

Amanda opened the KFC bag and said, "That's gross. I told you to go to Safeway."

D'Wayne looked up from his son. "I didn't forget, Mandy. We're a little short this month."

"Get tall. This is America."

Kasdan heard someone else speaking in his daughter.

"But I bought a ticket from the lucky Arab all-night store. Got a good feeling about this one, Mandy."

Kasdan believed the California lottery was not the solution to this family's financial problems, despite the television coverage of gleeful security guards and welfare mothers. Fair to say: it was too chancy.

Ferd grinned at Kasdan. "Three's a crowd, goodbye."

Four in this case, Kasdan thought, doing the arithmetic.

Without looking at them, touching Sergei's cheek with his thumb, caressing the silky skin, ready to help Sergei back down into sleep or up into wakefulness, D'Wayne said: "Five of us here, man, if we countin'."

"Hey! Next time!" Ferd called, waving, in a hurry. "Catch you later, okay?"

He was out the door. D'Wayne picked up Sergei and was crooning softly to his son, his arms full of warm child in its halfway bliss between sleeping and waking. Amanda pulled the window curtain aside and was staring at something heading down the street. Kasdan waited a moment before saying goodbye.

– 10 –

Ellis, where Amanda, D'Wayne and Sergei had moved, was a Kaposi's sarcoma street, scarred, feverish, day and night. Kasdan lived only a few blocks away. "So now you can babysit on a moment's notice," Amanda explained. "Isn't that thoughtful of me, Dad?"

In this center of the city, which had been convulsing almost since Gold Rush times, the homeless wandered or crouched with their Styrofoam begging cups and slept on geological insulations of stacked litter. They dreamed of a better yesterday, a worse tomorrow. Ambulating no place, muttering vows of revenge, angry or tweaking, the agitated ones scuffed against last night's abandoned cardboard beds, sometimes kicked, clubbed, stabbed, or stole the shoes of those enjoying siestas in doorways. A band of Indians who used to reclaim their ancient lands on the steps of the old Main Library, now the Asian Museum, had recreated a Native American ancestral territory up Larkin at Turk, but retained their traditional name as the Library Tribe. Kasdan was accustomed to the hazy mumble, "Fucking Book Depot was our grazing land, White Eyes, so build me a casino or give me a dollar." Kasdan preferred the second option; he was a bringer of temporary peace, especially since they might recognize his Civic parked nearby.

A landlord named Patel, like many landlords in the Tenderloin, refused to recognize them as Indians – he was a true Indian, he claimed, almost a Brahmin – and set fire to the boarded-up Good Karma Hotel when they took it over as the Great Spirit Squat. Mr. Patel's heroic auto da fé was disputed by his insurance carrier, claiming he had committed what bureaucrats call "arson." His lawyer argued that there was no proof of crime by Mr. Patel since the leaky gasoline can found in his client's modest Ford Falcon was needed to prime his carburetor in cold weather. The matter was settled out of court. All-Star Insurance paid.

The faceless, heartless, friendly folks at All-Star considered it best not to litigate this case against a striving ethnic businessman with eleven children. Suttee was still a recognized Hindu tradition and All-

Star treasured its clients nation-wide as part of the All-Star family. Since Ferd Conway had accepted the Patel matter on a small retainer, large contingency basis, there was a nice payday for both the Patels and the Conway.

Kasdan admired Ferd's skill at hunting and gathering in the Tenderloin – tweakers at the thieves' market near City Center Plaza, selling shoplifted surplus from Kaplan's Surplus & Sporting Goods; crack and pill merchants; bargain-priced watches from mainland China, inscribed with names from *Vanity Fair* advertisements; and of course, the dealers in manual, oral and anal massage. Overhead, as Kasdan walked to his daughter's apartment, red-tailed hawks circled in the sky, mirroring the human hawks observing their girls at work from all-day, all-nite convenience store doorways.

Kasdan admired the tail finery of both the human and the hawk hawks. He admired the morning shift Asian massage employees teetering on their heels into "Beyond the Green Door" and "Deep Stroke." He kept his own apartment in the Tenderloin because he liked company and he liked familiarity, sometimes explaining to his fellow court translators that he was a creature of tradition, which sounded more upscale than being a creature of depressed habit. (His friend Harvey Johnson said, "What you like, man, is rent control.") Approaching Amanda's building (landlord: another Mr. Patel), he felt a delicate whisper of pigeon feathers slip down his shoulder. The hawk was sailing off with its takeout dinner. Kasdan brushed at the feathers unnecessarily; their quills and gravity steered them to the pavement.

"Amanda, I'm here."

"You're late, Dad."

D'Wayne defended his father-in-law. "Mandy, twenty minutes late ain't late. Hey man, we appreciate."

"We'll miss the show."

Kasdan told them to get on their way, but Amanda lingered, fretting over Sergei. Sergei had learned some life lessons. The maneuver of smashing his head against the bars of his crib if no one came to him when he wanted something right *now*, no delay, such as milk or a spoonful of honey or simply to share the pain of life, usually brought adult action and fingers tenderly stroking the welts on his forehead. Working in his favor, there was equipment everywhere, walls, floor, the noisy vibrating of his crib bars, all useful for summoning caregivers when screaming failed to bring immediate action.

D'Wayne winced at the sound. He tried to be philosophical. "They'll do that, my momma said I did that." It gave him grief. "But I don't anymore, do I, babe, so maybe he'll stop."

Amanda shook her head. "Like he'll hurt his brain? You have those headaches, you think that's kind of why?"

"Only my me-grain when you tell me things like it's my fault."

"Nothing's your fault," Amanda said. "Let's go, we're missing the Coming Attractions."

This may have been just another normal young parent conversation, something Kasdan had missed because he had missed marriage. D'Wayne was trying his best to be a right-on husband, rarely replying, "Don't need this shit from you, babe."

There was silence all around as they contemplated their shared fact, Sergei Mose. The grandfather had arrived to give the young parents a time out for themselves. It was unnecessary to name what all three were thinking: Sergei is bruised, born bruised. Someone had to break the silence. Amanda pulled D'Wayne's arm. "Come *on*, we'll miss the feature."

Sergei seemed to understand the limits to his power over others when negotiations by means of head-banging failed to produce the desired result, often because neither he nor the others understood his wishes. He stopped thumping his forehead against the crib bars. The welts on his face may have distracted him; perhaps the terrified bustling of parents stirred reptile beginnings of pity in his soul. His grandfather hoped so. Everyone, judges, jailers, executioners, and infants should develop that instinct. This included Sergei Mose.

Or in the middle of the banging he just forgot to continue. He flooded out like an overpumped engine; there were little sobbing explosions, hints of future or past spasms. The convulsions just stopped.

Smart, smart, smart. A lizard with a lizard mind catches a moment of rest before leaping at a gnat. At times, Sergei seemed almost to care for himself. The life force pushed through his brain stem; health might be glimpsed as an option, if there were an attentive God. Kasdan wished it were so. Learning to care for himself (good Sergei!) could be an advance toward caring for his mother, his dad, his grandfather. Way to go, Sergei Mose! It was the evolution toward moving in the world as a human being. Since Sergei was already loved by three persons, it was called upon him to join them and love himself. Oh stop that head-banging, dear child, it's a torment.

A plastic paper-napkin clip slid off a table and fell to the floor with a soft papery and plastic plop. What marvelous vibrations you produce, grandson, which ricochet across a room, accumulating force, knocking over napkin holders when you stop your flailing and sobs. Sergei's shadowy baby eyebrows arched. He must have heard the sound or been listening for the next sound, which was the voice of his grandfather murmuring, rumbling in his chest, humming a deep note, the song of wordless soothing as he rocked his daughter's son.

Kasdan's eyes hurt when he gazed upon the child. He squinted against the invisible glare beamed from the child's skin, *blood of my blood, flesh of my flesh.* He disapproved of this blinding, these tears; it damaged his easeful passage; he said aloud, "Allergies." He would have needed to offer his daughter, who had escaped to the movies, thanks to the babysitter, the variety-pak of explanation: "Sinus... an eyelash... got a Kleenex?"

"Here's a paper napkin, fresh off the floor." That would be his daughter.

"I think I might be coming down with something."

"Dad, if he catches it, I swear I'll kill you."

Homicide might run in the family but unlike Kasdan she wouldn't mean it. In the grandfather's case, as a cautious person, he awaited the proper time, in due course, no hurry, and with appropriate rewards. *I'll kill you* from Amanda meant she was teasing, something a daughter might say if she were kidding on the square. He blotted his eyes with the napkin which had only briefly rested on the floor, surely not long enough to pick up microbes or cockroach droppings.

Kill was a thing a daughter might say to a longtime absent, nonexistent father whose existence she was getting used to, too late in her life to ever name him Daddy.

From outside the building, an advancing boombox, best buddy of a street-dwelling Vietnam veteran, bass turned up, roared a rap recitation which Sergei was too young and Kasdan too old to appreciate. He would have preferred the Rolling Stones' "You Can't

Always Get What You Want," which dated from the time when he was sure he could get what he wanted.

After Sergei Mose was born, the attending pediatrician at San Francisco General, with a watchful young medical resident in psychiatry trailing behind him, came to visit Amanda, groggy after a difficult birth, the episiotomy accomplished, D'Wayne holding her hand at bedside in a room with a curtain separating them from other new parents. Stately and solemn, a true professional, Dr. Farley leaned over Amanda, making eye contact no matter how fatiguing it was for him to do so. He wanted to make sure she understood him. The resident, his hand across his chest, touching his stethoscope – a gesture of sincerity – was fully invested in this learning experience. It was an opportunity to broaden his perspective on the issues of unusual parturitions and births.

Sergei was born with a high fever. Discreetly, the pediatrician noted that the medical personnel at the Haight-Ashbury Free Clinic would have induced birth immediately if Mrs. Lincoln...

"Washington," said D'Wayne.

"... if Mom had gone to the clinic at once when the placenta broke. Premature release of waters generally calls for prompt intervention..."

It was not his place to blame anyone. Sometimes these things are not fully explained to Mom, given the shortage of time and occasional lapses of training in volunteer staffs at the Free... but it was not really waters in the sense of H_2O, but rather, a necessary insulation and source of nourishment, indicative and causative of infection when... The pediatrician, Willis Farley, M.D., according to his badge, had found there was no point in rushing with bad news about the limited resources for keeping moms fully informed in outreach medical situations.

So to sum up, here were the matters to consider at this point in time. On the one hand, a nurturing institution with trained personnel could give proper custodial care to little Sergei Moses...

"No!" Amanda shouted, and D'Wayne stroked her damp hair.

"On the other hand, it will be difficult, of course at this preliminary stage we can't be certain, every case is different, development can take an exceptional course in the nurturing process. For reasons we don't fully understand, the body of an infant sometimes shows remarkable powers of regeneration..."

"Training, stimulation, and exercise," the resident murmured, and the pediatrician glared at him to shut up. Dr. Farley was handling this.

"Sometimes the mom and dad situation seems to influence part of the brain, which is not fully mature anyway in the developmental stage, and the amygdala, for example, can be guided... governed... sometimes. The limbic system may be mostly intact, partially. Damage in certain cases can be largely overcome, at least in part. Medical science, despite all the promising advances in recent times, still registers unusual and unpredictable outcomes, if mom and dad choose to devote yourself fully..."

"A hundred per cent," said the resident.

"And you are obviously a close, concerned family," Doctor Farley noted, patting Amanda's shoulder and nodding approvingly toward D'Wayne. His look was congratulatory, on the edge of fond, although tired of making eye contact. The resident, with an effort, managed not to echo Dr. Farley with "a close concerned *inter-racial* family."

Dr. Farley's judgment was correct about Amanda and D'Wayne and also conformed with the protocol for expression of opinion concerning relationships on the part of Staff at San Francisco General. A white mother, a black father ("Please, Doctor, *African-American*," he learned seven years ago from a Filipino, make that Filopin-*a* nurse), the mixed-race couple legally married at City Hall and still living together: Dr. Farley had seen an increasing number of similar cases. He had adjusted. The Lincolns or Washingtons, whatever, were determined, probably; loyal, perhaps, for the time being; maybe foolhardy with the rushed decision-making of young irresponsible hormones.

"But you should understand," Dr. Farley explained, "although damage may be, to a certain extent, ameliorated..."

The resident, a tall young man with stringent blue eyes, unflinching, surely a star in his college sports programs, perhaps a quarterback, both a scholar and an athlete, was gazing keenly upon the young mother. He intended to be more than an observer gaining useful experience. He was a born leader. He already had his degree. He would assist the pediatrician in charge of the case whether the older man wanted his help or not. He felt it like a personal responsibility, also an opportunity, from the perspective of a healer at the beginning of his career, soon to be in private practice, to suggest, urge, point out a more desirable outcome for the young couple. It was incumbent on him. He planned ahead. "You can arrange to visit almost as often as you like in the early years. Later, as little Sergei Moses matures, there are excellent advanced custodial institutions, more like a school, where they have really great programs. If you like, you can plan visitations on a regular weekend schedule."

Amanda was crying. D'Wayne was crying. Amanda, who had been removed from her father, would never let her child be taken from her. D'Wayne, who had never met his father, shared her determination for his own reasons.

As a leader of men (and, on wine-tasting weekends, women), the resident sensed it was time to inject a note of optimism into the game plan. The former quarterback was chafing for action in the huddle. Aware that the pediatrician was in charge, like a coach, the resident stood on the field, bedside in this case, bearing his own insights. These unfortunate parents should be fully informed, no holds barred.

"The fusiform is less active. Technically, it's diminished. There are recent developments in dealing with the situation. Let's visualize the mini-columns that extend through the layers of the neo-cortex – in layperson's language, stacks of neurons…"

He extended his hands to bring them along with him. Now that he was putting into layman/woman's language, he paused for acknowledgement from the African-American dad. D'Wayne stared. Dr. Farley was jotting notes on a pad, probably something about an overly aggressive resident. Finally D'Wayne nodded.

Encouraged, the resident proceeded with a relatively optimistic scenario. "In some cases, an overabundance of myelin presents…"

This was not a complete thought. It was developing without the good cheer the resident had intended. He was distracted by Amanda's steady tearfalls. He was wondering how her amygdala would present if they could MRI it. Flooded, most likely, showing red on the scan. He cast his sincere blue gaze upon D'Wayne. Couldn't he tell his wife to shut up?

Dr. Farley glanced at his watch. Actually, he lifted his wrist and frowned closely at it. He had rounds to make, and he really needed to have a word with the resident. He said to Amanda and D'Wayne: "I respect your first impulse. You have time to review your decision. There is much we don't know yet. Science is not an exact science, so

I'm only offering you an overview. Consult, get other opinions, that's your option. Much can be done in some cases if you are bound to proceed on the path you have indicated as a first frequent reaction."

An unspoken *maybe* was left in the curtained alcove as the pediatrician, sighing, patted Amanda's shoulder, shook D'Wayne's hand, and left. The resident lingered to give D'Wayne an athletic, non-multicultural handshake. No high fives today, no "Peace, bruh." Both doctors were relieved that a painful duty had been accomplished and now they could move along to better moments in the turmoil of San Francisco General on Potrero Hill. Furrowing his brow, the pediatrician was considering how to remind the resident that he was there as an observer, not an interrupter, and that he should only butt in his stupid two cents when he was invited to do so.

Dan Kasdan was giving Amanda and D'Wayne an evening respite at the multiplex; they deserved it. Alone with Sergei thrashing and shrieking, a grandfather couldn't do what Kasdan frequently did in his own flat – screen the call with his answering machine, answer it later or not. If Amanda were there, he could turn toward her and the shamed mother would run to respond, not wanting the grandfather to be upset. It was Amanda's duty to attend to the thrashings. When he was home, D'Wayne did his best.

It was not only for Amanda that a craving for cash stirred in the court translator who seemed to have been permanently remade as a layabout by San Francisco's decades-long Summer of Love. He wanted it, he wanted it soon, he was old enough to remedy the delay caused by prudence, carelessness, layabout habits. And then, if all went well, he would ease himself into age and prostate results with no more shame for what he had done and not done. As to conventional conscience about the Ferd Conway matter, he could handle it alone in his rent-controlled apartment; there was plenty of company in the neighborhood for handling matters of conscience. He followed a philosopher's rule, justifying hatred because, without hatred, there was no joy in revenge. And if somehow he made an error and the police came for him, hey, he was just a crotchety old guy with no previous felony on his record who happened, due to family stress, to slide off his rocker. A clear mental case. He knew a motherly psychiatrist who would be happy to testify about early-stage dementia, Alzheimer's only provable upon autopsy, but elements of rage, failure of impulse control, and paranoia definitely indicative.

Harvey Johnson would testify to his previous stable nature, even excessively stable, followed by abrupt personality changes.

A possibility occurred to Kasdan amid Sergei's din. Another of Ferd's clients, for whom Kasdan translated, had only been trying to upgrade his equipment when he was arrested. He had tapped a piece of pipe, rag-wrapped so as not to disturb the passersby, against the window of a parked Miata, so why did the (word deleted) cop have to handcuff and pat him down, pinching his private parts, Your Honor? If all he was doing was tending to business, reaching for a purse left on the seat of her two-seater by a Mill Valley dummy, why was he carrying a Smith & Wesson Model 10 .38 caliber revolver? Answer: Because he wanted to get rid of it. Question: How did he plan to do that? Answer: Trade it in. Question: For what?

Answer: Because his sainted mother raised him never to lie to a man in robes, even a judge, even if Your Honor is not a priest... pause for confession to take effect... for a Glock 19 9-millimeter semi-automatic. Question: Who was going to sell it to him? Answer: A cop, dude never mentioned his name, wearing a blue uniform or maybe it was green, but it wasn't no (same word deleted) robes – "Strike that, Your Honor." From the bench: "Objection sustained. Please try not to libel the San Francisco Police Department. The park police wear green, son."

And why did you want that Glock?

"Man, I live in a rough neighborhood, you call 911, you don't get no protection before your kids is shot, maybe you too when they spray pretty good..."

Kasdan tried to translate idiomatically, sometimes succeeded, sometimes omitting inessential disruptive language.

"... and the mother-fucking Glock is light, see, so you can reach quick and protect your loved ones."

Under pressure Kasdan couldn't always use state-of-the-art idioms, but the essence of explanation and plea was always clear. Like this devoted father, he too wanted to succor his family. There were difficulties in his projected single use of a Glock or another small pistol. Kasdan wasn't familiar with guns; he didn't even own a weapon yet; they made noise, didn't they? Aren't silencers mostly valid only in gangster movies? Weren't the walls of Ferd's condo of somewhat flimsy dot-com speculative construction, therefore alerting Ferd's neighbors to a despairing bankruptcy or domestic dispute?

Yet-to-be-determined was how to go about matters.

Sergei was shrieking again. In this exercise he was tireless, never bored with the typhoons that wracked his body. Tempted simply to cover his ears, Kasdan could not allow himself to do this; he said, "Oh dear son, please, please;" a turmoil like his grandchild's wracked him with alternating chill and fever. Oh, the child was suffering.

Someplace within these nervous explosions, too wild for him to feel anything but the storm, a belief must have been hidden within the human creature Sergei that he deserved better. He deserved a better fate. The mashed nose, the lips that bled although only a few teeth were pushing through his gums, the rolling bloodshot eyes demanded something better. In recent times, Dan Kasdan also bit his lips in his sleep and awakened with blood on his pillow.

Kasdan's role was not to be a counselor studying birth injuries and genetic malfunctions. His place was that of a grandfather holding firm until the parents returned to relieve him. He brushed the child's face with his fingertips, trying to channel health and comfort into wet skin, slippery with malfunction and fathomless resentment, things gone wrong through no fault of Sergei Mose – this child, this grandson, this baby, this damaged beloved message to the future.

Street sounds no longer existed; nor did the weed tree in the alley, bending in today's steady winds off the Pacific. Only Sergei and Dan were present together in the universe. There were sounds of eruption, these were Sergei sounds; sounds of swampy boilings, risings, overflowings – Sergei's sounds. The firing of ganglia in meat circuits seemed unstoppable, fed by furious life forces. Kasdan marveled at this. Sergei seemed to recapitulate all the accidents which resulted in solar systems, planets, a moon, Spanish interpreters. Kasdan's own universe would not come to an end with this red-faced child of his child, this turbulent proof that even Kasdan could never be alone in the world. It was a gift he knew he had not earned.

Since the best thing was not available, he looked to find redemption by doing the wrong thing. Perhaps it would not be the worst thing.

So he told himself.

The child slept. Kasdan held him in his arms, flared nostrils, flattened nose, lolling tongue, the child at peace. Sergei could count on his grandfather.

Now the rest of the universe returned. Sounds so penetrating they were almost visible pierced the walls. Like a crotchety housebound retiree, Kasdan pulled a curtain aside to peer into the street. Boys were tottering under immense drums, slapping at them; banners held aloft on wooden poles almost reached to the second floor; girls, doll-like in red and white plastic boots, were marching down Ellis while parents, uncles, and aunts expressionlessly admired them and non-Cambodian kids rushed to gawk and jeer and debate about which of the girls they would be happy to push into an alley. Whatever the community was celebrating, their neighbors also wanted to be out there and joining in; like gay and proud, black and proud, Hare Krishna and proud; Americans and not ashamed, whoever, no matter. Noisemakers clacked, slammed-down firecrackers popped under feet like tiny grenades, sparks flew, and families dug chopsticks into rice arranged with shiny pink and green dyed items on little white paper boats.

Smells of caramelized soy and burnt sugar wafted through the Tenderloin along with this carnival gaiety. Sergei shared the excitement by jerking his legs. He smelled a set of stinks he liked. He extended his arms and legs and shrieked. Whatever it was, he wanted some.

Kasdan carried him to the window. The wide-brimmed hats of tiny grandmothers made them look, from above, like humanoid mushrooms, sprouting from a cement terrain without rice ponds. Brave mini-gangster kids were chanting – no, rapping – but if it was a community prayer rap, it now included homegrown USA elements, *motha-fucka motha fucka,* absorbed into their ancient language from the world they had entered. Non-Cambodians were also out in force, some selling the Street Sheet. A social work graduate student was trying to hand out copies of the Tenderloin Times in English, Spanish, Vietnamese, Tagalog, and Cambodian on separate pages. Having traveled here to share the San Francisco multicultural experience and learn to better appreciate Syracuse and Dallas, tourists stared at the Tenderloin Times and shook their heads. It was free, but they knew there was a catch someplace; and anyway, they preferred cuisine to periodicals. There was no such thing as a free whatever-it-was.

A proud boy of ten or twelve, hair slicked down, a leash made of intertwined red, white and green nylon strands clutched in his fist, was tugging, to keep it in order, a small, shiny-coated white piglet. Although meant to be in a parade, it darted from side to side. At that age, piglets are anarchists. A cluster of kids chased it along the sidewalk. The piglet kept its nose to the street, having better things on its mind than the admiration of children. Where there is the smell of food, there is often the incidence of food. "Look, Sergei," Kasdan whispered, "You never saw one like that before, did you?"

The parade passed. Kasdan had always wondered why the Tenderloin Times included no Cantonese page. The crowd began to thin out, leaving behind the normal population of runaways, last-stop hookers and panhandlers with Styrofoam outstretched and eyes perished long ago.

Kasdan shut the window. Sergei was being good. Kasdan dipped a spoon into the open jar of Safeway honey (didn't remember opening it) and let Sergei gum the spoon. He had been good for minutes in a row; he was still busily calm. Kasdan hoped he would draw the logical conclusion: When your limbs stop jerking and you give up the screaming and you allow your grandfather just to hold you without threatening to fling yourself onto the floor, sweetness comes into your life. There were juicy sliding sounds and a couple of new teeth clicking against the spoon.

Peace be with you, dear Sergei Mose.

Later Kasdan fed him from the Gerber's cornucopia, an open jar of something proteinal, smelling like peanut butter, an open jar of mashed prunes, an open jar of apple sauce. A veritable Gerber's feast, my grandson.

Kasdan lifted the apple sauce jar to his own face and darted a tongue inside. "Mmm, good, want some more?" He held the spoon to Sergei's mouth, but the lips were pressed shut and Sergei dribbled out an oozing sample. Oh, excellent, you make your non-wants known. "Okay, okay, no problema," Kasdan said aloud. There was something comforting in carrying both ends of the conversation. Communication was pure.

Sergei stared unblinkingly at his grandfather, then blinked slowly. Maybe this lazy unblinking regard, like a lizard's, followed by the slow blinking, was some kind of Morse code developed back in reptile times. "Good, good," Kasdan said, "want some honey?" He was beginning to interpret the child like one of his court-assigned clients. Honey made him blink and almost smile. Kasdan dipped the spoon into the jar and Sergei licked, his teeth clicked against the spoon, and surely that was a smile. It was a burp. Sergei shut his eyes. He slept. A sleeping child nestled against his grandfather's shoulder.

Kasdan touched Sergei's forehead. No fever, no chill; calm and a slow breathing. "Good boy, good boy," Kasdan muttered, as if he would hear, as if he would understand, as if the words could do justice to Kasdan's despairing love for the first offspring he had known since birth.

Mommy loves you, Daddy loves you, and as long as I live... Oh, if only you could remember in the years to come.

This was his America as Dan Kasdan found it. Care and remedy required cash or ready credit in case of trouble, and in the case of much trouble, much money. Kasdan knew where the cash could be found; Ferd Conway had it. Was it fair to say that Kasdan would be helping Ferd redeem himself, whether he wanted to or not? No matter; Kasdan was ready in this special case to leave fairness behind.

"Duh... Duh."

"Is that a word you're saying, Sergei? Daddy? It's a start, boy. Now try *grand*-duh-duh."

"Duh-duh."

"Good! Almost splendido!"

Kasdan lifted his grandson into the air. The tiny buttocks squirmed. The czars of Russia kissed the behinds of their offspring, but Kasdan was shy about family love. He was new to it. He was only learning about dynasty. Nevertheless, he smacked his lips a little, meaning kiss-kiss, and Sergei wriggled as if he understood. Soon he might be screaming again, surely he would be screaming again, but just now, just now! When Kasdan turned the boy's face to his, he found a heartbreaking gummy smile.

– 11 –

It was not easy for Dan Kasdan, lifer in the City and County of San Francisco legal services system, to be somewhat older than he used to be only a moment ago, as was the City and County itself, as were the visitors and the marooned, having bought their wars but now liberated from distress by medically-prescribed grass (formerly Maui Wowie) or optional brain-feeding LSD, speed, crack, or tried-and-true, old-fashioned, high-octane wines. The boys and girls still trickled in from all over to find Utopia last Tuesday or tomorrow. The Summer of Love persisted through many summers.

The communes mostly vanished. Kerista, devoted to polysexuality, all men and women fathers and mothers to all children, no longer had a telephone number. Crash pads were condominiumized and degroovied. Most of the flower people went home, or elsewhere, or moved on to middle age. Still, some didn't.

Amanda, Dan's daughter, child of Margaret Torres, grew up in Mendocino and Napa because fathers were a waste of Margaret's time; but the child decided to dig up her father anyway and present herself ("I'm your daughter, here I am."). The father proceeded from ignorance to astonishment to discovering that his daughter seemed to complete his life. Of course, a life was only completed when it was over.

Other children of the children who lived through daily revelations also came searching for ghosts of the past on Haight Street or, if they were less lucky, in the Single Room Occupancy hotels of Eddy, Ellis, and Turk. The Tenderloin was nearer to the Greyhound Bus Depot. A helpful Vietnam veteran might lead a tired girl there, having just seen her daddy – what was his name again? – only the other day; offering to carry the backpack, provide a briefing on the terrain and a place to rest up, honey. Mom had said, "I met your father... I think it was on the corner of Ellis and Taylor, the cafeteria there," so it made sense that Pop might have stayed on to let his hit-and-run accident find him.

Little did these daughters from Stockton or Denver realize that the groovy jobs starring in porn films, as Mom did, had mostly gone to the San Fernando Valley or become ungroovy, due to the Mafia, AIDS, herpes, and excessive competition. Recently, even the dot.com catering jobs for parties had dried up. Perhaps that was why this young seeker of something was taking black coffee in a glass at Katie's Meddle of Honor Tavern on Taylor, although a shot and a beer was the normal fare here. Perhaps she wanted to be alert in case her Pop happened to drop by.

Instead, Dan Kasdan dropped by. A beer in a back corner of the Meddle of Honor was the respite-seeking court interpreter-translator's custom at the end of many days. If he did it every day, it would be called a habit, if not an addiction. Since he only did it three or four or five days a week, skipping now and then, it was more like a custom. On this traditional, customary afternoon, his table at the back and in the corner, the gangster's seat, looking out, was already taken by a young woman. These were rare at Katie's Meddle of Honor.

Katie called her bar the Meddle of Honor because president Harry S. Truman had pinned a Medal of Honor on her dress uniform pre-Katie, when she was still Karl, a sailor who had galloped around above decks, caring for the boys, during the Korean War. She still disregarded "incoming fire," paid it no never mind, administered loving care and CPR when necessary to sailors on shore leave, and was also pretty shrewd about attempted entrapment from the Tenderloin Task Force of the SFPD. A good business lady, Katie tithed the Trannie Task Force, an association of former men and women, and did it with gladness, which was not always the case when dealing with the SFPD.

Katie, né Karl, liked to ride her pony from the back room to the bar proper; Kasdan enjoyed the pitter-patter of tiny hooves along with his refreshing brew. The Meddle of Honor, with its traditional San Francisco martini glass in purple neon signage outside and reflected inside, was singular in several respects; a straight bar with transsexual owner, a jukebox with Puccini and popular Italian tunes, a well-groomed pony occasionally trotting through the premises.

Generally speaking, runaways performed their rituals of hanging out elsewhere. Nevertheless, this flower throwback child, wispy dark-blond hair hanging lank as anti-dreadlocks, eyes heavily outlined by some kind of ghostly grease, was perched at Kasdan's back corner table, one more late arrival auditioning for the movie to be titled "The Summer of Love Never Died." (As yet, no camera or casting director on the scene.) The girl's eyes were downcast, staring at a spiral notebook in which she might soon be writing: Mom, I copped a ticket to San Francisco, so I get to see the place where you put the orange robes on your back and met Dad and panhandled for the Hairy Krishnas... Years after earning her Medal of Honor, Katie was still living dangerously. Now she ran the risk of losing her liquor license for underage sale, not even bothering to ask for the photo-copied and glued driver's license collage.

"You don't use a laptop," Kasdan stated.

The girl looked up and grinned. "No connection plus no batteries." Okay, maybe she was of legal age. "You don't happen to have some batteries on you, do you, mister?"

"No."

She waited a moment, offering a space for something flirty to move events forward. "You're a live one, aren't you?"

He anticipated the continuation of this conversation before he sat down. When the age difference came up (he would bring it up, preempting reproach, unlike other old farts), he would point out that in a hundred years he would be an alert dude of a hundred and fifty-seven and she would be a faded beauty. He also had the option of falling to his knees right now and asking, Will you be my widow? But he had always been cautious in the matter of true love. If he were a few years younger, theirs would still be an inappropriate romance. Old as he was... he might delay mentioning the daughter... old as he was, their romance was ludicrous, not merely inappropriate, and therefore all she needed was a sense of humor.

Do you appreciate the ridiculous, miss?

But before he could launch his lightning campaign in pursuit of a person who wanted to be caught, he saw the blue scars at the crook of her arms. She noticed his noticing and slid her hands up to her elbows. It didn't make the marks go away. Kasdan came out of his dream. Sergei was more important than suicide sex. Amanda was more important than an evening in the company of trouble.

While he was deciding to drop a bill on the table, a five or a twenty – "Here, get yourself some batteries" – she was saying: "I get what you're telling me. I really, really, really..." She stretched out her hand and took a fistful of his jeans because this would surely make him forget the dark blue elbow freckles. "... dig you."

"Sorry, sorry..." He pulled away, awakened, regretting.

She smoothed his pants where she had pinched them. "Hope springs eternal," she said. "Or immortal."

So he sat down anyway – no harm so far – and she shut the spiral notebook. No matter what else he did to her, she didn't want him to read what she was writing in the journal of her voyage to San Francisco. Startled, she asked: "What's that?"

"It's Katie."

The pony's tap dance clatter parted the curtain to the back space. Katie came riding through, danced up to their table, asked, "You folks fine?" and didn't wait for an answer. Of course they were fine. Katie rode to the only other patron at this hour, slumped at the bar in that late afternoon grief which precedes evening good cheer, and asked, "You fine?"

The pony snorted delicately. Katie's bartender, fresh on duty, tattoos revealed, reached a lump of sugar across the bar, but Katie trotted away. "You're spoiling her! She'll get cavities!"

"But she'll like me better," the bartender shouted fondly, and then with tempered tone, "You bitch."

Kasdan resolved to put his daughter and grandson out of mind for an evening. It was the right of an older guy to accept his fun, assuming that he deserved it, with the excuse that he would be gone forever sooner than others; not just the right but the duty of an older guy with a serious plan. Amanda had no right to judge him for what she would never know.

The girl, Petal, seemed to like him, no doubt for reasons that must have seemed good to her. Whatever her real name was, Petal was the name now and she was sticking to it.

"I told you mine, so what's *your* name?"

He hesitated.

"Hey, you didn't have a fallback? Make something up, that's cool, just so I can call you something if you say something. Or I can just say Mister or Dude."

"Dan," Kasdan said.

"That's a good one. So we're in business, okay? Dan, Danny, Daniel, rhymes with Dude."

It was nice to laugh. Kasdan didn't do much of that. The body and spirit were lightened. "Petal... it's not a rhyme just because they all begin with a D." He enjoyed that he told her his real name, because why not? Was she going to blackmail him? Extort? For what? And she was sure it wasn't his real name, even if it was.

He was still grinning until she said, "Danny the Dynamo Which Laffs," and then he erased the smile. "You tweaking?" she asked. "Dudes who do stuff make me nervous even if personally, sometimes I can use a liftoff..."

No answer. Often his clients were tweakers, busy motivators using meth, ice, crack, coke when they scored and were trying to travel luxury-class. These clients were twitching, erratic, warning systems. After a brief exercise of pills years ago, he realized they weren't the cure for his well-practiced distraction. The time he shared a couple lines of cocaine with a young woman who really wanted him to because he was sleepy, he was still sleepy afterwards but couldn't sleep. The young woman gave up in disgust. He had been okay with that.

"So what do you use, Danny Dude?"

"For what?" Already he felt nostalgia for the memory of the laughter which had surprised him only a moment ago. He was lucky so far today, and it wasn't even nightfall yet. He had heard men say, Got lucky in this joint, and now it happened to him, proving that he was a man with good luck like some others.

If he had been unlucky, Ferd Conway might have floated in, although Katie's Meddle of Honor wasn't the kind of upscale lounge or hotel corner which a man of Ferd's distinction preferred. The one time Ferd had joined him there, he claimed to see pony shit next to a booth and advised Dan to find another venue for his moping. Ferd aimed higher.

Petal too was sunk in rapid thought. No accident of bad serendipity marred the occasion. It was a reward young people deserve, and what the young deserve can also serve as a special memory for the less young. Biological years, wheels, clutches were working the ganglia of Petal and Dan; synapses were colliding. Soon she would share with him what was on her mind.

Her mouth, small, fleshy, slightly protuberant at the middle, would be described as heart-shaped by a man who found her perfect; otherwise, he might think she should have her front teeth fixed. Kasdan liked her heart-shaped pouting mouth. If she were his daughter (she was not), he would send her to the dental school on Sacramento near Fillmore to see what the faculty or advanced students, under qualified supervision, could do about her front teeth. Without damage to that delightful heart shape.

"Your last name, Petal?"

"Smith or Jones, what do you prefer? This some kind of third-degree type interrogation? I reserve the right to remain silent, Officer Dude. Petal Johnson from Muncie, Indiana, how about that? My mom went home from the Avalon Auditorium and got her degree in Cosmetology. That part's the truth – satisfied? She always told me, growing up with a single mom, she was first in her class, so why don't I take up skin care?"

"I don't suppose that's a heritable talent."

"Hair *what*? You bet. On Mom's side, prob'ly. Never met my birth dad personally, whoever the asshole was, but he must've been a friend of Mom's. She said she had zits at my age..." She sipped at her bar glass of black coffee. Katie's alert bartender filled it because he didn't want the customers to run on empty. The smell of burnt coffee appealed to Kasdan under these interesting circumstances. "... those little pink volcanoes, you know, on her nose? But I don't, thanks to whoever he was, my dad's skin. Plus, stay away from chocolate."

"Now they say it doesn't cause psoriasis –"

"Sore what-sis?"

"Acne. That was a thing people said because it tasted good."

"It's the American Way, Dude."

"So you like chocolate?"

"Depends. You buying? The dark kind, not that milk shit?"

Katie's Meddle of Honor was the rare tavern with a clock beyond the display of bottles, a relic of U.S. Navy discipline. Katie felt certain that her clients on watch here wouldn't be deterred from their drinking by the round face with its moving second hand in the dusk near the Cabin Boy's Room, No Handicapped Access, where her pony grazed. Sometimes Kasdan studied the clock to remind himself that his time on earth was limited. Good Lord, nearly six in the afternoon already, unless you were the sort who thought of it as six in the evening.

Dinner for two was on the menu tonight, maybe a chocolate pudding called "mousse" for dessert, because the lady liked chocolate and didn't fear pimples. Whatever her heart desired, because Dan and Petal, like everyone, deserved a good break now and then.

"Don't you think maybe I'm a little starved, you know, hungry for some spicy food?" Petal asked. "Something *real*?"

Romantic Dan Kasdan said, "Spicy, Indian," and steered her by the elbow up Leavenworth to the Good Luxe Muhammad Dining Restaurant with its "Best Buffet in the Tenderloin Lunch Only $7.95," although at dinner they would be ordering from the menu, not the buffet, and it was Pakistani, not Indian, and the Lunch Only Buffet no longer included Your Choice of Soda or Chai Tea. Nothing was too good for this Petal. (But not to overdo things.) The pinkish glow of Muhammad's molded glass lighting fixtures reflected the pink of Muhammad's Extra Special Melon Juice and contributed a purplish tinge to Petal's cheeks. Kasdan hoped it also worked its magic on his own gray-flecked face with its long crevice indentations, deceptive laugh lines on a man whose laughter had been sparse.

She frowned over the epoxied menu bundle after a quick smile of advance appreciation, idly scraping her fingernail against a dried sticky stretch of tassel. Someone had been too eager to reach for his melon juice, causing purple tassel tangle when it dried. After Petal scraped it clean and crisp, she nibbled at her fingernail to get a preview of coming meal attractions, items crisp and curried, plus a possible creamed rice and raisin pudding to add sweetness to the repast.

A mural on the back wall of the G.L.M. Dining Restaurant depicted the Riviera of Pakistan, a beach with women bathers in burkas, borne aloft rather than sinking waterlogged in the artist's creative imagination; a complex of chimneys belching black smoke; and a mysterious windowless cinderblock structure with a question mark painted on it and soldiers in kepis patrolling alongside; all proving that industry can thrive along with godly vacations and development of the Pakistani nuclear deterrent.

Muhammad himself, founder of the G.L.M. Dining Restaurant, took their order. Although he wasn't a Sikh, he wore a turban for additional ethnic atmosphere at non-buffet hours. He tapped a finger against his order pad, a proud Sikh-like dinner warrior. It wasn't so much an impatient tap-tap as an eager one. "I'll have the... Nam?" said Petal. "That fried bread thingie? And the lamb glop right here..." – melon-flavored fingertip pointing to a paragraph describing rare and exotic spices – "... but hold the garlic?"

"It comes with," said Muhammad.

"Come without," Petal said, her smile softening the command. The temporary Sikh was charmed; beamed; didn't necessarily understand what she was saying.

Petal was hungry and Dan was glad. No mousse on the menu, but in her present mood of contentment with procedures so far, Petal was okay without whipped chocolate goo. She wiped up sauces with bread-like folds of flat dough. A hungry child ate like that. If Kasdan was destined to put his face close to her mouth, there would be mint, garlic, and curried lamb gravy smells, and cauliflower cooked and steamed, left over like roadkill from the $7.95 buffet lunch. Dan was okay with Petal's potpourri. It inspired him to tell her the story of his Bolivian client whose wife tried to poison him with pumpkin soup, but was too parsimonious – "That means stingy" – with the rat poison, so he survived, due to insufficient arsenic.

The wife was judged psychotic and sent to Vacaville, where the devoted husband visited religiously and the couple reconciled. She was released by recommendation of a blue-ribbon shrink committee. But then, after all, her husband asked for a divorce because she refused to cook for him. He loved her cuisine. He longed for her pumpkin soup, a tradition in their household. "Didn't trust herself," wise Petal said. Her eyes were shining; she liked entertainment of all sorts. "Can I have a dessert?" She turned to the tasseled menu, humming to herself. "I'd like something really sweet, with sugar."

Kasdan raised his hand and Muhammad advanced with his order pad and his suggestions for sweetness, including off-menu options. His smile displayed many teeth, both gold and silver. Fleetingly, Kasdan wondered if he were selling more than his $7.95 lunch buffet at month's end when the welfare checks came in. A person could buy property abroad, not necessarily in Haiti, or open a restaurant in San Francisco to wash away the stains on drug money, safely returning it to the international trade economy.

"For you," Muhammad proclaimed, "just the halva or baklava is superlative, for the digestion very good, my dear, honey, nuts, pressed leaves of home-made pastry. I recommend."

"Right, right," Petal said, "and seeds. Is there chocolate? I've been around the block a few times with Indian..."

"This is Pakistan," said Muhammad, mitigating his hurt with a smiling bow. He hated the nearby competition, that Mr. Patel and his poisonous nest of mouse-droppings in the buffet trays.

"... Asian-type food. You come here often, Dude? Speaking of that, you like a nice haircut?"

They weren't speaking of coiffeurs, but okay.

"... and a massage? I do a monster haircut. I'm practicing my Shit-Sue massage and you can help me map the pressure points."

Muhammad took the hint. The conversation between the girl and the older guy was not meant to be shared by a patriotic Pakistani with only a Green card.

"Or say you buy the eggs, you got a skillet? My omelets are awesome. I won't poison you like that lady, What's-her-face, the Brazilian, but my massage kills, guaranteed..." She winked. She must have had previous success with winks. "... or a painless throat slit when I'm trimming the hair in back where it makes your neck look tired and hairy."

"Thanks for the heads-up." (*Old* and hairy.)

She stared at the swinging doors that led to the kitchen. She could see Muhammad's sandals – he was wearing crew socks, so she could also see fleshy ankles – and judging by his body language, he was scraping halva out of a bin. Dividing her attention to the oncoming halva, she murmured, "A Western omelet maybe? That sound good to you? I put in the chili sauce, it goes with my green peppers, my cheese, sometimes I call it my Denver omelet. Or just what's left over – a Sacramento frittata? Isn't it the thought that counts, Danny Dude?"

"Funny."

"I don't know you well enough to want to poison you. Wouldn't even occur for a passing fancy."

"I have every confidence. Please inform me when you do."

Silence fell. Both of them participated in this silence. If teasing was a part of foreplay, they had made progress. They were both thoughtful – forced smiles, pressed lips, grim lines between the eyes – the silence an edge around deeper considerations about how their previous lives were contributing unshared memories to an occasion of feeding together. The world was in the state of its usual distress; the curry-imbued air here glowed pink and purple; two peculiar new acquaintances sat confused, needy, and less alone on Leavenworth at the bottom of Nob Hill. They were quick to lie to each other, to tease, pretend, and be stupid, as was fitting for how they met. Kasdan dreamed of a truth beyond this ritual foolishness. So much hope deserved a chance to redeem Dan and Petal-she-called-herself.

She broke the silence first. She was making her way in life by taking initiatives; lifelong, Kasdan's habit had been to watch and wait while initiatives were taken. Where the hell was that halva? Muhammad's hands suddenly appeared beneath the doors to the kitchen; he was yanking up his crew socks. A person with compassion in his heart could appreciate the annoyance of crew socks with tired elastic sliding down over the heel in sandals. The doors swung apart and halva arrived, set down with a scrape and a flourish. Muhammad's socks were completely pulled up.

This young Petal had a graspy hand. It had found his thigh again. She was saying, "Don't you get tired of restaurant food even if it's outstanding? How about soon I cook something for you? You could watch me bustling around, that be cozy?"

She was firing off energetically, scattering whitish and brownish halva shreds, bits meeting her teeth and spraying outwards. On her, it looked good.

"As a healthy old dude who lives alone, not that you're *old*, Dude, don't you get tired of that outside cooking? I could make one of my stews, whatever you got in the house, and you could sit there in your tee shirt, I hope you don't wear one of those strappy undershirts, and you could be telling me the sad story of your life, how you got to be an orphan."

"It's not that sad. My parents died."

"Probably. But the downward slope, man, and no loved ones to live after you..."

"A daughter. A grandson."

"Hey, whatever! Awesome! But everybody should have a good time before they go. We tsigane believe that."

Kasdan was startled. "You're not a gypsy."

She pressed the tines of her fork against the remaining shreds of halva, trying to make them stick. Didn't work too well. She picked at it with her fingernails. She was a young woman whom God had given long fingernails with the intention that she use them. Dan could barely see the halva, or the traces of it, as she licked her fingertips against her small, plump, heart-shaped mouth. "My grandfather on my mother's side. Or maybe my dad's. I don't exackly recall. Not exackly a gypsy, but a Traveler, the Irish kind, with wagons – now they use trucks, just like anybody."

Whatever, Kasdan decided.

"And I bet I can shock you with a surprise you'll never guess – only one tattoo on my bod! Boo!"

Whatever.

The radiator in her room at the Minerva Hotel on Turk was cold, but rust indicated occasional heat and steam leakage. Curtains decorated with a vegetable motif, tomato, carrots, bunches of radishes, hung over a window looking out on a street of castaways which Kasdan knew well. The curtains had been designed for a kitchen and may have been an urban renewal effort by a previous occupant who didn't take them with him when he moved up to a flat, down to a shelter, or died. Kasdan wasn't ready to trust Petal in his own apartment a few blocks away. He trusted her enough to call her by that name even if it wasn't hers.

Three stained paperbacks lay on the radiator, *Siddhartha*, *Stranger in a Strange Land* and *The Thinking Woman's Guide to Enlightenment*, passed along by her doting mother as goodbye presents. Kasdan was curious about such things even if they were extraneous elements in the current situation.

"I'm a klepto-scopto-bibliophiliac," he explained.

"Wha?"

"Means I like to steal looks at other people's books."

"Awesome. But if you're being clever, there's something I gotta tell you. It's not working out." But then she grinned, removing the sting and leaving only a little venom behind.

Circle designs on the book covers had no mystic significance; the books had been used as coasters. Street flicker from Turk through the

carrot, tomato, and radish curtains distracted him, though it was not
the worst problem he faced. Out of practice, he anticipated that the
climax of his visit to Petal might be giggles and hollow reassurance:
That's okay, you're a nice guy anyway, I appreciate the effort.

He said: "You're pretty young... Petal."

"Right, but actually you're not that old." She gestured toward a
choice of chair or bed. He sat on the chair, which turned out to have
room for two when she darted onto his lap. "Hey, what you're thinking? Like everybody makes that mistake. Mom named me."

"I guessed it would be something like that."

A moment of mutual meditation.

"... Petal," he added in order to show complete faith, the weight in
his lap squirming.

"So, French?" she asked. "You like kissing with your mouth open?
Just curious – French?"

"Do you?"

She shrugged her sturdy shoulders. This was one of those life
decisions about which she had yet to make up her mind. Her mother
had taught her to level with herself and others about both certainties
and doubts. Like Amanda, she did not utterly reject her mom. It was
touching, those shoulders, which were in the process of evolving
from waifiness to sturdiness. She was still thinking about the French.
"Dunno, I dunno. They say there's like a lot of bacteria in spit unless
you're a vegan. You're not a vegan."

"No."

"Me neither, but someday..." More thought, silence, dreaming of a
future of ingesting rather than eating, oxidizing only products which
support the beauty of Planet Earth and encourage fulfillment of it as
a bountiful, pesticide-free, planetary space. Veganism would give a
person abundance to share, fruit, vegetable and grain protein, all
created under sunshine and rain with the help of God's green chloro-
phyll. It would lead to germ-free French kissing, including unlimited
tongue action. Would it involve bad-vibe discussions with non-
vegans? This was a problem grass and cows never face, unless you
consider mowing or slaughter a kind of bad-vibe discussion.

He tried to relax while she followed the lonely winding trail of
rumination. Better to let matters unfold as if everyone in the entire
solar system, Dan, Amanda, Sergei, D'Wayne, Petal, even Ferd

Conway, really did have all the time in the world; and why not? It should be so.

Finally she came to a conclusion, sighing, "Well, a blow job's okay, I guess."

"No worries about..."

"Right. It's marginal they say, health-wise. I really appreciative you're letting me work this out for myself and not being an asshole about it."

"Thanks. This is the twenty-first century, no problem."

"Right, right, I've got a calendar. So you do a lot of Thai, Mexican, Hunan, like that?"

"The spices," he said. "A taste treat in many cultures."

He was trying to communicate with this stranger, just as he tried to adapt to his Hispanic miscreant clients (Hispanic or Latino, whatever they preferred). He shouldn't be here in her room at the Minerva. His precarious grasp on his own future didn't reduce his obligations as a careworn imminent senior citizen.

"Spices," she murmured. "Since you do, when they're filtered through the body..." Kasdan was thinking: liver, spleen, gall bladder, prostate. "... but I like you, so never mind."

"Appreciate."

"But probably I won't swallow."

"Thank you for sharing."

"Hmmm." This was humming. "You're very polite, dude." Her following silence called a time out for silent courtship. He accepted guidance. There was an implication during the silence of tenderness, trust, a closeness between strangers who had discovered each other by happenstance in the eddying gusts of the Tenderloin, the coziness of Katie's Meddle of Honor, on ground hallowed more than a hundred and fifty years ago by the tramping of miners from the gold fields, out to get blasted; then by immigrants from the far East, sometimes selling, under the terms of art, "massage" and "outcalls;" by runaway adolescents offering what they called "great shit;" by mumbling veterans of wars to bring democracy and freedom to the world; by old folks who had failed to make adequate arrangements for their sunset years. Also by Dan Kasdan.

He played his part, the loser with no visible hard feelings about being a non-winner. Aiming toward murder soon, he welcomed whatever came along today. In the matter of Ferd Conway, this was his secret and treasure, and if all went well, no one would be in a position to complain.

"Penny for your thoughts?" Petal asked.

"Make a better offer."

She did so, but he remained stingy with his thoughts. Dust, curtains, shiny orange carrots slowly and rapidly fluttering in the winds of Turk and Ellis, lifting the peeling plasticized curtains as if someone were spying through the window and asking, *Dad, what the hell you doing with her?*

She filled his arms with warmth. Oh, how long, how long? How long since, how long for? This flooding was not yet finished for him. His blood and hers were joined although she belonged to that stranger, herself. The truth could be forgotten just now.

"Who are you?"

"Shush, why ask questions? Take what there is, sweet man."

After they lay there silently awhile, letting the slick dry, hands lightly touching with that creature fondness which is everyone's due, Petal decided to read his mind. She read incorrectly, a clairvoyant with cloudy vision: "I do too have a sense of humor." She sat up, bent over, kissed, sat back up, observed the rising. "Magic," she said. "Hope springs immortal."

"Hope isn't what it's called. I wasn't thinking about your sense of humor."

"You weren't? Can't distract you?" She bent, again did what she had just done to incite what she called hope and encourage its ascension. "Right now, the wrong thing to think about is your wife or your ex or your kids if you've got some."

In fact, a thought of Sergei had floated through his haze. Here with Petal, he was firmly based on terra incognita. Despite Marvin Feldstein's urological pessimism, the little gland had consented to do its traditional job. Thank you, agreeable little gland. "Watchful waiting" was one of the options Marvin had offered; watchful coitus was one of the byproducts. Veteran Prostate, You're My Friend.

Fondness led to murmured confidences. Petal was a self-taught massage therapist, but rejected invitations to do, yucch, the kind of massage those Asian girls, they don't like to be called Oriental, or those former boys now proudly trannies, or all those others in the neighborhood were selling. "Yucch," she murmured into his ear, "that's so degrading. I might give somebody a handjob if I want to take a day off for shopping, not have to pick around at Goodwill for my stuff, but no... you know," she added shyly.

Kasdan thought he knew. No deep soul-to-soul tantric celebration of oneness.

"But I like whatever you like. Tell me what you like. I'm just a girl, so what else you like?"

Kasdan was open to her suggestions. She waited. After a sigh, warm breath in his ear, she commented, "Whatever." Kasdan inclined his head; it was a gesture like piety; his ear tickled. How could he ever repay her compliments? Well, first, not to take them seriously. Compliments were a kind gesture, a validated ritual in love-making, even after short acquaintance, part of the interplay of hormones and civilized tradition, like a companionable back scratch or nuzzle.

He raised his head off the pillow; prayer concluded. Her breath still warmed him. Prayer not quite concluded; he added a codicil: And thanks also to Doc Feldstein for the concept of watchful waiting. As she opened to him, her eyelids drooped in lonely abstention; and then they widened with the luxurious blank stare of arousal, fright-ened, her eyes rolling back into her head as if she had fainted. Briefly, she was present; then she escaped. She seemed to have fled in panic from her body. Kasdan should have been happy; he was lying there with a warm, beautiful, and strange young woman; a marvelous turmoil had come to him; but he was not happy. There were regrets.

She sighed and shyly smiled. All these accidents were more than he deserved. Now he knew what he regretted – that it was no longer 1969 with the Grateful Dead playing a free concert under pine and eucalyptus trees in the Panhandle of Golden Gate Park, when marvel-ous accidents and turmoil seemed to be everyone's due.

Dan Kasdan was far away; he had been there before, he no longer remembered the time, the place, the life, himself; he was gone to Dan Kasdan. He must have slept.

"Was that nice?"

He opened his eyes. The curtains with their vegetable patterns, tomatoes, peppers, the ferocious orange of the carrots, were still stirring and lifting in the winds swirling down Turk. Grit had eaten at the curtains. Night had come and a streetlamp flickered. The bulb needed changing. It would be replaced someday, when the city bureau in charge of filaments took notice. Here in San Francisco, it was generally not urgent either to close the window or to open it, but grit had sifted through the curtains, the plasticized fabric eroding, and only the carrot dye stood out in its bright, bright orange. For a moment, Kasdan, flickering like the filament in the streetlamp, returning from his brief elsewhere, that blessed nonbeing convulsion, feared that the spirits of past loves, uneasy and unremembered ones, had lifted the desolate rag of curtain. They were spying on him. They were ready to take their revenge. The wind down Turk found him.

"Are you happy now?"

He turned onto his side and bunched the sheet between his knees, drying the stickiness. "I'm not sad."

"Just not sad, that's all? Dude, you are sickening."

He leaned up into her anxious face. "I'm fine, I'm fine."

"Learn to be polite, okay? Just lie when a person asks you, okay?"

"I'm sorry."

She shook her head. She was used to disappointment. "People never – I'm a person wants things my own way, always was, always will be – but people never... They don't do what I want them to do or say what I want them to say."

"Not an uncommon problem. My experience, too."

She seemed pleased by this. Despite the age difference, they were tight, like brother and sister, even if brother and sister wasn't the kind of tightness going on. She wanted to talk. He owed her some confiding conversation. He ran his finger along her eyebrows, smoothing them – they were damp. It had always been trouble for him to lie. The social ramble was difficult and it was more comfortable to keep it to a minimum. Okay, Harvey Johnson, his Roma pal, sometimes a dinner and a brew – that was about it. Marriage, children, long friendships, the prospect of these arduous matters had made him uneasy and he chose a life without them. No doubt it was a life that chose him.

But now that Amanda had chosen to find him, Sergei had come upon him, a daughter and a grandson fallen into his late years, he was determined to manage what he had not intended. It was easier to translate his Hall of Justice clients' lies than to tell his own. Ferd Conway was helping. Of course, Kasdan hadn't informed Ferd that he would be drastically ripped off, but this wasn't exactly deceitful – also didn't tell him he would *not* be ripped off and killed.

Kasdan touched Petal's cheeks as she had touched his. "You're different. I like you."

"Really? You mean that? I think you're different, too."

A pair of different people in a room on the third floor of the Minerva Hotel with vegetable curtains billowing at the window. For a time, their arms wrapped around their unshared dreams, they slept.

"This other guy, this black dude, African-American, you know?" Petal was murmuring near the ear of this present guy, this white dude, offering the words *this black dude* as if jealousy might be a sealant to their connection, "He has an idea for me."

For Kasdan, jealousy was more of a distraction than anything favorable toward something like, what was it? Love. He was too old for his stomach to churn over the words *this other dude*, spoken by a stranger whom he happened to be lying alongside, his hand over her breast. Nevertheless, of its own will, his stomach twisted a little, due to an ancient peristaltic persistence of desires for exclusive possession.

"It's sort of weird, but Mom always said a woman's body is my own. I can get a leg up, really save a nest egg, which I dearly need, plus free medical checkups, work a little and have a nice room all to myself, maid service, linen service, I don't dearly need all that, but it would be awesome, maybe not all my weekends free, but if I keep my looks, and I don't see why not, special dates in heavy-duty restaurants..." She stopped for breath, due to rapid naming of dearly awesome options; her lovely lips were damp and parted.

Next move, Dan Kasdan's.

"Enlighten me," he said, startled at what came out of his mouth. Usually what startled him came out of the mouth of Amanda or Ferd or one of the perps he helped to give their accounts of what really happened. *Endarken us.*

"Huh?" Petal asked. Even Kasdan's perps had better evasions when interrogated.

He sat up and leaned against the headboard, which creaked and hit the wall. He jammed a pillow against the small of his back.

"What're you talking about?"

"A clinic kind of deal. Helping guys like you, really nice guys, not hit them up personally for the money, that's so gross. The nurse in charge, you call her the attendant, takes care of these details..."

"A whorehouse," Kasdan said.

"Shush, you're rude, dude. Hey, I just made another poem, didn't I? Rude... dude? It's a nice clean safe place and let me tell you I could use some nice clean safe in my life."

"A brothel," Kasdan said.

"That's better. I like that."

"What's his name? The dude with the business opportunity. How do you know him? What's his deal?"

She pulled his nose. She kissed it better. Her lips pouted over the protuberant front teeth. Her mouth was soft, which he already knew. "His name, that would be telling, wouldn't it? Way uncool. Really rude, dude."

"Tell me anyway."

Stomach, be still, slow down. The evening swirls of fog were blowing down Turk. There was a crustiness of the sheet against his leg. Her abstracted, considering, confiding face; her breath warming him. "Big strong dude makes sure everything is copacetic, he's like a doorman, no trouble allowed, and he says, 'Welcome, thank you for coming,' like a greeter for the guys, stuff like that – a really responsible position for an expert in the street smarts field."

Had she gotten up to slip into a plasticine of crystal while he dozed? No fresh spot of pink near her elbow; no hit to be smelled on her breath, although curry and halva and mint toothpaste could disguise a late-evening pick-her-up which caused the motor to run on ahead.

"This gentleman gets a commission for bringing you in. Did he audition you first?"

"I told you already, it's just a job. He's got a wife, a baby, but he can see I'm sort of cute and he doesn't mind telling me."

Kasdan asked, "What's his name?"

"Man, you keep after a person, don't you? You always wanna know what's my real name, now it's *his* name. Okay, I think it's his real name, it does sound like that, doesn't it? D'Wayne," she said.

D'Wayne. Heading home from Katie's Meddle of Honor, home from their Pakistani experience, home from the Minerva Hotel, Kasdan was thinking it over. What were the chances he would find himself in a hotel room on Turk with its window decorated with inappropriate kitchen curtains, carrots, tomatoes, and squash, on this day or any other day? It had happened. He thought it over further. What were the chances a longtime court translator would murder a close associate in order to steal his illegal money, therefore making the money twice illegal? It would happen.

It was midnight and, at the corner, two dealers were treating each other to high-fives. Peace, brother; although competitors, they meant each other no harm. A cat was worrying a dead pigeon at the curb outside Kasdan's apartment building. The cat cuffed it, the clawed body budged, a few feathers dropped off, the cat snarled and attacked; the pigeon didn't fight back. The cat crouched and made an ominous non-purring rumble, a low-pitched whine, cuffed the pigeon again with velvet claws.... This cat and pigeon show wasn't played out near Kasdan's entrance every day, but on the other hand, here they were and it was happening.

So she had met D'Wayne. San Francisco was a small town, walled by the sea. Why wouldn't a lost waif find a friendly, fleshy, smiling black guy hustling to support his family as best he could? It was almost logical.

Go on from here. Shit happens to pigeons and people. Deal with it.

– 12 –

Amanda's face was hot when he put his arms around her and laid her head against his cheek. No matter how often he did this, and he did it when any excuse presented itself, the lost years remained their lost years. "Are you running a fever?"

"Dad, it just feels like that to you. Maybe you're just cold-blooded."

Which didn't answer the question. Margaret Torres had used "cold blood" as one of the explanations for why Amanda's father never appeared during her childhood. (Other explanations: died, in prison, on the lam, turned gay and then transsexual; take your pick, sweetie.) Balancing out the cold blood, Amanda burned at a high temperature; as did Sergei, because of his different bruising. Kasdan's own thermostat was set as it was set. Today Amanda happened to wonder if the grandfather would like to stay awhile with Sergei while she made a quick trip to the Safeway. She waved a shopping list in his direction. "Hey Dad, it'll be a bonding experience, that's what I read in the hospital dealie they gave me." She needed to escape for an hour or two. It would give him time to practice his grandfather skills.

"Keep Sergei from..." Amanda shrugged. There was a long roster of things to keep Sergei from. "Bond," she said. She grabbed a purse and a sweater. "Bond, okay?" A torn pamphlet fell from the edge of a folding changing table when she slammed the door. It was "The Modern Mom," an instruction manual with pink and blue colors, gender neutral, probably including a section of advice on how to persuade apprehensive grandfathers to perform acts of family responsibility. Bonding, okay; here goes.

"Sergei, what should we talk about?"

Scream.

"Let's discuss, Sergei. I hear you. We're busy bonding, but could you specify more exactly?"

Spasms and kicks, red-faced fury, distraught rolling eyes.

"I get it, you miss Mom? She'll be right back. Hey, come on."

He held the twisting body close, swaddling him, and a miracle occurred. The throb of Kasdan's heart was transmitted through his chest. Before he was born, Sergei lay curled in his mother, attending to her heartbeat. There must have been a remembrance of vibrations. The child sobbed with subsiding wet gurgles. And then, abruptly, silence. Like a healthy child, Sergei slept in his arms.

"I'm thirsty," Kasdan whispered.

Sergei sagged, fitting body to body, his hand curled against Kasdan's shoulder. Kasdan could wait for the glass of water until Amanda returned. This light curling of monkey paw on shoulder was drink enough. The sour smell was part of the babysitting grandfather dealie. He knew that all babies spit up and drool; enzymes and valves haven't learned to synchronize yet. Another part of the caretaking which he had missed with Amanda were these stains and stinks. He held the child and practiced one-sided conversation with him. "Now, now... All right... Good boy, nice boy, settle down... It's okay, Sergei." The child was breathing through his mouth, pushing smells around. Kasdan wanted to kiss him anyway. Perhaps that would encourage the enzymes and mucous and kid drainage systems do their work. Later, if Dan Kasdan was still present on earth, he could watch Sergei learn to crawl, the gurgle signals changing to syllables; learn to smile, as a child should, digesting accurately and with pleasure; attending to those lovely ordinary matters along the trail of years even when Kasdan would surely be absent from his life.

Sergei despaired of the world. In a moment he was again trying to scream and drool simultaneously, and succeeding. "Please," Kasdan began – not the way to go; he wouldn't understand *please*. "Don't overdo the tantrums," he pleaded, stroking the child's shoulder, knowing that a baby with storms raging in his body couldn't understand Overdo, Tantrum, or Don't, although he had been surrounded by Don'ts and Can'ts since his irregular feet-first birth.

Not expecting favorable results, Kasdan received none. Sergei screamed, pissed, shat, and threw up. He choked, then breathed again. His convulsions were difficult for his grandfather, but Sergei wasn't in the business of considering other people's comfort. Kasdan lifted him and tapped his back in the *now, now* gesture, a parental, grandparental reflex. Not all evolutionary instincts are productive. The child was spilling fluids upon his grandfather.

"You're not trying," Kasdan said.

He wiped; he tried to clean. He smeared. He wished Amanda or D'Wayne would return. He had never experienced the many orifices of a convulsing child. "How will you..." he began cajolingly, not losing his temper, caressing a miniature summation of all the griefs of the human race. How will you ever qualify to criticize others, and make stupid mistakes, like me, if you don't behave yourself? Silent advice was sent into unconnected receptors.

On the other hand, Sergei – Kasdan still trying for good-humored silent transmission – as an American, in the tradition of freedom and compassion which makes this country more than great, beyond superior, superb, Sergei – more silent patient grandfatherly thoughtwave labor – you have the right and privilege, nay, the duty to ignore your own imperfections while demanding service from others... Sergei bawled.

Aloud, Kasdan said, "Oh please shut up."

Sergei's twistings and spittings, the mashing of his gums together and the bleeding where a tooth raked them, the spasms of legs and arms and little shoulders with their quivering pads of baby flesh, were accompanied by intervals of a very grownup squinting, a staring look of terror. Sergei didn't choose to fling himself into these dances. His soul knew it was not right. His immortal soul understood and mourned.

"Shush, shush, shush," Kasdan said, the boy kicking and screaming into his ear while the desperation in his eyes begged: Help me! Save me!

"Shush, child, I'm just holding you, I'm here, it's okay."

One of the pediatricians at San Francisco General had suggested, "Try to keep his limbs from striking hard surfaces. Think of it as something like childhood-onset epilepsy or a form of Tourette's. Try to shield him from throwing himself off his crib or against a wall. Call my office if you have further questions about little Sergei Moses."

Kasdan pressed him tightly against his chest. Tiny arms jerked as if a reptile ancestor wanted to fly from a predator but hadn't yet grown wings. Kasdan's heart was breaking. He said: "Listen, there's this Pasqual, he's only a client, but he can make himself clear, Sergei. He's not even a relative except that all human beings are brothers and sisters, grandchildren, whatever. Please, dear. Please."

After the storm, after soiling himself, after screaming for no reason to be grasped by anyone, desolate and inconsolable, Sergei subsided. He was exhausted. He slept. The hot head against Kasdan's heart burrowed a nest and the person under the nest took joy in giving shelter. Even Kasdan felt himself slipping into a doze, his arms around the pain of this small creature. The sour smell was one of the perfumes of family. A place in Kasdan's chest was communicating with a place behind his eyes in the desire to weep with joy. Sergei urged him along the path. He was happy to learn from his grandson.

Kasdan glimpsed a tiny shadow flickering across the kitchen floor and disappearing into the wall. It was a tenant he had not met. Within this household, already complete enough, a mouse had sublet space between plaster crumbles and a shaggy wooden strut, its edges shredded by insects who liked fiber, rodents which liked to sharpen their teeth. Kasdan thought he might mention it to D'Wayne. He thought not to mention it to Amanda. Kasdan had not yet decided whether to mention it to anyone.

He was struggling with a plastic-coated disposable diaper, tabs that were supposed to be pulled together and then stick. Sergei was squeaking, not screaming, as Kasdan tried to keep him from falling off the table while he undid, wiped, fastened, worried, felt sure he wasn't doing it right. He noticed a scatter of mouse droppings near the wall; he kept his arm on Sergei so he wouldn't flip off the table. Amanda and D'Wayne probably knew about the mouse but hadn't yet gotten around to doing anything about it.

Kasdan's daughter wouldn't worry about a mouse running up her leg and disappearing within. Some women would. Kasdan had heard of a woman who saw a mouse in her kitchen and called 911. When the police rejected her plea, she called the Fire Department.

Once Kasdan had been in his bathtub, a relic raised on cast iron claws, sharing a nice hot bath with a new acquaintance, when she saw a mouse, said, "Eeek," and threw herself, splashing and giggling with both the fright and the fun of it, into his lap. So mice didn't always have deleterious effects. He had felt exceptionally stalwart about saving her; he rose sturdily to the challenge.

"My hero," said his bathtub companion.

Later, she asked if he scheduled periodontal checkups every year and he realized that he was having mouse-assisted sex with a dentist.

When a person is a lifelong bachelor in San Francisco, he never knows what may ensue from a casual meeting at the Caffe Roma.

Best to let Amanda and D'Wayne discover and deal with their mouse without counsel from the formerly absent father of Sergei's mother.

Tending to Sergei felt like wrestling with a burst plumbing pipe. There was no good way to take hold. He was shoved and drenched, near to helpless, while the convenient bio-degradable diaper hung crookedly from soft, fat, uncoordinated legs. When keys rattled at the door, Kasdan's first two thoughts were, Am I locked in? Is the jailer here for my interrogation? But it was Amanda, arms loaded with Safeway bags, paper products spilling out. A baby seemed to consume forests. Kasdan's arms were tumbled with paper towels, toilet rolls, plasticized disposable diapers. "Thanks, Dad, really appreciate – you had fun, right? Was he good?"

"Fine, fine, fine."

"Man, I needed that. Shopping for shit is like a vacation for me."

"Oh, we had a terrific time," the grandfather said. This about covered the bases without dealing with panic, anxiety, doubt, isolation, conditions which didn't need futile elaboration for his daughter.

Now Sergei was asleep, mouth parted, gums wet and darkened with congealed blood. Amanda wasn't planning to press on, although she did: "He give you a hard time?"

"Had a ball," Kasdan repeated. "Fine."

Sergei's lashes were glued shut. In the abrupt way of a child, he had checked out. His eyes behind closed lids, still wet from previous tears, were stirring in dreams, but of what? Of darkness or light, of an earlier iguana or monkey life, or of nothing at all.

"Like a vacation at the beach for me," Kasdan said, "lounging with my grandson."

Amanda kissed him for this lie, and for the sarcasm added a little bite on his cheek, a mere nip which didn't break the skin.

And they said goodbye for now. Despite Kasdan's diminished hearing, the determined voice from the street came through clearly: "White horse." Due to insistent reiteration, he could make no mistake about it. A vendor, wearing a long black overcoat despite a climate which did not call for long overcoats, chanted his offer to passersby: "White horse, white horse, white horse." He was tireless. His chant would only be interrupted by the consummation of a deal, money exchanged for glassine envelopes. Kasdan had a plan for moving Amanda's family to another neighborhood.

The vendor in the long black overcoat didn't see Kasdan heading his way through the vestibule, but recovered in time to ask the man moving past him: "Hey... White horse?"

"Not today."

He had succeeded in putting other matters out of mind while he attended to his daughter, his grandson, and the evidence of previous inadequacies. It was only right that he do so; he tried to give himself a little credit. Dan Kasdan was making his way like a young man, or like an old man, or like a wise one; like some kind of man.

Here, on Ellis, it seemed like a betrayal to be thinking of Petal again, her lips pushed entrancingly ahead of her front teeth, a flaw that charmed the some kind of unwise man that he still seemed to be. It should have been enough occupation for the day to be in a house of love and betrayal; Amanda's of D'Wayne, actual or imminent; Ferd Conway's of Dan and his family; Dan's of his future victim; all these lovers, needing to be lovers, on the way to betrayal.

Petal's lips on his sealed them with a kiss, then opened with his kisses.

"Hey Sir," said the man in the long black overcoat, "you look like you can use a little pick-up or calm-down, don't you? Can't quite afford Colombia white today, I got you some righteous Thai brown... Sir?"

The merchant, his overcoat flapping as he followed, treated Kasdan's gray hair and eroded cheeks with respect.

"Sir? Make a first-client deal on special today only?"

– 13 –

Dan Kasdan jump-started the journey through his next day with the comfort of anonymous companionship after the anxious dreams of Sergei which crowded his night, the dark thoughts of his destination with Ferd Conway that accompanied his barefoot treks down the hall to pee, shake vigorously, send a mental salute to Doc Feldstein. In the half light from the street, he sighed, sipped from a glass of water, bid anxious dreams to stay away, including the one about Petal, returned to his bed for another hour or two. It wasn't in his heart to pray for mercy to an all-forgiving God, so he only posted a To Whom It May Concern notice on the wall of night; then sank back down, if he was lucky, into renewed sleep without renewed dreams. He couldn't bring back the one about Petal. The film was blank.

Sometimes, during troubled nights, he imagined Sergei as a seventeen-year-old driven to find out what to do with an erection or, if he were a rational and ambulatory boy by that time, and perhaps he might be, heading out to pick up a raddled hooker on Capp Street, the last stop for raddled hookers. Kasdan might not be around to offer guidance. D'Wayne might be.

The morning bustle at the Caffe Roma across the street from the Hall of Justice served nicely in the jump-starting mode. Lawyers, defendants on bail, morose sheriff deputies, cops managing to look full of importance even when they took their coffee, confused conscripts to the jury pool, weepy spouse-equivalents and moms of defendants, all gathered amid the clang and whine of espresso machines, cell phones and each other.

Kasdan used to be certain of which were the lawyers, which the defendants, which the guards and plainclothes personnel, but now tattoos seemed to be everywhere in the criminal justice system. Piercings were not quite as contagious, but getting there. He waited at the counter for his very large latte, served by Marta to him alone, as a special favor, in a deep soup bowl which warmed the paws of Dan Kasdan, court interpreter. Since she had no time to do anything more to express cafe favoritism, Marta only winked.

In the crowd there were whispered consultations about strategy along with family tears; also irritable demands for justice or extra hot milk. When Marta was on duty at the espresso machine, Kasdan got the extra hot milk as a matter of tradition between them; nice Marta, pony tail, lip ring, multicolored butterfly etched into her back, and Kasdan would never risk sacrificing his extra hot milk by proposing to open the butterfly's wings. When Marta caught him eying the tattoo as she stretched her tongs to reach a muffin, separating the blouse from the jeans, she asked: "So you like my rear license plate?"

At this hour of the morning, extra hot milk, hold the foam, was more important. Nice wakeup smells of coffee, toast, and heated muffins were supplemented – you could say amplified – by spicy side dishes, such as the recent flock of teeny-tiny Asian graduates of pretty good law schools, teetering into their careers on dangerous high heels and carrying the new top-grain vinyl briefcases given them by proud fathers. It was the thought that counted; later, a boyfriend might provide leather. Occasionally, raving homeless souls pushed through, sent away with free cups of coffee, all the sugar and cream their hearts desired, by friendly Marta, she of the savoir vivre and generous spirit and agreement with Roma management that their coffee didn't come out of her pay. It was a civic responsibility for doing business in the neighborhood. The teeny-tiny new lawyers were already accustomed to not seeing the mad persons, who were everywhere in San Francisco. America was still a nation which held to the strong belief in kindness except sometimes.

A row of storefront bail bondsmen nearby, a pawnshop – conven-ient for a quick cash fix – bars with the traditional purple neon martini glass installation, although as at Katie's Meddle of Honor, martinis were no longer a prominent factor in San Francisco beveraging activity... the neighborhood offered all the services a criminal lawyer or defendant or significant other could ask for, including motels a block or so away if someone got lucky and didn't object to a four-minute stroll on behalf of a quality erotic adventure. Whether high or low quality was strictly up to the individuals involved. Kasdan missed taking his breakfast coffee bowl with Harvey Johnson these days. It was Kasdan's own fault for complicating his life; Amanda, Sergei, Ferd... Harvey and he could be having another chat about their prostates or Harvey could review his rap about the stories perps tell. "After the fact, therefore not caused by the fact,"

Kasdan would say, the way old buddies tease each other. "I know you're proud of your Latin, Harv."

"Yeah, so this corner boy says he was just boppin' on past the store, when this kid I never even knew ask me if I hold his gun a minute and it jes blew up in my hand. How was I to antici-perate the lady was gonna scare all up on me and drop her payroll?"

Kasdan nodded.

"Res ipsa loquitur Not, Ossifer."

Instead, with Harvey pissed with him, Kasdan sat alone this morning. The detective must be doing his breakfast elsewhere, or sitting in his car on a stakeout, or just offering an implied statement about old friends who make stupid choices in new friends, such as Ferd Conway. Dan wouldn't bring up the Petal subject, at least not yet. Alone at the Roma, warming his hands around the extra-large bowl (it felt Spanish to him, or at least French), Kasdan heard keys nervously jingling at the next table. A middle-aged, middle-paunched lawyer was leaning forward to explain the facts of life, what he hoped would be the facts of *her* life, to one of the cute, teeny-tiny, newly-minted public defenders. Perhaps she could think of his ardent key-jingling as chimes instead of an annoying tic.

With age, Kasdan had not become less nosy; eavesdropping was a bachelor's recourse, vicarious sociability, which used to keep him from speeding even faster on the downward slope. He was interested in what went on around him, across the room, and in the street. He guessed that pudgy key-jingling hand – the lawyer jingling his keys like a horny kid playing with himself – was accompanying a hint of options for the lovely legal waif: use of an upscale office and a fine German automobile if she preferred a quickie, a weekend stay at Tahoe or on his a neat little boat docked at the St. Francis Yacht Club if they really got along; various proposals in store for her, but only by mutual consent, this being the twenty-first century, although of course without any formal stipulation in writing. No letter agreement or any other feminist crapola.

Clash of keys against keys; a persuading baritone monologue; an answering stare out of almond-shaped eyes, exasperatingly unread-able, just as in the days before high-IQ Asian waifs entered the market.

Kasdan sipped his coffee, wiped foam off his lips. Thank you, Marta. He wondered if the bunch of keys, rabbit's foot attached, really unlocked all the many doors they promised. The waif only listened, but now was gazing intently into the attorney's eyes. She smelled of a good lotion, warmth rising around her; she smelled of what a Boalt Hall graduate might dab on her neck and wrists in the morning. She gazed with the concentration of someone who wouldn't mind career help, but wasn't sure this bozo could provide it. Still, let him dream...

Oh, no. Kasdan was late for Pasqual, once more his client, on the road to a three-strikes conviction, a life term in exchange for minor felonies. Kasdan, breaking professional standards of strict boundaries to his service, had tried to warn him the last time; Pasqual was a stubborn slow learner, like Dan Kasdan in that way.

He left an inch of his double latte in the bowl and hurried across the street toward 850 Bryant. Waste not, want not, but Kasdan also believed in promptness, the kindness he owed clients who weren't on the receiving end of many kindnesses in the legal grinder. As he hurried past Judge Gonzalez, stately Gustavo Gonzalez, the magistrate greeted him with a restrained multicultural salute – his raised pinkie with a bright stone shining, sending its glare into Kasdan's less prosperous court translator's eyes. Unlike "Speedy" Gonzalez (never called that to his face), Kasdan was the sort of non-outgoing loser who was incapable of finding a *chica* thoughtful enough to give him a pinkie ring on a religious holiday or personal birthday. Poor Pasqual didn't reach for the stars, probably because the stars were out of his reach.

Pasqual was waiting in the holding pen. At the elevator, a young woman with a black beret aslant on her head and a shiny black miniskirt, her legs stretched by too-high heels, an alert Fifi in historical Apache drag, greeted him: "Hey? Hey?" A crooked smile twisted the heart-shaped mouth, there was a chipped front tooth he hadn't noticed before, and her expression was wide-eyed and inquiring, as if expecting not to be acknowledged.

"Petal," he stated. But he had to get to the holding pen (poor Pasqual); duty called. "Petal Jihad."

"Awesome," she said. "You believe that name I told you." Not living up to her Apache costume, she repeated like a high school kid,

"You are awesome, dude." She was grinning and shaking her head. "But how could you forget?"

"Wouldn't, and you know that. What're you doing here?"

"So I got a new job. You want my telephone number, did I give it to you? No, I couldn't, it's my new cell phone. You want to call me?"

Sure do, thought Kasdan, and then said: "Sure do. Yes."

Amenities taken care of, her smile flashed off as they were jostled by the morning crowd pushing into the elevator. She handed him a torn piece of paper. "I got to talk to you, really. Are you up for it? Talk? I made a promise..."

"To me."

She wasn't looking at him. She was staring at the sliding elevator door. She seemed to be giving him bad news, saying, without meeting his eyes, "I stopped about the needles. I'm supposed to keep my promises, that's part of the program. Promised on my honor, God's honor, too. In the program. So I got to say I'm sorry..."

"Never mind – sorry for what? Petal, there's no harm in you."

She was startled at the judgment. Kasdan remembered the lava flow of warmth that had engulfed him with this strange creature from another time, this visitant from the Summer of Love; it was daytime in another century now, it was work time; and Pasqual, if he knew Pasqual, was probably still drunk and sick from last night, standing in the reek of a holding pen. Despite his limits in language and IQ, Pasqual always managed to find the means to get high, even when unjustly harassed by lying racist accusations that he was always getting high. The elevator door slid open again and Petal cried in a bereft voice, "Take the next one!"

"Got a client needs me, I'm late – we'll talk later – you have nothing to be sorry for."

She was shaking her head. She just gave up. He was not available; not available was something she knew all about. She could make her 12-step apology when he was ready to hear it. There was harm in her. She could break her promise another time.

He stood in the elevator and she stood outside and they stared at each other as the door slid shut. He caught a glimpse of her turning and running toward the security guards. He couldn't recall any promises to be broken by her. But just now he had to think about Pasqual and help to prep him as best he could; the public defender was there already, exasperated because Pascal's court translator, usually so reliable, was running late.

— 14 —

He picked the torn scrap of paper out of his breast pocket, his "office pocket." He called her new cell phone number. Voicemail answered: "Hi! Petal! Shine on!" He didn't expect her to pick up.

It was dusk, not raining or gloomily cold, not yet anyway, and nothing especially worse than usual had happened today for Kasdan's client Pasqual, twenty-four years old, career car-washer and purse-snatcher, up for a possible third strike and life imprisonment – nothing unexpectedly bad and nothing especially good, either. My colleague, Kasdan thought about Pasqual, even if they weren't colleagues. The same nothing bad, nothing good applied to Kasdan, who left ladies' purses where they belonged and let his eight-year-old Honda Civic sit uncleaned except by the street people who occasionally wiped off the dust or pigeon droppings with their butts by sitting on it. Amanda, D'Wayne and Sergei were also doing okay at the moment, according to Amanda, Sergei waking to the sound of his own screams only twice today.

Kasdan headed for a brew. He was wondering what Petal had on her mind. There were ample unknowns in this stranger who had caused commotion, stirred him, for reasons of Kasdan and reasons of Petal, certainly different ones for each. Despite the dreaminess of great and authoritative poets, this was the case even when true, deep, and everlasting love is out of the question.

Now that his duty with Pasqual was done for awhile, and he had spent all the compassion he could spare, he turned to his own problems. There were a few. The late afternoon, early evening blues needed no justification, they were normal, but his newer worry, Petal-she-called-herself, added to his excuses for a cold glass in a quiet corner with his eyelids drooping just a little and the spool of his life stuttering in his head. Remedies were called for. The beer would ease him down toward minestrone, a hunk of sourdough bread, and early bed. There was always a price to be paid for an evening Anchor steam followed by another. He would wake to pee more often than usual, but when he needed a beer, it was useless to worry in advance about sleep interruptions. A price was demanded for every consolation.

He could try to sort out the long inconclusive day with a beverage session at Katie's Meddle of Honor. It had nothing to do with having met Petal there; he assured himself of this. Every man in any situation deserves a destination where he can take a corner table at the back and stare into the darkening street with purple reflections radiating off the purple neon martini glass, although not every man realizes this. Tough for them. Didn't they understand the concept of "home away from home?" The sign was a comfort. Random street noises – automobiles and trucks, dialogues by solo conversationalists raising their voices to be heard by the other half of their personalities, the sharp snapping of electrical neon connections, dim evening cries and scrapes – all that was familiar to him was Kasdan's familiar reassurance. It filtered his reality, which needed filtering. The world might be okay, even if sometimes more interesting than was desirable. The world had never asked for Kasdan's approval. Okayness would be a little more prevalent after his evening sorting-out procedure, aided by the single draft of Anchor steam beer, a prudent man's respite.

Even if Kasdan had to face the fact that, actually, after due consideration, he was imprudent and on the way to being more so. And then another single moderate draft.

Despite his fuller understanding of the day only a few minutes ago – no, an hour ago now – it had turned dark, rainy and gloomily cold. He was tired. He had lost track of time. He might skip the soup and torn-off sourdough hunks, have another Anchor steam instead. More than his past was on his mind. Both the weather and general life events moved in irregular lurches on the sea-bound peninsula of San Francisco. The city was enclosed by the bay and an ocean. This man, he decided, was not an island – he too was a peninsula. Walls of water separated him from the world, except at one corner. He was not fully cut off.

Tonight, during a gust of wet, the purple neon reflections sparkled in droplets sliding down Katie's front window. Kasdan sneezed. He was allergic to the hay stacked for Katie's pony, farm aromas blown in from the back room, which Katie called her "corral." Or the sneeze might have been a sneeze of compassion for Pasqual. Despite Kasdan's skill at translating abusive, obscene, pitiful Spanish into indignant English, Pasqual was looking at a future of incarceration until the three strikes law was repealed. Win hardly any, lose many.

A chilled half pint with beads like cold tears streaming down the glass was always helpful. Around the time of Amanda's conception, twenty years ago, Kasdan had learned that two half pints were not twice as good as one; learned in general, not always in particular.

In the "corral" Katie was cuddling her pony's cute little head, smoothing back its perked-up ears, tending its hooves, and then fixing her own makeup, which had smeared in the rainy garden. The biceps of Fabulous Frank, the tattooed bartender, were slowly deflating, like balloons – he did curling exercises before his night shift – as he polished fly specks, lipstick stains, or other adverse blotches off the glasses, protective of Meddle of Honor ambiance. The evening biceps display was part of his general keeping up of standards. Something was clicking in the martini neon, needing a replacement cord or a new switch. If the click segued into a sputter, it would short out – this had happened before when it rained. All was, if not right, at least normal with the world.

"The usual, Big Guy? Sure you don't want a shot with that, just for fun? Cure the damp? But the farmers are happy, they adore this weather."

There weren't many farmers on Ellis, Turk, or Leavenworth in San Francisco. Fabulous Frank winked as Kasdan took a nice swallow before carrying a rare additional half pint to his table.

"Feel better already, don't you? And let me grant you this, it do not tend to give you the downer blahs some folks get from crank or that shitty ice they were smoking couple-three years ago, but no more."

"No more," said Kasdan, which was about the extent of his polite banter with Frank this evening.

"You'll grant me that, Big Guy."

Their friendship was firmly rooted in an understanding of leave-me-mostly-alone. Frank was a bartender who understood the clients. He offered dialogue, an exchange of views, working up to philosophies of life; then the choice of either further ramification or benevolent silence was up to the person buying the drinks. Tonight, Kasdan chose an early halt to view exchange. No probing. Frank's biceps were deflating even as they spoke. His curling exercises were a strictly on-duty phenomenon. The gain in masculinity esteem which was achieved before they deflated lingered through the process of gradual beveraging by Katie's regulars. No hissing tire-leak sound betrayed the temporary nature of Fabulous Frank's outstanding biceps.

Kasdan sipped with slow concentration. He slept more easily if he helped the day decelerate, but it was a trade-off. Often he awakened exactly at the moment when his dreams were getting interesting. Before a person breaks familiar routines, does something drastic, such as a first murder, it was helpful to rest the spirit with reminders of consoling patterns: a brew at Katie's Meddle of Honor, a review of Fabulous Frank's fabulous inflatable biceps, the pitter-patter of pony hooves in the back garden or the room which doubled as the Tenderloin's only corral. When patrons opened the door to enter the bar, the draft brought fresh hay smells to mingle with aromas of hops and ale. Besides paying for her surgery, Katie had built a decent business with her discharge pay and pension, not pissing it away on drugs, women, and hunky power vehicles, like so many veterans.

The door to the Meddle of Honor banged open, startling even Frank. A gust of wind threw rain the length of a person onto the floor. When Petal entered, she didn't pause like a woman unsure of her welcome. She paused like a woman whose mind was made up, no matter what anyone else wanted. She knew her way. As soon as she saw Kasdan at his table, she came hurrying toward him, shaking wetness off her hair. Frank recognized the body language of No thanks, not yet, maybe I'll order later; the body language of We got business right now.

She had come in regularly at this hour to look for Kasdan. Just because he drank his beer on many evenings didn't mean he couldn't also skip many evenings. Having habits didn't mean that Kasdan was a creature of habit. But it happened that at this hour, tonight, when the weather kept many regulars away, she found him.

Kasdan stood as she reached the table. She sat and, impatiently, with a flat hand, gestured for him to sit. No flirting tonight, that was the business. Her business was to settle matters. Kasdan had no idea what matters Petal needed to settle; he had come in with his own plans for the evening – to do nothing, nothing, and then very little – and was not looking to accomplish anything else.

It was too soon to say she was pregnant by Dan Kasdan. And she wasn't drinking tonight. And she wasn't hiding the blue freckles at the crook of her arm. Registering her expression, it was only honestly apprehensive of him to be thinking it might be nicer if they met tomorrow or the day after.

"What is it?"

"He told me, 'Go deep. Go real deep.'"

"Who? Go deep what?" Kasdan asked.

"I'm shy, it's my problem, so I got to be a good actor. He said, 'Play like you're a call girl.'"

"You're not. *Who* said *what*?"

"Not yet, I guess. He said to put a leak in your boat."

Exasperated, Kasdan repeated: "*Who*? What kind of stuff you using? Are you tweaking? Act like you're clean and tell me what you're talking about."

"I'm clean," Petal said.

Katie hurried past on her way to figure out what was wrong with the purple neon martini sign. It was sputtering and blinking. Annoying fucking rain – wasn't this supposed to be Sunny California, orange blossoms and fun on the beach? – always did that to the tubing. Katie nodded to Mister Court Translator and his girlfriend; a free dose of charm, on the house, could come later. First she needed to tend to her non-sundrenched, non-beachfront property.

Petal was gripping the table with both hands. Her hair had been pasted down by the rain. "I don't know him, see, not very much, but he gave me a hundred. I had to tell you what I told you. A hundred for then, plus a hundred later, he said, when I put a leak…"

"A leak in my boat, okay – *what*?"

"… but I don't think lying is right unless you have to. I don't have to, I got principles, I can sell my ass…" She stopped. "But I never met any D'Wayne. I don't even know any D'Waynes. He just wanted me to tell you the story – funny, right?"

It wasn't all that funny. She gazed close to Kasdan's face, a habitual early-warning winsomeness which, this evening, in advance of whatever oncoming action was in store, he did not like. A soft baby-girl voice followed. He didn't like that part of it, either. He wondered if she was imagining that the rain on her face was tears and she was living up to tears that were not tears. She whispered, "Do you miss my goo?"

"Pardon?"

"My wet, my juice?" She gave up the baby-girl whisper. "I don't want you to take me seriously... Cowboy."

It was like a punch in the belly. It was a punch below the belly. She intended it. *Cowboy.*

Kasdan thanked her and was on his way. Just as he reached the street, the purple martini glass shorted out, sparked and went dark, and neon tubes splintered onto the wet pavement and Katie was running after him, calling, "You okay?" Glass crunched like wet snow underfoot, although snow never happened around here. Things that couldn't happen were happening.

"You okay, Mister Court Translator?"

"Fine, fine, no problema."

– 15 –

A hawk circled above the gulls, gracefully tracking its prey, estimating its best opportunity, unconcerned about whether these were really only just pigeons below, or, if gulls, why they flew over land and not water with its fresh salt sea products. First, the hawk followed from on high, floating, gliding, spreading its wings wide – a falcon? No, a red tail, it was a red-tailed hawk – and then it seemed to hover unmoving for a moment before it plunged toward a tasty whatever, gull or pigeon, and carried it off squawking to a nest where eager bald babies would squabble over the feathers.

A hawk is a hawk, Kasdan thought, a wide-winged red-tailed distraction, a legitimate predator; and a Kasdan is a man whose mind is at last made up.

"You got these nice pink cheeks all at once," Ferd said. "What's the matter, you feeling good? You gettin' some? I can always tell."

"Congratulations on your insight," Kasdan said. "All kinds of things'll do that – high blood pressure, say."

"So kudos on getting the blood plus the jism in circulation, pal."

Welcome to Ferd's shining condo with its shining down payment, welcome to lifestyle decor, to chrome and deep orange carpeting in materials especially manufactured for quality hassle-free care, welcome to the finalizing of serious business arrangements, Welcome, at last, to getting to the point by means of evading, testing, reconnoitering all aspects of the point. Due to sensitivity and discretion, Ferd started to extend two fingers but stopped short of pinching Dan's praiseworthy pink cheeks. He realized that matters had turned delicate. Their friendship was under stress. The shortest distance to his goal was a dotted line floating in space like silent San Francisco house flies, darting and playing, mating with quick midair collisions. But unlike San Francisco house flies, Ferd Conway buzzed at his play.

"It's no fun toting up a lot of cash if you can't share it with somebody, and I don't include the government as a somebody, Cowboy. I'm sharing with you because you're a professional performing a professional service – you deserve is what I mean – but also because, well..." Downcast shy eyes. "... frankly, sharing is in my nature. Not always, but sometimes, like now. With someone I feel close to. I'm just a human being, right?"

"Granted."

"Right. After all. Do you have to use a term of legal art when I bring up our friendship? Are you so uptight? You might as well say 'Stipulated.'"

"Objection sustained, Ferd."

"Okay, like my clients say, 'Yo! Ah respeck you, man.' That's not racist, it's more like realist." His pale eyelashes fluttered. Kasdan wondered if now he would take it all back. "Course, some of them are Latino, so they say, 'Yo, tu bueno hombre' – go ahead, correct my Hispanish, you're the expert."

He was testing. He needed to see if covetousness conquered all because, face it, a few distractions had come up (Amanda, Petal) which could turn Kasdan away from their foundation in good feelings and the deal. Ferd placed his trust in a large spirit, one which understood where his true interests lay.

Ferd's hair shone in the light, the effect of a recent crème rinse. Although Kasdan's expertise didn't extend to such questions, he had occasionally watched television and therefore guessed: Clairol. Maybe so, maybe not; the low-level fluorescent gleam off Ferd's hair, especially the new hair, might look good in a station break advertisement. Here it reflected a low-level fluorescent gleam against the pale pink of scalp. Along with mood swings, Ferd was subject to hair plantings, coiffeur designs, and home treatment in the never-ending quest to be up-to-the-minute.

No saintly yearning for peace and forgiveness was active in Dan Kasdan. He crooned to himself a song of vengeance, an anthem of spite; his entire body was keeping time and his cheeks were surely pink, just as Ferd had observed. He couldn't have wanted all his life to carry out his plan for Ferd Conway because he hadn't known him all his life. No wonder he had passed the years in a becalmed state. Nothing had occupied the space for hatred in his heart.

There was also the new space for Amanda and her way of holding her arms around herself, as if she were cold, and for Sergei, thrashing and bruised Sergei Mose. Love was a distraction which had suddenly come his way. He wasn't yet certain of the consequences; such was the nature of the thing. His late greed for lots of cash, tax-free, as Ferd promised, excluded sharing with its provider. He had found reasons for not sharing. The pleasures of hatred filled his heart with eagerness. It was crowded in there.

How interesting it seemed to Kasdan to become the proprietor of confused passions at his time in life. These novelties tended to make him somewhat emotional.

But care and calm were in order. Ferd was watching intently, tuning in to his own thoughts and how they might tune into Dan's. "Probably you don't want to hear any confessions of weakness, they call it fallibility, you and me both know that word, Dan, but here I go anyway."

"Right. Again."

"Yeah, okay, bear with me. I fully realize, without saying it, we got some issues – you do, anyway – and some a my behavior needs explanation."

"Explain then, Ferd."

"I'm not saying justification. Some things are hard to understand. But let me hope with all my heart, I can build here an explanation..."

He paused. He put one hand over the other, and then the other hand over the first one. He was building the explanation in the air. The motion was like kids choosing up sides, but just one doing all the work and doing it on an invisible baseball bat. Kasdan nodded. Ferd took this to mean, *Go ahead*, and in fact it did.

"Before I accepted myself, self-esteem-wise, I gotta tell you, 'cause I tended toward scrawny as a kid, then middle-age-related pot plus scrawny, not the greatest combo – before that – I tried exercise, Dan. Pushups hurt my back, that's all it did for me. So I got these weights from a client couldn't take them with him to the federal pen, and he also deeded me, so to speak, his whole shelf of bottles, the muscle medicine, the no-boobs-hanging-there medicine, takes care of your body image issues, they call them steroids now..."

"Did then, too."

"Called them? Okay. I wasn't cognizant with the medical term." Ferd paused to acknowledge past vocabulary deficits, also for the next thought and breath. "I'm telling you all this because they say confession is good for the soul and sometimes gets you a lighter sentence."

He curled his fingers toward Kasdan, beckoning, come here, come on, laugh with me.

"And?" Kasdan asked. No laugh. They were now in a conversation, a regular dialogue, two old friends communicating, one explaining, apologizing without actually apologizing, explaining hard. Kasdan had duties, too. His job was to help. Ferd nodded gratefully because at least Dan had contributed this *And*?

"And the result was... You know what the result was from this medicine they started to call steroids?"

"I give up. What?"

"Pimples! Pimples on my back!" Ferd twisted his shirt collar.

"Don't show me," Kasdan said.

"Plus couldn't get it up jacking off, pardon the expression. You don't want to see?"

Kasdan hoped his set lips clearly stated, No, don't get funny.

"I just mean the pimples, buddy. They're gone now, but I scratched so much I got these bumps. And those stinky biceps, triceps, quadrosepts, they just went away with no goodbye – they dwindled, Dan! Like someone stuck a pin in them! I tell you all this in confidence because I never tell anyone. As if I have anyone but you to tell."

Kasdan lowered his eyes. Ferd looked away. Guy talk was difficult.

"I think God," Ferd said reverently, "really wants me to be lean. Plus maybe this little pot, which there is no remedy for – just have faith that what will be really is. I shrug it off." He shrugged to illustrate the point. "So accepting myself, I'm now fully self-esteemed – you notice?"

"It has come to my attention," Kasdan said.

Ferd was on a roll. "Okay, the business. You'll head off to glamorous Port-au-Prince, Haiti, where the sun shines all year round, and hope the hurricane doesn't blow the cash up your nose – you don't do blow, another reason for my self-esteem for you. There's hardly any paperwork, just a minimum. You'll talk to a lawyer, a *notaire* they call him, but he's higher on the scale of command than any notary public in fucking San Francisco. You sign a few forms. You can read French, can't you?"

"Yes. It's close to Spanish."

"That's my boy."

Kasdan was thinking: Amanda deserves more, Sergei deserves better; a more better deal is what I owe them. No one will miss Ferd.

"So do you have any questions?"

"Yeah. Exactly what am I going to do?"

Ferd extended his arms, smiled benignly, welcoming the confusion of another. "You're going to have to go through all the ticket hassles, pack for the tropics, ask around if you need malaria pills, but you know what? You only have to do some of that. I've arranged for the tickets myself, a deal with a travel agent, legitimate tickets. Making it easy for you, Dan..."

Ferd was all heart.

"... because I like you, not to speak of to everybody's advantage."

The process of easing Kasdan into their business, a procedure of testing and urging which made it even more appealing, filled Ferd's hours with figuring how Dan could really get into it. If it were too easy, what would be the fun? It wasn't merely business; it was like love. Now was the time for Ferd to reveal his soul to his buddy Dan in more of its depths. "You know, I still talk to my mom every day. I got yelled at by my dad, but now I get to yell back. That's because they're dead, you know?"

Kasdan knew. Sometimes he too dreamt conversations with his parents. Ferd was promising that he was of that breed, the ones who remember. Ferd dabbed unnecessarily at his eyes. "Do you yell back at your dad? Do you call him Pop, like I do?"

In fact, Dan had not shouted at his dead father in years now. The memory tended to fade. Learning that he was himself a father, then in a jiffy a grandfather, filled the places formerly occupied by his dead mother and father.

In the alley next to this steel and glass spaceship landed south of Market in a newly developed, newly depressed district – once ware-houses and muffler, tailpipe, and body shops, then promoted by high tech enterprise into credit-rich real estate, then demoted by the revenge of dot.com into a terrain of FOR LEASE FOR RENT FOR SALE FOR ANYTHING PLEASE MAKE BEST OFFER – the traditional alley weeds had quickly colonized with their seeds, roots and sun-seeking leaves. Ailanthus sent its green shoots skyward. Heliotropic pinchweed and screw-you grass poked out of new cracks in third-mortgage construction materials, doing the work of vegetable vultures, burrowing into hastily laid plaster. Advance parties of rats had discovered a field of opportunity. Too bad Ferd would miss so much of the interesting history of the future.

"Welcome once more to my humble condo," he said.

Kasdan's attention was wandering, a habit Ferd frequently noted and deplored. Well, perhaps he had things on his mind. Ferd hated to interrupt dreams of what? Ultimate prosperity? Probably. "Like to peek under the furniture, see where I bought it? Copenhagen Life-style, man, where Danish modern is always in good taste." He squinted shrewdly. It was difficult to radiate trust and confidence while simultaneously glowing with suspicion. Ferd's dearest friend Dan had something unexpected in mind for him. Other people talked when they were nervous, talked a lot; Ferd talked a lot also when he was not nervous, but on certain occasions he could fall heavily silent and watchful. This was one of those occasions. Dan didn't peek under the couch to see the labels, Cost Plus Do Not Remove or All Natural Fibers or Made by Shaker Craftsman in Hokaido. Still, Ferd felt that something here was unknown.

Something was up. Kasdan was already experiencing future nostalgia for the good old days when Ferd had been alive, thriving, his eyes with their pale lashes glinting with expectation. Kasdan would have shared feelings of human warmth with his colleague, but unfortunately that was out of the question. It was inappropriate to deepen bonds with the victim on his last day. Still, Ferd had brought value and focus into Kasdan's life. Gratitude can't always be expressed.

A spider was clambering in its symmetrical skeleton structure at the window. Look again: the spider was outside, clinging to the window, blowing slightly in currents of air. Although the building was new, conforming to earthquake and termite specifications, it had no defense against spider webs. Mind my own business, Kasdan was thinking, not that of the rodent, ailanthus and arachnid worlds. If the web tore and fell in the wind, the spider, toting her eggs in her sac, would still be at the center of things, her eggs intact.

"Hey?" Ferd asked. "Pay attention in class, okay?"

Kasdan was wondering if spiders could sense that the always imminent San Francisco earthquake has ripened. If the building falls, even if it isn't supposed to, does the web sway and bend but not break, due to spider architectural skills?

"Hey, hey, we got business here, you look uncomfortable. Not comfy, pard?" There was much goodwill in his concern, with the implication that Kasdan should reciprocate with goodwill of his own. Instead, Kasdan was busy sniffing out the mold finding its place in the shaded alley along with weed saplings, the trees of purgatory; sniffing out what he couldn't smell. "Dan, I need you to care, not just do a job like it's only a job. Pay attention. I'm human, you read me? Just like anybody else, I want to hear the bitch, strike that, the *lady* say my name after I come. Maybe she'd come too if she said my name and then I'd say hers. But no – dumb cunts! So friendship in a not faggot way is what I really count on, now that I feel sad because the bitch always lets me down, it's what they do. Might as well use a greasy pillow, toss it in the trash, know what I'm telling you, Dan?"

"I do."

"Then pay attention."

"I am."

"Okay then..." Ferd relaxed. He gathered his strength. He adopted a dramatic old-time television voice, growling, "Our story continues..."

"I'll do it," stated Dan Kasdan.

Ferd responded with a wide wet lippy smile. It had to go like this. Dan was coming through for him. "You know what, Cowboy?"

"Don't..."

Ferd's hand flew up. "Okay, okay, I won't. Peace, brother. You're my partner and a cowboy partner has his own dignity, but okay, okay, you don't like the tribute. I'm just asking your undivided... I was going to tell you all..." – another dramatic television voice – "Prominent Lawyer and Business Man Tells All! How I used to earn my daily burrito with extra salsa trying to help our Hispanic Latino Chicano brothers from the other side of the law make something better of themselves, upgrade from perpetrator to, I don't know, dishwasher, sell some white powder around the back entrance maybe, buy an SUV maybe – no, scratch that – a Buick Skylark convertible from the lot in Daly City with the gizmos that make it hump and jump when they're cruising on Mission the hottest day of Chinko de Mayo, they

like that, pumping the tar up from the street because the stupid
Skylark's rusted all the way down, what-the-fuck..."

"Ferd?"

"Okay, okay. But just let me mention Pedro probably got the
sound box turned up maximo maximus... You know those Latino girls
with the skin like brown silk and the shiny ass till they're twenty,
twenty-one? That silk is mucho-mucho, hombre. But then the ass
starts to wrinkle and droop from too many burritos in lard, plus their
natural born genes. So Pedro dreams about the white girl he could
really love and *respeck*. Personally, I ask him: what's wrong with a
firecracker from your own kind? He doesn't answer cause I only ask
him in my secret heart. Meantime, you can hear him spinning, doing
wheelies, blasting his music all the way to the Indian Alkie Happy
Hunting Ground, you know that sidewalk between 16th and 18th on
Mission? And then he pulls up 'cause he sees this pair of tits
bouncing down the street... Do I get your undivided attention?"

"No," Kasdan said. "Cut to the chase."

"You'll be amply funded to jet off to Hong Kong China for R and R,
come back with white linen suits from that tailor there. Shit, you'll
wanna fly to La Jolla California for a quick weekend, wear your new
linen suit to the La Valencia, sit in that bar where all the stoned rich
hotties drink down the sunset. You won't even need one of the rich
ones. You can embellish your suit, man, with a beautiful cocktail
honey, no Botox in her face, doesn't need it, not yet – wrinkles up her
skin adoringly when you say, Dinner? Course, her mother probably
bought her the grandissimo hooters across the border in Tijuana
Mexico for her sweet sixteenth birthday, couple years ago. Mom and
her both got the blond hair dark at the roots, up for anything, both of
them together – Mom's just a big kid herself, but built, muy built."

Kasdan's eyes were closed.

"You can, let me emphasize this, you can do anything your heart
desires. I don't feel your pain, man. I feel your pleasure."

"You know what I want."

"Right right right." Ferd was impatient with Kasdan's impatience.
"Right, take care of your daughter, get little Sergei the best of custodial, the nursemaid, the docs, the helps, not need D'Wayne to do
what you know he can't... There you go, right. But sometimes a fellow
needs to work off a little mischief, you're picked up shitfaced..."

"Not me."

"... you can just pay the fine, apologize to your buddy Harvey, say Judge I needed to work off a little, well, you'll call it something, how about 'stress'? Not criminal mischief..."

"Is this where we're going? Blah, blah, blah?"

And suddenly the spigot turned itself off. Ferd blushed. He had revealed too much exhilaration. His cheeks revealed a pale stubble. He seemed to remember he had to take matters step by step for the man who worked for him, not just fire off words, not just spending adrenalin and nerves, self-inflamed, to demonstrate that the universe did the bidding of Ferd Conway. He stopped emitting. He looked about himself confusedly, waiting for the words to die against walls, decay, fall to the floor. He accepted being called to order. Silence happened. He said: "Profit is where we're going. Gain."

A telephone was ringing two steps away. Kasdan had already noticed this phone, a novelty item with a pig snout and hair painted on its muzzle, a Chinatown special. He hadn't considered it a working object. This was not the first mistake in his association with Ferd. It was a working pig snout. The pig rang and rang and Ferd committed the grim little, shy little, shrugging little smile that stated: You are so important to me, and our deal is so important to us both, that I'm not even going to answer this phone. It rang once more, half a ring. Ferd shook his head. He gazed silently upon Kasdan while the drama of the unanswered pig snout filled their lives.

When it stopped, he continued. "Hey, things go as good as they're bound to, you can have a par-tay, dress up, meet some rich person with her own real estate, even marry her, why not? You can fuckin pool your resources, Dan, hear me?"

He had Kasdan's divided attention. Kasdan was thinking of Sergei and the diapers he would need for too long. He was seeing the lost and found Amanda smiling at her dad, which she did sometimes, although the conditions of her rearing were defined by his absence. He could make up for it. "Yes, I'm listening," Kasdan said.

"Not planning to step out on me, Dan? Not planning, I don't know, what's that I smell? Duplicity?"

It was a big word, but after all, Ferd had passed the California Bar and only been suspended from practice, due to no fault of his, twice.

"In that you need some ready cash money, free of the federal claim, also the state's cut, and in that I need a partner I can trust and to whom I can give all my fiduciary confidence..."

"Be it resolved," Kasdan murmured.

"... and in that I personally prefer furthermore a partner I value as a human being albeit at times a sarcastic asshole..."

"Let's get to it," Kasdan said.

"You're awesome!" Ferd held his hands up, palms open and out, nothing to hide. "Lookit," he said. He pulled a stained vinyl suitcase from a bottom shelf which otherwise held *San Francisco Chronicles* to be perused at some future date. "This is what you won't carry!" he said. "You will pass through Miami International with dignity, man, along with all the other fun-lovers, only a little sweaty. Those security hassles after that fucking nine-eleven, it's natural. I'm paying you for not showing it. Apply an aluminum compound, dries the flopsweat pores, maybe irritate your skin a little, but don't set off no detectors, plus you get to meditate about the extra percentage I lay on the top for pain and suffering, whatever blood pressure might ensue."

"Ferd..."

"Wait." He held up only one hand this time. "I'm getting there in my own time. We need to cover every step of the way. This is for your own benefit, feel secure plus *be* secure, okay?" As if it belonged to someone else, he blinked at his right hand, which was still suspended in air, did his wincing grin, pulled it down with his left hand. See how concerned he was, so that even his body's coordinated limbs were uncoordinated?

So afterwards, he continued... and there really wasn't that much heavy lifting involved, just carry the cash to Port-au-Prince, Haiti, buy a little property there, a nice house on the seashore in Jacmel, this pretty little village – okay, it was a rough trip by a bad road from Porto – and okay, plus you have to deal with a *notaire*, they call him, make sure the papers were all in order, the deed... okay, there was a little *light* lifting going on, it's the Third World after all, but the beauty part – Third World records and computers... like Pong machines!... and then afterwards Dan could settle back home in a better-living condo and not have to talk jive with illegal funkybutts in County Jail, but instead... help poor little Sergei with some special ed? Make Amanda proud by acting like a real dad?... Ferd paused for breath; he was only human. And added: "Take a trip to Vegas or Paris any day, any time, think nothing of it!"

Dan's choice. One little deal, maybe a follow-up if he wants to increase the extra affluence. All he had to do.

In addition, Dan and Ferd would be forever bound together by chains of deep mutual self-interest. Together, they could grow old gracefully (Dan ahead of Ferd in the grow-old department, of course, but it makes little difference after the first hundred years).

All Dan had to do, right?

"... like the grown-up prosperous ma-choor individuals we both aim to be, are we on the same page, partner?"

The stare of Kasdan's partner was like that of a contented but wary cat across the ruins of a meal of newborn mice, the mom having been saved for dessert, sticky pieces of her not yet cleaned from his claws. Then Ferd did a little curtsey, not anything too extreme, not sinking to his knees, just enough to make it clear he was being cute.

But hadn't Dan already agreed and agreed and agreed?

"The first of the month," Ferd was saying. "A nice two weeks is ample to settle in, relax, buy the *notaire* a couple drinks and dinner, see for sure it's straight down the line. In the Third World, you got to make extensive nice. Your passport's up to date, right?"

"I'll make sure."

"Summer clothes. Pick up some Neet at Walgreens, they say it's good for mosquitoes."

"I can slap them."

"What a hero. So we are all set, Cowboy? After I make a few more collections? Just one or three little details?"

– 16 –

He was receiving the news in segments. Either Ferd wasn't ready, or he didn't trust Kasdan, or the deal about the deal was like Coming Attractions at the movies, encouraging interest with a loud soundtrack. But Kasdan needed no further wooing. He was ready to buy into it.

Foglight, that lucid sun-suffused San Francisco glimmer taken from the ocean, the bay, thermal rising and falling, swept brightness along the street. Even as the winds slowed, the town was not like other towns. On a day like this, through no fault of Kasdan's, his thoughts slid toward the lips of Petal-she-called-herself until the father and grandfather reminded himself: No! There's a daughter. There is Sergei Mose.

Waves of sound emerged from Teletubby Midway, Shoppe Supreme for Happy Kids. The noise pushed Kasdan backwards onto the sidewalk. He re-gathered his strength. He forged onward. He wasn't accustomed to shopping for happy kids, sad kids, any kids at all, but he knew this was something grandfathers do – head up from home in the Tenderloin to Union Square to find a smoochy, fabricky, squeezy, trademark-registered product for Sergei. He had money in his pocket and soon, thanks to his caro amigo Ferd Conway, there would be more.

He braced himself. He rode the surf of clanging, arfing, chiming audiotape straight into the maw of kiddie purchasing opportunities. He penetrated the interior of Teletubby Midway. Now he recognized calliope music, the sounds of lost love, lost childhood, sweetness embedded in the genetic code, as if he had sped backwards through time on a merry-go-round, and perhaps he really had, finally arriving at this place. Time to get off. The music merely occurred; it wasn't really played, it *occurred* on some computerized loop. He guessed carousels were being evoked simultaneously in every Teletubby Midway, Shoppe Supreme for Happy Kids (Trademark Registered), in shopping centers and malls across the nation. Sound environment engineers adjusted for time zones at World Headquarters in an industrial park in Burbank.

Buy a toy and get the hell out.

He tried not to trample the young mothers, a sprinkling of fathers, and less young grandparents seeking items for their beloveds. Well, now he was one of them. He slowed down at Aisle Gretal, between Goldielocks Strasse and Rue de Hansel. He was tempted by a pig-like wolf, a wolf-like pig, a fuzzy-wuzzy towel cloth creation not yet stained by spit and piss, soon to be treasured by Sergei. Grampa read the instructions. It could be hand-washed in hot soapy water. It should be air-dried.

He bought.

He hurried to the door.

An alarm buzzed like an electric chair. A security guard stopped him, shoved him, demanded, "Hey, Mister." He ran a wand over his body; no toys secreted in his clothes. Kasdan presented the receipt. The cashier had forgotten to remove the chip. The manager apologized and presented him with a ten-dollar chit toward a future purchase, not valid for sale items, in return for his not seeing his attorney, not suing on the basis of public embarrassment, just because a crew of clerks and a crowd of young mothers and fathers, less young grandparents and ethical toddlers, were pointing accusatory fingers at him. "Plus, I'll put a notation in the cashier's file," the manager promised.

"No, don't, why bother with the paperwork," said Kasdan. "But you could cut off her hand, would you do that?"

An appreciative audience of gawkers, formerly witnesses at the crime scene, snickered in styles appropriate to their ages. This absolved shopper was joking! This was like Reality! And as in Reality on television, sometimes all was forgiven and profitable. It was a form of Reality which included both Absolution and Justice, a winning combo. For the jostle of fond adults and children infused with pre-caffeine sodas, flooding their arteries with sugar derivatives, what had started out to be just another purchasing expedition had been transformed into a thrill ride followed by poignant redemption. It was an incident to share later while the kids explored their battery-powered robots, space ships, submarines, lasers, child-safe massage units, a choice assortment of implements for contemporary junior living, except for no dildos. Mom would need to double-park at Good Vibrations on the way home if she wanted the latter. It would snow in Union Square before Dan Kasdan returned to use his ten-dollar chit.

Union Square had already experienced tickertape, Presidential rallies, earthquake, fire, bankruptcy, franchise food, and credit jewelries, but snow? Not likely, although according to myth, supported by archival photographs, it had happened. He passed through the front door again without incident.

On this fine autumn day in San Francisco, the tourists in their shorts and sandals, their flowered shirts and their maps, cameras banging against their navels, were, momentarily, in good luck. They found themselves in a California with real California weather, although the major orange blossoms and movie stars were only to be discovered hundreds of miles to the south. This California was the one with the fog, the cable car, the Crab Louie, the hippies and the homosexuals.

The few blocks from Union Square to the Tenderloin always gave Kasdan a brief sense of youth and vigor, thanks to a descending slope. He was young, he was agile, he only saw Doc Feldstein to complain insincerely about their shared bachelordom, he slept through the night without interruption. Now, on Ellis, a narrow strip of wind swirled between store signs boasting about products whose prices ended in 99 cents. Harvey Johnson, the judgmental cop, said that only hookers and crack dealers were straightforward enough to offer their goods with prices that ended, as in an honest world they should, in zeros.

Kasdan stopped briefly at Katie's Meddle of Honor, nodding apologetically at Frank, the bartender, whose biceps were freshly inflated by his curling exercises. No beer just now, only dropping by for a quick visit to the head. He wondered if his prostate was paying an extra toll, due to stress from the non-shoplifting experience, the security guard waving a magic wand of detection over his crotch. He proceeded toward presentation of the Smurfy object to Sergei Mose, who deserved some pleasure in life after being brought damaged into the world through no fault of his own. Receding adrenalin; rebounding weariness; if Amanda offered, he would gratefully accept a mug of coffee, no sugar, no cream. If she didn't offer, he would exercise a grandfather's prerogative to make his own (instant, if she stocked it;

the high-fashion kind that popped its little crystals, he hoped; if not, any generic brown sand would do).

A familiar vehicle was parked at an expired meter half a block from her apartment. Kasdan recognized the customized yellow and black Buick Skylark; most Skylarks had disappeared into junkyards or the Mission district, which put special wheels on them, fixed them to bow, dip, and preen for weekend paseos, and kept them running the way ancient cars were preserved in Havana. Ferd's was just temporary transportation, pending a good score. He had received it tax-free from a client with no need for a customized Skylark, yellow sides, black top, red Aztec arrows aimed at white targets on the fenders, while he served his time in Folsom.

What the hell was Ferd doing on this block?

Kasdan found himself making a new withdrawal on his adrenalin reserves. Some thoughts did that to him. Although he lacked direct personal experience in the matter, he believed in the sanctity of marriage. He also believed that the contract could properly be voided through divorce, because marriage was holy and blessed promises to love should not be blasphemed by strife. The marriage between his daughter, fatherless during her Mendocino commune years, and D'Wayne, who had passed his childhood with a single mother in the Valencia Gardens Project, was a sacred union between two semi-orphans. D'Wayne took reliable employment as doorman and security guard at the Yerba Buena Foundation, "Sex Therapy Like the Doctor Ordered, Big Boy." He was a responsible young man. Together, Amanda and D'Wayne treasured Kasdan's grandson, who arrived along with difficulties – called "challenges" in California – such as being a mulatto child with irregular brain sparkings, nerve and muscular malfunctions.

True, Kasdan sometimes wondered why Amanda chose the husband she chose. But wondering about love was someone else's right. He was not an expert, inoculated against it until the time came when he found himself in love with his family. Amanda chose and loved; surely an excellent thing. A few years ago, Kasdan had gone to bed with a black court stenographer and she smelled good in the morning, despite the can of onion soup he left opened on the sink after a post-lovemaking snack. What was her name again? Some black name, Johanda, Jolamma, when Joanne would do well enough.

But she was warm, she smelled good, she teased him about his living arrangements with the right kind of tolerant amusement in her eyes, and he shouldn't have drifted away after a few weeks. Jocinda, that was it, Jocinda with the low sweet voice.

Amanda and D'Wayne loved, married. Kasdan liked Jo-whatever and was left with no idea of what had become of her.

He didn't buzz himself in because Amanda's apartment had a buzzer, but it didn't work; it had a locked front entrance, but the lock had gone unrepaired for months now; it had an elevator to get to the third floor, but the elevator was usually stuck between floors. Walking upstairs was good for a person. Mr. Patel, the landlord, promoted its health benefits, the life-affirming smells of curry, the powers of meditation, and harmonious rapport with city building inspectors. Kasdan prepared cheerful greetings for his family. By the time he reached the third floor, he was imagining Sergei wriggling in his arms, burrowing into the heat and heartbeat. Sergei's body understood about love, even if his limbs jerked without control when Amanda used a Q-tip to pluck boogers out of his nose. Someday things could be made better. Kasdan made and remade this promise to himself.

The door to the apartment was ajar. Amanda was careless about such things and shouldn't have been, especially with D'Wayne away at odd hours. The sign in front of the Yerba Buena Foundation on Pine said "No Walk-Ins," not being an ordinary whorehouse, although it did accept walk-ins if they seemed like sincere johns, not nosy cops.

Maybe D'Wayne had forgotten his key and Amanda left the door open for his return.

Unlikely. He could always knock. He could always reach for the extra key hidden against the wall above the door jamb. He was not only wide; he was also tall.

Kasdan heard the wet phlegmy snores of Sergei. It was careless of Amanda to leave the apartment door open while both she and Sergei napped. The door to the other bedroom was closed, but there were tussling sounds behind it. Kasdan asked, "Amanda?" And then, without thinking, without thinking enough, pushed the door open. The sounds of Dan Kasdan moving through the apartment hadn't interrupted the tussling sounds. The sight of Dan Kasdan in the bedroom stopped the tussling.

"Dad! What're you doing here?"

It wasn't the relevant question.

"Hey Cowboy, fancy meeting you so unexpected."

It wasn't a relevant statement. Ferd was pulling the sheet between his legs, as if to dry or subdue or hide.

Kasdan said nothing.

"Dad, you got no business barging in here..."

Ferd waited and Kasdan stood at the foot of the bed without moving. Ferd said, "Dan, I really like her."

The flesh of his flesh, the voice of his daughter: "Don't blame anybody, Dad, he didn't do anything, we're just messing around..."

"Don't say that! Folks shouldn't cast the first stone, Cowboy. I really like her. Mandy, I really like you."

"He's good to me, Dad. He doesn't need to bring me things. He's good to me, have you heard of that?"

Kasdan tried to understand the gleam in Ferd's eyes. Maybe it was pride; his eyes were wet. Kasdan succeeded in not understanding.

"So sometimes it happens, people get together. Good things mean don't blame anyone and you take a shower afterwards, you know? And no harm done. Am I expressing myself? A little soap, shampoo, the conditioner, all gone just like that, am I right?" Ferd wanted to snap his finger to drive the point home, *all gone, over,* but he needed the hand for discretion. He held the sheet.

Kasdan said nothing.

"This don't change anything, buddy? We're kind of family, so to speak, am I right?"

Kasdan said nothing.

Amanda said, "God, now I have to explain. I hate this. Okay, so my whole life changed, Dad. I didn't know what was gonna happen. You see how I started to sag? My boobs, my butt? Oh, God, Dad. I thought Sergei would be this perfect... Oh, God, my whole life changed."

"I like her just like she is," Ferd said.

Kasdan said nothing. Amanda may have repeated, Oh God, Oh God, and Ferd may have repeated, I really like her. Kasdan wasn't certain.

"You want to talk?" Ferd asked.

Kasdan said nothing. Dust was stirring in the air, motes rising, one color for panic, one for confusion, then another and another, motes stained for his old failures to focus and his late decisions. Amoebas wriggled across his eyes; time and macular degeneration were stealing his vision. There was a roar in his ears, a silence behind it, a tumbling chaos. Ferd sat forward, bony shoulders hunched, irregular patches of hair on his chest partly hidden by the sheet. He was waiting. The tumble of noise and silence made Kasdan dizzy. He said nothing.

As if it were winter and the thermostat had churned wildly, heat flooded through Kasdan's body and clothes, his skin was on fire. He stood silent. The force of rage, boiling instinct, kept him fixed there, burning. Dan Kasdan, at an hour and in an address, San Francisco, 4:30 in the afternoon, remained wordless.

On the chair near the bed lay pants with a belt hastily pulled half out of the loops. On the floor near the bed lay red shorts with the words Bill Blass or Tommy Hilfiger or Johnny Chan on the elastic. Kasdan's eyesight seemed to be smoked over. It registered Ferd's slack skinniness, loose male breasts. Kasdan wondered what women found to value in men; surely, they must look at them sometimes. If Kasdan had tried to speak, he would have found his voice hoarse and unmanageable. It didn't occur to him to try to speak.

Amanda was still staring at this stranger who happened to be her father: *What are you going to do?* Ferd Conway observed Dan Kasdan with great care, his own question hovering busily but silently in the close, cooked-mushroom smells, along with the swift and silent San Francisco house flies churning in the air: *So, Cowboy, now what?*

Nothing, I'll do nothing. I'll do something at the right time.

Amanda's unblinking gaze of unanswered question. Ferd's concerned frown. He was not sure of what emotion he should offer at a time like this.

The inevitable was now even more likely. Kasdan brushed his forehead with his hand.

"Hey, amigo." Ferd could explain everything.

"Dad, you don't know what it's like..."

What *what* is like? His daughter was in bed with a very large insect, covered loosely with skin. What could it be like? Their souls meeting, was that the appeal? Their souls meeting in a marriage bed and making a smell liked overcooked mushrooms?

"What you thinking, amigo? Bam? You thinking *Bam*?" Ferd cocked his fingers and made a shooting gesture, his other hand holding the sheet. It was annoying for him, Kasdan just standing there silently.

"Dad..." Amanda began again, meaning, You don't understand, you can't, you don't understand me, you *can't*...

Ferd let the sheet fall; why bother? He said, "Okay, I don't expect you to be totally happy about this."

What Kasdan was presently considering was why those feet in their thin black socks were poking up at him from the end of the top sheet. He was trying to recall ancient history. Someone's father had taken him to an Elks Club meeting when he was still in junior high school, now called middle school, and there had been a 16-millimeter film in black and white clattering in the projector and the story of a salesman delivering ice, eventually wearing nothing but black socks. The motel room in Newark or Cleveland or wherever they made the film must have had a dirty, probably cold floor. The actor kept his socks on.

Amanda's father did not ask Ferd why he didn't take off his socks. Ferd's perturbed frown indicated he would have avoided this meeting if he had been offered a choice, but he knew how to deal with distressing meetings. He reached his hand out to cup Amanda's shoulder. He preferred that she not have to make explanations to her father. For Amanda's sake, he wanted this moment to end. It wasn't the right time for Kasdan to ask Ferd about his socks.

Ferd was tired. His buddy had created a stressful situation. His voice came in a resigned drone. Perhaps he didn't even hope to convince. He was staring at Kasdan's nose, not his eyes, in a best effort at sincerity. The voice was also the best he could do. He didn't plead his case; he wasn't really explaining.

"I've never been married, see. I never had a kid. Now there's just you and Amanda. She's a beautiful person, Dan. This might be difficult for you, I understand that, but life is difficult for her, too. The kid, no money, the post-partum. If somebody doesn't watch out, time is going to pass her by. It's hard for her, amigo. I really like her."

Shut up. Kasdan didn't say it aloud, but Ferd seemed to hear. He leaned against the headboard, pulling the sheet up to his chin. The two of them lay there, hardly moving.

Nobody seemed to be thinking, What if the husband happens to come home unexpectedly? Husbands do unexpected things sometimes, just like wives.

And then there was another rush from Amanda, an avalanche of explanation, falling over itself with blame and panic: "Dad, he's right, I got this post partum, you don't know anything, I don't suppose you ever had it, but I have this baby and this husband and this father just turned up on me, and I can't just dump them all, maybe I could dump you but I want to give you a chance, and some girls get divorced or run out on their babies, so don't get all social worker on me, like I'm some slut, I'm not a slut. I'm not going to do what you did, Dad, run out on my baby, are you listening? Ferd's nice to me. He pays attention. Ferd's my friend, like he's your friend..."

But Ferd doesn't slide into bed with me.

"... so since you didn't do nothing for me growing up, how about you try to figure me out now, okay, Dad? Cut me some slack? Is that something appeals to you?"

Amanda was holding the sheet tight against her body, propped up against crushed pillows, the two of them, Amanda and Ferd, in the bed of Amanda and D'Wayne with a cooked mushroom smell. Someone had better change the sheets.

Kasdan was thinking: Quick! Don't delay! Now's the time!

Kasdan was thinking: Change the sheets, change the sheets.

Kasdan heard the rattle at the door before Amanda and Ferd did. He hurried out to greet his son-in-law.

"Hey man, you up for a brew? Sergei asleep in there?"

Kasdan put his hand on D'Wayne's shoulder and steered him toward the kitchen and found his voice. He didn't usually drink in the afternoon, made him sleepy, but it's a hot day, dehydrates a person, and that Hetch Hetchy water – I read that someplace – might have chemicals from the runoff, so yeah, D'Wayne, let's do a cold one. I could use a cold one. I could sure use a cold one.

"On account of brew is the best kind of water," D'Wayne said with his large happy thunder of a laugh which must have thrilled many a cute woman before it got around to thrilling Amanda. But what was past was past. He loved his son, he loved his wife, he meant to do his best to change their histories, his and hers, of no father and no proper family. He intended something different for his son who was Kasdan's grandson. "I got the light ones, ain't no good sense in them, I got the darks, I got this ale they call it biker brew, mikerbrew, some shit like that – micro? – extra foam mess up your face. So to what do we owe the pleasure?"

Noise of their footsteps, noise of refrigerator opening, noise of Kasdan talking, raising his voice, and D'Wayne welcoming him and chuckling like a proper host, a proper son-in-law; chink of bottles against each other, a toast to family; scrape of chairs pulled to the kitchen table; no noise from Sergei Mose, who was still asleep, so no hurry...

Again D'Wayne touched the neck of his bottle to the neck of Kasdan's frosty ale, this time for good luck and appreciation. "Hey, fine, you know what I'm sayin?"

"I do."

"So gimme another knock at that microshit, man."

Kasdan wondered if D'Wayne noticed how he raised his voice, scraped his chair, made every plausible clumsy noise he could think of.

D'Wayne stretched out his legs, cracked his knuckles. "Time, man, say a big wet hello to my wife in there..."

"She's sleeping. You aren't going to empty your bottle?"

"What happenin, they turn on the gas and they sleepin away the day?"

"It's been hot. The weather's changing, so..."

Kasdan followed D'Wayne into the bedroom. Nothing else to be done. The window was open wide and the curtain was blowing. Amanda was lying there, blinking awake. Shoes, pants, and most of the cooked mushroom smell were gone. Kasdan ambled to the window and shut it halfway. He could see where the alley weeds had been trampled.

D'Wayne said, "Where's he at, man?"

Amanda seemed to jerk wide awake, then sank back into the pillow. "His crib, where you think? *Man.*"

"We gotta get him a big boy bed any day soon now."

"Right... *man*."

D'Wayne gave his forehead a noisy slap. "Okay, I forgot, you my main dude, but you a mama don't like to be call 'Man'." Leaned, grinned, kissed wet, kissed again, reared back. "Better now, fee-man?"

He ducked out, in a hurry to proceed with further kisses, this time for Sergei, to whom he could say Man without reproach. No need to say goodbye. He would be back in a moment with his son.

Someplace, probably in his two-colored Skylark, Ferd was pulling slivers out of his hands and feet after shimmying down the drainpipe, bracing himself against wooden slats. He must have ripped his skin on rusty nails and rotten siding. If he didn't have a current tetanus inoculation, he would need protection against lockjaw. Kasdan did not want to be robbed of his plan by tetanus.

Sergei woke in D'Wayne's arms, making baby gurgles, and Kasdan took the child, cradling him, leaving D'Wayne and Amanda to finish greeting each other. As a man who had never been married, Kasdan didn't know the procedures for a wife to say hello, hi there, what's up, to a husband who returns home unexpectedly before the normal day's work was done.

– 17 –

"Mama! Mama!"

A shrill voice penetrated the morning sound surf crashing against the walls of the Caffe Roma, eddying back over tables, chairs, coffee, bagels, muffins of blueberry, bran, oats, or chocolate marble for those seeking a fast start on the day's sugar. "Mama, I'm getting off this time, promise, Mama! New lawyer got us a plan!"

Both Ferd and Dan, also Marta, who was working the espresso machine, knew the dude was not getting off and probably the mama knew it, too. The new lawyer's plan was a miracle alibi pro tem to get the grieving mother off his case. She wore a headscarf; her tears were dropping down her cheeks, unblotted; bluish veins stood out on the son's face; persuasion was hard for him. He was not persuading his mother. At variance with the high pitch of his appeal for confidence in the simple justice of his cause was the jail-made pentagram on his neck, intended to intimidate jurors and frighten judges in case simple justice did not suffice.

After recent unfortunate stresses in their relationship, it was good for Ferd and Dan to meet again at everyone's home away from home, the Caffe Roma, kitchen central of the legal system's maxi-family – chiming and hissing breakfast equipment, small tables on which to balance shots of espresso and plates of quick fuel, a swarm of lawyers swapping brags and lies, perpetrators muttering exculpations, mothers, wives and girlfriends sullen or resigned or sobbing, jury draftees reading their morning *San Francisco Chronicles* until the hour of summons. If they made bail and their lawyers were okay with it, Kasdan liked to meet his Pasquals or Jesuses here for get-acquainted discussions before their court appearances. He could explain that panic or surliness were not helpful with most judges.

As usual, Ferd inspected the teeny-tiny Asian public defenders on their precarious heels, recently initiated into the profession, often not yet fully Americanized, taking tea instead of coffee for breakfast. "Lookit that one, amigo. She is one upward mobile from Nam. Before law school, I know her, graduated Phi Beta in Manicure School – still does pedicure for special friends. You got a slew a parking tickets? You got feet with pedi problems? I can arrange a package deal. Only for a friend would I do this."

Kasdan was having difficulty with his muffin. It wasn't the abrasive bit of bran stuck in an overtaxed swallowing reflex. Previous matters clotted his throat. It was rage choking him; it was suppression of rage choking him; it was the problem of waiting until the right time to do what he needed to do that was making difficulties with his swallowing and his digestion. Complicating distractions had led to a frontal lobe headache. He lifted his bowl of coffee. His hand was steady. Good, good.

Kasdan gave himself a vote of approval. In this case, one vote was a majority.

Ferd was observing him with concern. He wanted to acknowledge, in his own way, the little problem that had recently come up. "Sergei, I was noticing, you think he'll ever learn to go potty, like on his own? I mean, the changing of his diaper, the older they get, you know, kind of messy... a kid like that, do they learn?"

Kasdan occupied himself with keeping his hands quiet. No Parkinsonism. No pseudo-Parkinsonism caused by desires to do damage. Okay so far.

"Jeez, watching the mom change him, maybe he's having fun, the nice mommy touching him, you think so? I mean I might have fun too, somebody like that wiping me..."

Not making a fist tight enough to break anything, Kasdan was gone. No twisting of one hand against the other. Good. He was elsewhere. He was absent, but not just from this wire-backed chair opposite Ferd Conway. He had departed from himself. He had fled.

"Hey? Dan? Talking so softly, I can't even hear you?"

Kasdan noticed that his mouth was open; he shut it. He cleared his throat. He wouldn't cough with his mouth open, not in public. He said: "I was just seeing that's Harvey over there. Let's finish our business, should we?"

Relieved, Ferd grinned. "Getting greedy, right?"

"Something like that."

As Ferd Conway would surely say, given sufficient energy surges, if he happened to think of it, his dear amigo was in a situation never seen before or since in the history of mankind, unless others had found themselves in a similar situation. And as Dan Kasdan would surely respond, this situation happened to be his own (plus, don't call me Cowboy, okay?).

Both of them were early for today's meeting. Promptness suited serious intentions. Kasdan neatly folded into four squares the front section of his *Chronicle*, a habit he had learned from Harvey Johnson. Normally, he liked the morning prelude – coffee and a muffin alone, *Chron* alone, the warm Caffe Roma bath of getting ready alone for the oncoming day with the help of caffeine, international disasters, and company he didn't necessarily have to acknowledge. Today he wasn't alone. Ferd stared down Harvey Johnson, Kasdan's old pal, across the room, then asked Dan a general question: "So?" Harvey caught the stare, returned it for a concentrated three seconds, then raised an eyebrow; the stud in his ear caught a stray early morning sunbeam. He shrugged and snapped open his laptop.

Having asked Dan, "So?" Ferd answered his own question. "So," he stated.

The steam machine was banging and hissing, foaming milk for lattes and cappuccinos. Caffeine gaiety crowded the air. Sometimes the room was stuffy for patrons afflicted with sinus problems or illicit remedies for them. Rushes of optimism about getting money, getting acquitted, getting laid, these things cleared the nose almost as well as cocaine. Generally speaking, the Caffe Roma lifted the morning for everyone except most defendants, their dear ones, and resentful citizen conscripts to the jury pool. The griefs of others deepened the satisfaction of working lawyers, assistant DAs, clerks, bail bondsmen, guards, sheriffs, cops; in rhythms of grief and dealing with grief was how their world turned. Here and there, incipient flirtation made inroads on crossed-arms confrontation postures, narrow-eyed yearning over the rims of thick latte bowls, designed for comfort after last night's excesses. Crumbs flew from lips, paper napkins sopped up saucers where unsteady hands had puddled coffee, fingers plucked daintily at sticky and chunky food products. Despite some engorged conjunctival disturbances, many eyes were ready to rise and shine in the new day. Before court went into session and the briefcases flowed out, tugging at their bearers, a bloat of last-minute predictions and advice raised the Roma's temperature.

"Chill, man." It was not a mere request. A pissed-off advocate was shedding toughness onto a client; showing teeth, moving heavy shoulders in a well tailored but too tight jacket, seething, pretending to be at the limit of controlling his seething. He was demanding the balance due on his retainer before he would act any further on his client's behalf, not in a mood to employ the musical Latin words of art handed down through a tradition which extends back to the Magna Carta and earlier, back to the origins of faith in the rule of justice compounded of both mercy and revenge, to Roman juris-prudence, to Greek meditations upon humankind's place under the sun. He had already extended himself, out of sheer good nature. He got to the point: "Where's the mon, hon? Or find yourself a new shyster, okay, shitface?"

But Ferd and Dan were – that is, Ferd was – making progress. He felt this most sincerely. They were moving past that embarrassing glitch with Amanda. Probably Dan had completely forgotten it, and anyway, as Amanda said, they were just messing around. So he *should* forget it.

Ferd was overcoming by charm whatever hesitations infected his timid friend. Counting on this, plus money, plus offering his amigo a needed adventure to spice up a life spent mumbling back and forth in English and Spanish – oh, maybe a few hasty sexual encounters along the way, but doesn't God grant everyone a couple of those? – Ferd was confidently rushing forward into both caution and precision, like the wary attorney he was. He built his case; he nailed it. He marshaled his offer. Personally, besides money and a taste of adven-ture, Ferd wanted more, and not only for himself. He wanted to share. He wanted to prove his friendship.

He also wanted no fuckups. He would hold Dan by the ear, but carry him to the feast.

Distraction from what mattered, or should matter, had been Kasdan's traditional procedure for getting through the complications that always came up, no matter how he tried to simplify his life. It was more a sin than a mere habit. Now that Amanda, Sergei and the complications of age had come along, he was regrouping, trying to welcome complication. He thought of Petal drinking coffee from a mug, looking up at him questioningly, undecided about whether he would speak to her or she should just go on drinking coffee, but this moment had not actually taken place. Yes, it happened; no, it didn't. It was another relapse into distraction. But then he was deciding to help her find the child she had abandoned, a boy – this mother had abandoned a boy as Kasdan had abandoned a daughter..." News to him. Petal and her lost son, which she did not have (did she?), were clearer in his mind than the specter of Ferd Conway, waiting there before him in trim and tan flesh.

Ferd stared. No Kasdan present, just his body. A wakeup call was in order. "Okay, your buddy, the black dick..."

"You can call him Harvey Johnson."

"Sho nuff, Detective Johnson, the equal opportunity promotion. One of my boys told me he interrogates in his unmarked vee-hicle and bends the suspect, who is just loitering on the corner with no dime bags on him, just hanging out, he bends his fingers back: 'You have the right to remain silent.'"

"You're bending my fingers back, Ferd."

"Haha. Thought I lost you there, so thanks for lightening up with a touch of sarcasm. Now I can proceed..."

"Not yet. First, Harvey's probably the best cop on the street. Second..."

But he was thinking of Petal again. Her lost son. No second defense of Harvey.

Almost gently, Ferd murmured, "You're abusing the right to remain silent, partner. I'd prefer if we could have a frank exchange of views, go through our deal together, like leaders of the world."

"Except you're still blowing smoke at me."

Ferd grinned and poked Kasdan's shoulder with one finger, finding the nerve that hurt. "A frank exchange of smoke, okay?" But in an instant, as changeable as the San Francisco weather, Ferd's sunny cajoling gave way to a weary sigh, an interlude of pain. He challenged his partner. "Be nice, please. You ain't giving much to chew on here, Cowboy."

"For me there's enough."

"So why keep it private? Share, like I do. I share, don't I? Fully?"

Ferd was making an effort, yet Kasdan still seemed distracted, due to his own error. He had barged in on Amanda's privacy. But what was past was past, in Ferd's opinion. Events tended to complicate a friendship, okay, so get over it. He took a deep breath, pushing the memory into ancient history, like yesterday's shower. More sighs, and then Ferd decided to avoid useless hyperventilation by continuing their summit conference, just as if Dan were being helpful.

"So as I was extrapolating, I'll handle the airline tickets." Soon it would be impossible for Dan not to be helpful in return. "I'll hit you with some spending money so's you don't stress out your Visa, your MasterCard, and including a deck of dollars in an envelope, breast pocket, so you can hand out tips. Do it. You'll be everybody's favorite in fine grills, lobbies, the porters, the maids'll fight for your room and put candy on the graves of their madres in your honor. She sews a button on your shirt? Give her a couple bucks. Wakes you up with a quickie?"

"A couple bucks," said Kasdan.

"Topple her, bend her over a chair, give her a twenty. You're God!"

And all Kasdan had to do was carry the larger bills nicely wrapped, contact the *notaire* in Port-au-Prince, fill out a few papers, and then relax by the pool. (Don't forget the stamps on the deed, a few other details we'll go through.) Kasdan would agree, how could he not? The hotel has a pool. Even if he sometimes acted like a zombie, Kasdan was still, on a temporary basis, alive.

As were they both. Kasdan had already come to this conclusion. Amanda instructed him, Sergei proved it to him – he was alive with a plan. Ferd stared into his eyes as Kasdan said nothing, revealed less. Ferd willed their conversation to continue, their understanding to deepen. He fell back on a sure recourse: "She gives you hot tongue, you give her cold shoulder – you won't have to beg anymore, ever again. Finished with the niggling and begging! I see a future before you, partner."

Ferd's breath was camouflaged with Altoids, but his strong feeling came through. "Few days, a touch of red tape, nothing too much, you'll pick up that pidgin they talk..."

"Creole."

"... eat some rice and beans, try to avoid the girls with AIDS, and come back nice and tan."

"Sunscreen."

"Hear me out, a little tan doesn't poison you. How many folks you see walking around with skin cancer? The sunscreen companies are in business to sell you a scare story."

Kasdan fell silent. It was a habit. Ferd fell silent. It was hard dealing around here, but Ferd could overcome Kasdan's bad personality. "I can't use electronic transfers, don't favor them. Traceable. Also don't like cash rolled up in suppositories for constipation – yucch! I want you to be all comfy with this. But I can tell you, Port-au-Prince International Airport, they don't give a shit."

"Suppositories..."

"Naw, Dan, that was just my scare tactics, make you smile. You're gonna be the Olympic champion for Long-Distance Outdoor Money Plant."

"Is this the best way for you to launder it?"

"Cash and carry, and an oppo-tunity for you and I to work together like the friends and brothers we are. I'll model the carry-on for you, a strap, no metal, large bills won't strain your iliac. Time will pass."

Time will surprise, Kasdan did not say aloud, and Ferd now watched with amusement his friend's lips moving. This was power, Kasdan rendered speechless, stunned by the careful detailing of Ferd Conway.

"I'm here, maybe God put me here, to get some pep into your life. Even some good sex for the first time in awhile, due to upward-bound karma, am I right?"

Kasdan wasn't saying.

"Don't wanna cop, okay. I'm fine with that." And just at this moment, over the ruins of a breakfast which emphasized the sugar and caffeine groups, Ferd poked him gently in the belly, not hitting, just stroking a little, and then a tug at the belt, as if testing for pregnancy. Kasdan sucked in his stomach and pulled back. Shrewd Ferd caught his self-consciousness about the perfectly normal pot a guy develops in later years; not much to be done about it. A pretty Petal appreciated something more than flat abs.

Soon there would be real money, an important secret, and good-bye to stingy caution. Once when Kasdan was a boy, long ago, so long ago, he noticed a beat-up Chevy convertible with rust holes in the body cruising around town, looking for a customer: ANTIQUE AUTO. SWAP FOR GOLD MINE OR B.O. Kasdan was too young to make a deal. Then he didn't see it anymore, so someone's B.O. had been accepted. Kasdan needed Ferd to pull him into enterprise. Wouldn't it be better to live large? Late desire had come to him, thanks to unwilled, unplanned events.

He considered just doing the job, earning the reward for his cross-border risk, probably leading to a continuing sunset years career in the felony line. Ferd would be happy, Ferd and Dan the pals Ferd wanted them to be. Sharing. Sharing. Partners. In time he might also travel to Costa Rica, Baja, maybe even Argentina, following Ferd's instructions and benefiting from his careful preparations, accumulating property, seeing the sights, cathedrals and iguanas, and while also living well, providing steady sustenance for Sergei, Amanda, and D'Wayne, who was trying his inadequate best to be a good husband and father. Nice hotel sojourns for the grandfather. Nice casual encounters in hotel bars. Maybe meeting someones he trusted and giving up condoms.

Why not? Others did.

Ferd was explaining, reiterating, recommending, cementing him in. "Buy expensive books, you like looks, read them if you want to!"

Dan could live large, way to go. This was America, California and San Francisco, where it was never too late if you had a friend like Ferd Conway.

"So let's think bigger'n you used to, Dan. How expensive does a watch have to be before it stops being a watch and starts being a collectable? An heirloom? A timepiece for Sergei, he might straighten out someday, due to the best professional care? You'll be making decisions about purchases, all goes well, based on..."

"I don't mind Timex, Ferd. I'm not usually late..."

"...and no more Chef Boyardee dinners, partner. I bet you even eat it cold from the can."

Kasdan had never sunk that low. Ferd was exaggerating his case, due to native mania and cappuccino rush. He shrugged, turning thoughtful, caffeine metabolizing, mania intact, and confessed: "I did. Lincoln Night Law School when the fuckers wouldn't give me a student loan. Straight from the can, like drinking ketchup from the Foster's table, with the free water, makes tomato juice. Not a taste treat, so let's just say: Never again."

Jerry Barrish, the bail bondsman and junk sculpture king, a San Francisco institution – elsewhere, bail bondsmen were not also cutting edge artists – stopped at their table on his way out to ask Kasdan if he'd heard about the dyslexic forger. "No time for jokes just now," said Kasdan.

"But I just saw Ferd smiling! Anyway, this isn't a joke, it's a riddle."

"Okay, but tomorrow, okay?"

Barrish noticed Ferd's disapproval of the interruption, eyes averted, thumbs twiddling. That made two who didn't need him, a majority of those present. After picking up a bent napkin dispenser, examining it from three dimensions with narrowed eyes, deciding it didn't inspire him, deciding the pause proved that he wasn't simply being chased away, disappointed both in good fellowship and stressed metal, he trudged off to his storefront office down the street, Open 24 Hours. It was hard to be an artist, plus hurtful to be a friend to friends who didn't appreciate friendship.

When he was thoroughly gone, Ferd said, "Private discussion, Jerry." Had he said it during his actual presence, Jerry would have suffered. *See what a sweetheart I am, Dan?*

"You've got enough money," Kasdan said.

Startled, Ferd showed delight that the threads were being followed by his taciturn partner. "Sure, my condo, more than enough, so it's natural I want more. Not just the loan, the mortgage, but *you*."

Now it was Kasdan's turn to look startled.

"Want to lift you from the dol-der-ums, Cowboy. Plus, you never really win in this life. The most, you can get ahead if you're smart before you catch what I like to diagnose adult death syndrome, which I don't prefer, but hey."

"Deep waters, Ferd."

Again Harvey Johnson was glaring at Kasdan across the room. The detective was allowed to tote around his big belly – an exception to SFPD fitness regulations – because he toted it gracefully and he also toted a heavy brain. He was not at all pleased about Dan's company, his new close associate, and in Harvey's opinion – an opinion which was heavy, like everything about him – Dan was spending too much time with the sleaze lawyer. Harvey made his own judgments, believing in fingerprints and DNA, believing in blood tests and careful monitoring of undue sweating, but not believing in polygraph interrogations because psychopaths had no trouble with them. He also did not believe in Ferd Conway as a proper breakfast buddy. Again Harvey raised one finger to Dan across the room, both a warning finger and a fuck-you finger. It was not a bid to join the discussion.

Ferd sensed Harvey's finger. "Hey, since old Harv lost the kid in that driveby? In Newark?" he asked, needing no answer. He sipped the last of his coffee and sighed. "The first cup is the best, you notice that? Funny thing, the swartzer's kid must've been in a gang, wore the blue bandana. They can't seem to get civilized, that's the problem."

Harvey's raised finger was more than a punctuation mark, less than a right turn signal. Kasdan was a better reader than Ferd, translating from the Spanish and also from the middle finger air-flick. Harvey's finger stated: *Asshole can change his rap, man, but not his natural-born DNA...* The stud in Harvey's ear was new, larger than the previous one, because a paltry little silver lobe decoration would be a disgrace to a belly moving forward inexorably with the years. On a different overweight plainclothes dick, a single stud might have looked silly; in Harvey's ear, it didn't. It went with his ever-fresh manicure (clear polish) and his regular consolation for the day's travails provided by a Vietnamese darling wise beyond her years and miniature size.

Back when Kasdan was having breakfast more often with Harvey than with Ferd, Harvey explained that a whole subcontinent supported itself through the nail parlor and pedicure industry. Despite world trade agreements, manicures weren't going offshore.

A confused status system prevailed in democracy as practiced at the Caffe Roma. Defense lawyers dressed better than legal aid lawyers, sometimes going all the way to French cuffs. Assistant DAs sometimes sat alone with laptops open, arraying their artillery for the day's battles. Defendants, perpetrators, and their tattooed buddies, heads in ponytails or shaved or merely with hair spit-slicked down, huddled, whispered, and dared the pretty young Asian court-appointed attorneys to meet their eyes. A uniformed black woman with a badge that said COMMANDER (of what, Kasdan still didn't know, perhaps of Parallel Parking) sat with her Palm Pilot, rigorously playing a computer game, bureaucratic frown fixed upon her countenance even in this hour of breakfast relaxation. She commanded; she judged; she looked as if she were in a mood to condemn.

A court translator, or at least an old-timer like Dan Kasdan, escaped the rules of hierarchy when he sat here with Harvey, who could easily have made Captain if he ever bothered to want it. He preferred the streets. Harvey and Dan ruminated to each other about their troubles: Harvey's son shot for no reason by a gang wannabe who thought he had a reason; Dan's daughter kept out of his sight and knowledge by Margaret Torres, who thought that her couple of nights with a Summer of Love veteran practicing his Spanish skills gave him no rights of fatherhood.

The lawyers had been shading the truth since law school; most of the perps had been perpetrating since childhood; for twenty years Harvey and Dan had taken the measure of each other, which meant forgiving each other.

A reader in secret, Harvey once asked Dan if "your ventrolateral preoptic nucleus" was keeping him awake nights; "You look kind of depleted."

"Huh?"

"The word 'depleted' not familiar to you? Okay, next question, I got a lunch date, can you lend me a condom?"

"No need to return it," Kasdan had answered.

It was time for Dan's pal to head out with his new ear stud, his organic bellypack with its cholesterol-storage reserves, and his unmarked Ford Something. He shrugged little apologies to the jury pool conscript whose chair Harvey's responsible-leader paunch had nudged. Detouring to amble past Dan and Ferd, he muttered only one word of greeting: "Asshole."

The non-audible movement of his lips was directed at Kasdan, not Conway. Harvey may have been lying in wait at the Caffe Roma, but on the other hand, since he had a perfect right to his morning routines, unless he was on an all-night stakeout, maybe it was Kasdan, taking meetings here with Ferd, who was daring Harvey to try to be his conscience.

A little anxious, not quite hearing the word which was not quite directed at him, Ferd asked: "Hey? So the deal, it's firm, am I correct in assuming?"

Kasdan grinned. A Kasdan smile event was a rare pleasure for both of them.

"Tomorrow, nine o'clock, chez moy unless I meet you on the way like one of those limo guys you see at the airport. You're a celebrity! You need an escort! Maybe I'll hold up a sign: MISTER KASDAN."

"I'll be there."

Ferd was still amazed. "Hey, that smile on your face? On you it looks good."

"I'll try to do it more often."

"You're learning, Cowboy."

− 18 −

He awakened that morning with a wisp of foreign matter between his lips, not old guy petrified drool, but what was it? A hair. It was long, not gray, not his. How had Petal's hair been transferred to his clothes and then somehow to his pillow on its migration to his lips? She had not been here. She was not a sneak, although truth was not a dominant element in their friendship. She was someone invisibly carried to him during the night. It would have been a mystery and a sign if he believed in signs. He believed in mysteries, such as Petal's presence between his lips and on his tongue.

Or it may have been Amanda's hair.

He brushed his teeth with a vigor that would delight his dentist. The imprint of the hair on his tongue faded. He prepared himself for the day's action. A punitive white southern California light, frequent in Los Angeles despite the smog, rare in San Francisco because of moisture and fog, poured down over the Tenderloin, illuminating the dust which swirled like fireflies. Today, unmitigated like the sun, Kasdan would burn through distraction and have his way. Resolved.

He walked south across Market toward Ferd's apartment. He followed his usual route, this time to keep their final appointment.

All the other times of his life, he had been practicing for what he was about to do, except that there had been no previous times. If there were times to come, he might do it differently. Today he was determined not to worry about the past or future. As a practical matter, no record or pattern, no confidence shared with anyone, not even any hints to Harvey Johnson, meant that no signs would lead to him. Step by step, he would follow to the end. As he crossed Minna, a zonked "Vietnam Veteran" with his soggy corrugated cardboard sign and a Styrofoam cup, but relaxed and lacking initiative, failed to ask for spare change. He must have sensed Kasdan's momentary pause. He called out, "Have a nice day, asshole."

Despite living through the Summer of Love years, Kasdan still didn't believe in karma. Yet, without asking to see the veteran's discharge papers, he turned back and dropped a quarter in the cup. If not for the last word of the veteran's salutation, it would have been a dollar, in memory of the idea of karma.

On Mission, sometimes known as Mission Boulevard, a surprise awaited him. "Hi! Hi there, big guy!" Ferd had anticipated his route. He jumped up grinning from a sidewalk table at the Granada Cafe where he left half an espresso for whichever street person got there first. "One of the things I deeply admire about you is now you're taking the best way to get where you're going. Counting on people, knowing them through and through – very essential, n'est-ce pas?"

These were qualities to treasure. Kasdan didn't always take the shortest route, but today he did. They proceeded to business in the brightness of morning. Ferd also treasured the chance for a business-related stroll with his dear friend and colleague; ambling like the good pals they were, but also insuring that Kasdan would not back away during their final arrangements. He escorted his colleague toward his condo where airline tickets would be presented, via Miami to Port-au-Prince, also the address and telephone number of the *notaire* and instructions about the peculiarities of the telephone system in Haiti, and a complete agenda of the details concerning purchase of land and house. The money was already packed and guaranteed to be invisible during various customs inspections. "Sub rosa," Ferd murmured, in a Latin mood today.

Appreciatively, he sniffed deeply of the air. Two good pals and partners, marching along. Things were in the final stage despite the normal glitches that always come up in a human procedure. Ferd was a happy man.

A leather queen on a butch holiday swooped past on rollerblades, pads at the knees but his pants cut out behind so that a few stray hairs waved enticingly from the heart-shaped rear window. Ferd meditated upon this performance. "A few years ago, it would have been skateboards. I guess he's too grownup for kid transportation."

Remembering the success of yesterday's smile, Kasdan tried to join Ferd's good humor. "He's put away childish things."

"Like a big girl, he's into rollerblades. So what kind of future do you suppose? Nada, that's his future. Couple years hence, sit in a bar, maybe the Katie's place, sneaking a smoke and hope he can rent a nice boy at closing time, tell him about the time he skateboarded, got into rollerblades, used to be was a stud everybody wanted..." This sad prediction trailed off. He and Dan did not cut out their pants behind and were not losers.

Trucks were parked and double-parked on Folsom, drivers and helpers hauling crates into clubs and bars. Later, not much later, the bars would open, sending heavy rock, hip-hop, and disco out onto the street as San Francisco's leather central stirred into action, using up the beer, snacks, toilet paper, and vending machine items of rubber, creams and plastic. Ferd noticed out loud that the alleys were named for long-departed hookers, Minna, Jessie, Clementina, thus showing that he too, deep down, in his heart of hearts, was a caring and noticing guy. If Dan wanted to go there. "You're showing Grade A composure today," Ferd said. "I mean that in the best possible way. It's progress. I could almost say I admire it."

"Go ahead."

"I admire it, next to genuine affection..." It was a struggle. "Which you already know about... I admire you. You wouldn't venture any risky type of gig, not even for me, am I right? So here we are." He sighed. "Home."

Before the Nam-brand panhandlers and the leather bars, the Stud, the White Swallow, the Belly Up, there used to be marsh grass and willows, humming with insects and the small mammals scurrying to eat them, on this low-lying tract of San Francisco near the bay; then it was rapidly filled and firmed and the Indian footprints were obliterated by ballast from Gold Rush sailing ships and by the abandoned ships themselves; then came the time of light industry, slaughterhouses, storage tanks, and swift-shack housing. Now dot.com real estate speculation had taken its turn in the rotation. The willows and salt murk were gone; condominiums floated on the fill. Ferd believed in financing a snug nest with a favorable prognosis for capital appreciation.

Good conversation had shortened the journey home. Ferd's condo was built by a developer with a checklist of selling points. The structure, beyond modern, was *moderne*, its glass skin supported by exposed steel beams and excellent mortgage arrangements. Ferd's personal taste included occasional privacy, so he had sprung for curtains on a pull rod. He called these curtains "drapes" because they kept the sunlight and street snoops under wrap. He had his glass, he had his light when he so desired, he had his airy position and his view; but he also had protection against transparency and excess airiness. An expansive welcome-to-my-humble-domain gesture hinted to Kasdan about the benefits of affluence: CD player with small but powerful speakers; leather furniture to sink into with a sigh or, when lucky, to fuck in; open bar standing in the middle of the hospitality space where dusky sunlight turned the "drapes" a purplish black. When Ferd awakened at night or during what he called "the wee-wee hours" of the morning, he could find his way to the bathroom by the glow from the street.

Ferd lived most of his life elsewhere. Sometimes he grew lonely even in his way-of-life condo. He had sunk his ready cash into the down payment. But the loans? The mortgage? Life in general? Not to worry. Destiny was flowing toward copasetic for both Kasdan and Conway.

On a low table painted black and shellacked in a version of Chinese teakwood stood a device recognized by anyone who traveled through the once and forever San Francisco Sixties. The hookah's tube snaked out in the general direction of Ferd's guest. Its mouthpiece, like that of a whistle or a flute, was invitingly spit-stained. "Want a hit of some water-cooled herb, amigo?" A Barcalounger waited with open arms for Kasdan to fling himself down and inhale a civilized ommm experience. Barcalounger in brown vinyl didn't really match Chinese teak knockoff in contemporary lifestyle design, but a really advanced self-decorator knew that any one thing a person likes goes well with any other thing that person likes. No point in asking about the light caramel smell wafting off the curtains, the "drapes;" Kasdan wasn't here as an air quality inspector. He wasn't here to search out distractions. He was here to overcome his temptation by distraction.

Flourishing a long fireplace match, Ferd lit the hookah and took a first hit to assure correct bubbling through the water. A punctilious sommelier also tastes the wine after de-corking. Then Ferd moved the wet nozzle on its hose in the direction of his partner. He added a strained, held-breath invitation. "My food delivery system primed for the munchies, partner. Open fridge, go ahead, there're boxes, containers, bottles, and try the freezer..." He exhaled with a gasp. "You'll find the ice creams, the frozen yoghurt chocolate bars, the other shit I forget what. Brownies for an emergency. Anti-oxidant, that's what they are, bars for a fructose pickup in case you're not into dairy! Flavenoid phenols to improve your immortality, or at least get a shot at viral old age... Did I say *viral?* Hey, I happen to know you're a *virile* old fella, but it's a special time down south where the conviviality is..."

"You're high already, Ferd."

"... a cute chick when you're in the realm of prosperity like I intend to bring you, a sweet baby to fetch for you when you say, 'Bring me a beverage, bring me a little blue pill will you, bring me a round-the-world licking including darkest Africa like that stewardess I met once before they invented flight attendants and now they're all business stead of..."

"Get to it, Ferd."

"Okay, okay." He shook his head vigorously, shedding imaginary droplets of cold shower. He blinked away the exaggerated high. He lay down the nozzle of his hookah, careful not to nick his teak. He slid the curtain and checked out the street. He turned back to Dan. "Okay. All clear."

He pulled out a blue plastic document case. "So here's the ticket, American to Miami, you stay in the airport hotel, next morning wake up fresh and a quick shower, a short flight, hour and a half, voy-la! Port-au-Prince! I upgraded you to Business Class."

"I don't travel much."

"Don't blame that on me, Dan. They got toilet paper and everything in Haiti. You'll sleep comfortable when this is over, so a little stress comes with the territory, just fade into the background, you're carrying this other item in your belly pack. A tight deck of hundreds. I'll give you the name of the *notaire*, but best you memorize it. You can write down his telephone number, probably on – how old are you? – that very page, eighty-five, haha, a hundred ten, whatever, of the book you're reading. The phones there... just keep trying. There's this nice hotel. You speak French?"

"Spanish. I can make do."

"He speaks English, the *notaire*. Besides, you point to the menu and say Jumbo Omelet and they give you eggs with ham. You'll be fine."

The briefcase, new, unscuffed shiny leather, was not showoff top grain but not vinyl, either. "They'll ask you to unlock it, unless you don't have to, but you're smiling inside. It's not in your shoes. You do like to read on board a long flight, don't you? Study your French?

Only this book is not exactly a *reading* book. It's a transportation book. They ask you unlock the briefcase – no pharma-cuticles, am I right? – they spend ten minutes fiddling with the briefcase. By that time, other good citizens and aliens in line, they're too dumb to try reading your book, French book because you're studying, always studying, underlining the words you want to learn, the way you are, Dan – a scholar and a gentleman."

"Not exactly."

"You said it, I didn't."

The briefcase was still locked. Kasdan stared, leaving it on the table. Ferd gave him a tinny little key. "You can fumble, waste their valuable time, you're an absent-minded professor, understand?"

"You're not that hard to understand."

"Scholar that you are. They ask you to open, you do so. They rummage. They say, Sorry Mister, because, you know, that's in the T.O., Table of Disorganization, for when they're too stupid to look in the right place. You stand there patient, reading glasses maybe in your hair, you can get them at Walgreens, super-scholarly, and this study book tucked under your arm. They can see you're a professor or a court translator or some other kind of dummy..."

"Thanks."

"Now they've done their job. You're free to proceed to your seat, upgraded to Business Class. My advice: bring a nice sandwich for lunch. The stuff they serve you was always shit and in today's no finesse world it's *really* shit."

Ferd paused for a thank you for the dining advice. No thank you forthcoming. He waited for something else, a word about Amanda, about Petal. A possible reproach... A flicker of concern crossed Ferd's face. His partner wasn't sharing.

Okay, good, the partner's greed and the prospect of a nice payday took precedence over Amanda, Petal, and affiliated reproaches. This was America, wasn't it?

The flicker of concern was now a flicker of relief.

They were concluding their friendship south of Market in Ferd's condo on the former marsh, but Kasdan felt as if he were still at home among dogwood, ailanthus, alley trees and weeds and the scrambled debris outside. In the Tenderloin, a junk tree, seeking the sun, almost reached his window; swaying and rustling, weed trees stretched out their shoots like amphetamined bamboo. Here with Ferd, there was a faint naphtha smell of mothballs, Ferd fastidiously protecting his woolen clothes.

He was finally presenting Dan with all that he needed in proper order, travel documents, money, the name of the contact in Port-au-Prince, the *notaire*, a Monsieur Jean-Pierre Jean Pierre, who had legal custody of a seafront house for sale in Jacmel, a lovely residence for a cocaine transporter when he was at home and not transporting and also of permanent value because of its gracious garden, beach access, and helicopter docking space... Ferd full-heartedly smiled. He tilted his head optimistically. Kasdan was given a view of two narrow black caverns, nostril hairs waving with the tidal ebb and flow of breath intake and outgo.

"Prop-pity is always solid," Ferd explained. "Look, there's plenty in Nevada, and I'm not even counting the desert. I'm talking built-up, subdivided. In the desert, you take the wheels off your trailer on the outskirts of Tonapah – I thought about that, halfway between Reno and Vegas, they used to mine silver, they got a casino, the hotel has gold-plated faucets and you can flush with a gold nozzle..."

"That'd be fun," Kasdan said.

"Take the wheels off your trailer and what have you got? Real estate! Plus not that much government. They don't need no stinkin' zoning laws."

"Free at last," Kasdan said.

"But Haiti, there's loose dollars floating around, boats, airplanes, the Free Republic of Colombia practically next door, plus it's less government than Nevada even in the good old days before our time. It's the Wild West only elsewhere, so they need nice villas with beaches. Man, the whole world is full of real estate, that's how God made it. Even you should be able to figure that out, no head for business without me."

"Thanks."

"If the good Lord didn't want people to invest, why did He make the world out of real estate?"

Still and all, Ferd was uneasy. His friend and partner didn't seem fully alert. He wondered if he was losing his powers of persuasion, due to previous unfortunate events and loss of his powers of persuasion. "Okay, amigo, let's review just to make sure."

So here again were the travel documents, a few new details, paper tickets on American, don't have to worry about some electronic ticketing fuckup, and here was the faxed confirmation of your room at the Hotel Oloffson, did I tell you they call it the *Grand* Hotel Oloffson on a hill above shit-heap Port-au-Prince? Gotta admit, in all fairness, there's pollution from cheap gas and burning crap floats up, but it's cooler, papaya or mango or some kind of fruit trees in the garden, tropical birds showing off their butt feathers and they never fly away because what smart bird would ever leave this paradise and be taken for a chicken just because it can be cooked? Peacocks, fandangos, I dunno. Just like the birds, you can drink the water in the hotel but stay away from muggers in the street. When you go out, leave watch and camera back in the hotel – "Did I tell you that already?"

"I don't own a camera. My watch is a Timex from Payless."

"You had to tell me?" Ferd stared at this goofball friend of his. He had better leave nothing to normal good sense. "Get a little crazy, jetlag, try some a that good Creole coffee – turns a dull Kasdan into a crazy-ass Cowboy Dan."

"Is that what I need?"

"Sometimes we all need, partner. Let me amend that statement frankly: you more than anybody."

What was this dew? Ferd's eyes suddenly glistened. A secretion had occurred. Could it be empathy for people with needs, such as Dan Kasdan? Other people? Who were not Ferd Conway? He brushed the back of his hand over his face to clear away the moistness. There was hoarseness in his voice. "I've got needs, too. I'm like you, Dan. Wake up nights sometimes – longings where you don't know why or what for, that type of thing, you know?"

Kasdan stared. Ferd was telling God's honest truth; no, more astonishing than that, Ferd Conway's truth, his own, of which he had mysteriously taken possession. The thought that such a thing was possible had never before struck Kasdan.

"You think I'm just a dominant male unit..."

No, it wasn't what Kasdan thought.

"... but I'm more than that. Remember Big Sur?"

He didn't say Cowboy. He didn't add anything, although surely he soon would. Kasdan was busy judging himself because he hadn't imagined that Ferd might wake in the night and stare into the dark.

Ferd knew some things were amiss and was trying to set them right. But for Kasdan, no further revelations were in order. It was late. The program had been set. His money problems, some of his daughter problems, his grandson problems needed not to overwhelm him. It was time. Many puzzles, including Petal, Doc Feldstein's diagnosis, Harvey's judgment, were not resolved, maybe not resolvable, but action was finally to be taken, even by a man who had not taken enough in his life.

If Ferd happened to be a man of soul, compassion, true friendship, night longings, and not merely the male unit who thought he was a dominant male unit, fine, fine, fine. It was even more proper and fitting for Kasdan to carry out his planned mission. It would be a sacrifice, but that's a normal part of the struggle of life. So many would benefit. In his soul, now that he announced that he had one, Ferd should appreciate the stubborn facts of benefit. A man who lived for benefits could also vanish from the earth for some.

Dan Kasdan smiled at his colleague and friend and said, "I know."

"What?" It wasn't night, but Ferd was staring at the window, a man staring into the dark. He needed to awaken.

Dan repeated, "I know."

It was day, but Ferd was staring into darkness. There were creatures out there. He squinted as if this could help him see the invisible. His mouth moved, as if this could help him speak what he couldn't speak. "I was a baby, Dan. I bet we looked almost the same when we were babies."

"Probably. Babies tend to look alike. Why?"

"Just thinking. But they look different later."

"Tend to," Kasdan said.

"So I was thinking..." And again he used the back of his hand to brush against his eyes.

Then it was as if the time of soul was dismissed. It had never happened. It was not night. The light through the window, past the stirring curtains, was bright and Ferd was fully awake. "So," he said, brisk with his hands, making a dry noise as he rubbed them together, "so here are a few bonus reminders, in case I left out any details, which like any normal person I probably do..."

The seasons in Haiti were first hot, then hotter, but not to fret – never worse than LA in August. Plus, you come back a very prosperous individual, bordering on affluent, and there's a shining old age on the road ahead and lots of catch-up fun you'll have to learn to deal with. That's refreshing in itself! You can do it! Not to mention grateful appreciation from the family which lives after, treasuring your memory, generous, a good dad, a good grampa... He took a necessary breath and a refreshing pause. "Hey! Whatever happened to that smile I spotted on your face not so long ago?"

The smile failed to reappear. Ferd shrugged, continued.

So here was the French dictionary with the hollowed-out pages between "chat," which means cat, and "teinturerie," which means something like a dry-cleaner where they move you out of shitty colors. Dyeing, not dying, get it, partner? You with me on this? Mind not wandering? Look at this post-it: the address and telephone number, but don't count on the phones, you might have to keep calling, drop in on the *notaire*, Monsieur Pierre-Pierre, speaks his own kind of English... "Call him Peter-Peter, he might think it's funny. Try anyway, for kicks, or maybe not. Blame me, say the jetlag makes you crazy and you drank too much of that tasty Haitian coffee..."

"Ferd," Kasdan said.

"Okay, okay." Ferd swallowed. He didn't need that tasty Creole coffee. He appreciated being called to order; it showed initiative on Kasdan's part. "So watch it, open your French study book, and voy-la, as we say in English – a brick of fine layered paper fits right in where you look for 'cat' but the next word is 'dyeing.' Pretty cool, are we on the same page? With this brick tucked into your French dictionary you can peel off hundreds and avoid the hassles of a credit card, whatever those hassles might turn out to be, like the record of a monthly statement."

Kasdan had no questions.

"Ready to go then. Port-of-the-Prince, isn't that cute? Like it was named for Prince Dan four-five hundred years ago when you weren't even born yet." Ferd waited. No questions. Ferd said: "Not that old, are you? There's still time to upgrade. Personally, in my life, I'm always upgrading. For which I think I deserve a little credit, and let me give you an example – the buzzer for my door. The place, before it was my condo, came with a stupid buzz-buzz-buzz, so I just dip into my piggy bank and get these chimes, these authentic Merrie-England from Taiwan three-tone electric chimes. Voy-la! Soothing bing-bang-boing, Dan. Exceptionally restful if you're expecting guests, and then when you have additional guests, which could happen if you make friends, not just Harvey Jackson, the previous ones get to enjoy the bing-bang-boing, too. Why are your lips moving?"

"Harvey Johnson. Never mind."

Kasdan could upgrade Sergei, Amanda, D'Wayne, also, of course, and himself. Pituitary, adrenalin, and swollen amygdala sent their jolts into the proceedings. Kasdan tried to concentrate. He issued orders to his biology to do so. Ferd was a confiding soul as the deal entered its final stages. "... plus, you get to enjoy the dark clouds. Speaking personally, in my life, I don't like dark clouds, those furry fuzzy ones with all the precipi, call it, the precipi-tation."

"Pardon?"

"Between her legs. I tend, it's only my personal preference, prefer the blond clouds down there. How about you? You liked – what's her name again she calls herself?"

With a blandness, eyelids drooping, he awaited the answer. "Petal," Kasdan said. "You know that." He snapped open the blade.

"Right, right, right... What the fuck are you doing?"

The knife locked in place with a metal snap, a crisp biting sound. Ferd took a baby dance step backwards. "What the hell, I'm repeating myself, we're too old for games, partner."

Kasdan neither affirmed nor denied.

"Okay, okay," Ferd said. He was moving his arms in a steadying gesture, ready to explain whatever needed further explanation while avoiding the unsteady glinting of a blade catching the light. "Watch out for that thing, pal, it could hurt a person, say you slip, say you have an accident. Whyn't we go through a few details maybe on your mind before you make a booboo?"

No invitation from Kasdan.

Ferd went through the details anyway.

About that tasty little blond, since it seemed to come up as an issue (Petal wasn't so little and she wasn't all that blond; Ferd meant

to demonstrate that details were no reason colleagues should be distracted)... Still, about not so little, not so blond Petal, Ferd was happy
to fill in the details. It wasn't all that complicated. The whole
business was Ferd trying to bring some sparkle, some lip gloss and
glitter, some pre-reward into Dan's drab life. To remind him that
taking chances is part of any worthwhile deal. There's delightfulness
out there; there's herpes, too, of course. There's fun and gratefulness,
just like before herpes and AIDS came along. A person also has to put
up with stuff, okay, grant that, because life is a rocky series of woulda,
coulda, shoulda, my friend – was that the right proverb?

Ferd took a breath during which Kasdan did not give information
about stoic philosophy and folklore. Ferd continued anyway.

The thing about business was that surprises always come up; that's
why they call it busy-ness. Okay, Petal was cute, that was a plus, and
now we move forward. Nobody needs to go head over heels, your ass
bounces, because of a Petal – she wasn't that kind of awesome – just
the kind of sweetie anybody normal, carrying a normal boner, likes
just a little, little, – you speak Spanish – *leetle* bit. Was he right again?
"Hey, only a short while ago – a saintly smile. What happened to it?"

Silence. No return of smile.

Okay, so Petal worked out for the purpose at hand... Was the fine
colleague following the train of thought here? All Petal expected
anyway was here today, gone tomorrow, that was her modus
operandi, sufficient unto the day is the in-and-out thereof. Got it?
And no harm done.

Kasdan's knees felt tired. There must have been stress. He shifted
his posture.

Ferd believed in convincing, explaining, negotiating. A swift-
moving fog cleared everyone's mind, like a stroll on Ocean Beach
when the wind is up. Ferd's clarifications were coming faster than
usual, a bit of whiteness, froth it's called, gathering at the corners of
his mouth. It overflowed into the little notch of irony, the smile
notch. He snapped off a shriveled leaf from the spider plant in its pot
next to the hookah on the sort of teakwood table. He'd forgotten to
water. He was housekeeping absent-mindedly these days, due to the
pressure of business. "So?" he asked. "Whyn't you stop waving that
thing around, Dan? It makes me nervous."

Kasdan did not lower the blade.

"So can't I make it up to you, pal?"

Kasdan nodded. Neither of them knew if this meant *For What*? or *Yes*? or *No*? or *How*? What would constitute making it up?

"Whatever, brief me. You think I did you some harm, so consult with me. I'll make it right."

"Yes, you did. You did harm."

An insuppressible smile sped across the face of Ferd Conway, although he knew smiling was inappropriate at this time. He was happy to have helped. He brought clarity into Dan's life, Dan appreciated it, and that counted.

"So now you won't have to, you know," Ferd said slowly, awaiting sudden movements; and pointed his finger, just extending the wrist, not lifting his arm, toward the knife. "... since I offer you the gift of friendship and trust, plus money, plus – think about it – a whole truckload of dreams, Cowboy."

He took a breath, deciding nothing untoward could happen as long as he kept the conversation going. Kasdan moved the blade a few inches through the air, back and forth, pointing it. Ferd said: "The bureaucratics might not like me, screw them, but I always wanted you to be my friend, now more than ever, and not because – you're not turning into a bureaucratic, are you, Dan? But they won't be happy if they find the evidence, which they're getting good at, the prints, the DNA..." He was sure he was making progress. "I might be like a regular Richard W. Nixon, secretly taping the proceedings, in case of my unfortunate demise at the hands of a disturbed perpetrator..."

Running monologue with panicky language slippage.

Kasdan should have been sympathetic, but Ferd didn't look panicked, his eyes shining, lips quivering winsomely, smiles breaking through. On the other hand, yes, he did. He kept moving, dancing backwards, baby steps, nothing too sudden, nothing to upset a nervous fellow leaning toward bureaucraticism and irresponsibility. Kasdan followed. It felt like disco dancing. Ferd, still moving backwards, stumbled, bumped a drawer and it bounced open. Easy there, fella.

In the drawer, a pair of red panties of some limp petroleum-based fabric lay across the stack of boxer shorts. Ferd did his wincing smile. "I like to put it over the lamp, makes a rosy glow, reminds me of the first time I went, I went... remember when you first went all the way? With a girl, Dan?"

The slapped open drawer wasn't an accident.

"I could never forget her undies, Dan. It's like a sentimental thing."

Kasdan finally spoke. "Everyone deserves memories." This was encouraging for Ferd, suggesting progress.

"Listen here now, I might-could have a kid someplace, too. I could find her or him, as the case may be, and get to be an outstanding dad like you and Amanda and poor little Sergei. You don't want to foreclose all that. What dad ever knows or doesn't know about all his kids, guys like us, lived through those terrific young years, me and you, swingers, and you just happened to find out, man, got lucky, and it brought you into some psychological mix-up. I fully dig about that, but now you need to get organized. No more mix-up, hey? You with me on this?"

Kasdan held steady to the unfamiliar object pointing up, light glinting in little flashes off the blade, the handle warm in his fist. It was gradually becoming a known extension of his arm. Again Ferd backed slowly away, but he was urging Kasdan to pay closer attention. "Amanda cranks you up and well she should, Sergei's a big deal, plus I suppose Petal, well, you found room in your busy life, I'll grant you got a lot on your plate all at once, who'd have thunk, but then again – are you listening? Remember the fun we had in Big Sur? I wanted to get you running good, purring along like Dynaflow, partner, thanks to me."

Kasdan did not respond.

"All the nature there? Mountains? Ocean? That Lulu?"

Ferd wriggled a little, back now against the wall. He couldn't do his disco-moves anymore, but he didn't give up. He had faced hostile judgments before.

"You see that Ronson table lighter I got at the Re-Vue Consignment Shoppe on Larkin? Next to the Cambodian some kind of crap restaurant?" He reached toward it, a heavy, molded, antique-styled, non-antique, non-silver frequent wedding gift from the days when people still smoked and, on festive occasions, husbands were expected to offer guests a jet of flame from afar, graciously bringing ignition to their Pall Malls. Ronson's Buddha-like belly lay flat on the table with a lever to flip like a trigger, a fuse, a hidden flint, but at present no flame shooting out. Ferd snapped the lever and the flame shot out. He said: "Perfect working order, but who does nicotine anymore? People worry about cancer, plus the taxes disincent folks, except art students and Asians. But say there was an intruder – I could throw it, fracture his pea brain. Or say you ripped me off or I got sore at you for who knows why, not appreciating the kidding maybe, and couldn't find adequate words to express my disappointment?"

He mimed shot-putting the object. "Break your head, you know? Or shoot the fucker and singe you pretty good, hurting the guy in order to save him. Am I right, amigo?"

But then, having made his point, he withdrew his hand from the lighter and adjusted it back onto the felt patch which protected the table from scratches. Ferd nodded toward Kasdan's knife, winced, shrugged, offered selections from his full repertory. He grinned. Enough of this for now. Kasdan tested the knife with his finger. It was honed sharp enough to slice a hair sideways, not that he was an expert in hair-splitting. The handle had grown hot and wet in his right hand. He could pass it into his left hand and even out the temperature.

Surely afterwards he would keep it, this excellent knife. Disposal was not in order or necessary. First, he would clean it carefully. He understood about DNA evidence, but after soap and hot water, a thorough wiping, he could hide it nicely, never feel tempted to confide in anyone – before DNA, blabbing was the traditional risk – and then someday he would come back to its hiding place and retrieve this excellent knife for whatever further purposes might come up. Not that he anticipated doing today's work again, but for personal protection. Carried folded, retracted, wrapped in his fist, his heat conducted onto stainless steel, because the Tenderloin was a tricky place for a man of a certain age who might look like an easy mark. Unlike the unpleasant noisiness of guns, a knife split silently, sometimes even capable of slicing a hair sideways.

Ferd stared, trying to read the future in Kasdan's eyes. He thought it only fair to express his impatience. "You just stand there, you think you're all balanced or something, but I'll tell you what kind of a mood you put me in, Dan. Say something. *Give.*"

Kasdan made little circles in the air, a scooping gesture. The blade was not designed for this purpose, but it served. It could penetrate without gouging. It could slice upwards and deal swiftly with gristle and bone, not to speak of mere tissue; given determined pressure, of course.

"Hey, what'll your mother think? Okay, Mom's deceased these many years, I realize that, but still, in heaven, Cowboy?" Ferd's grin portrayed perfect ease, relaxation, enjoyment, except for the three bleeding dots on his lower lip where he first clenched and then bit. "How about the right to life, what about that? I'm not some abortion you can just flush down the shitter – skoose my language – the *toilet*, am I? I'm like you, a lonely individual with hopes and dreams, your buddy who just wants to do business with a pal who really needs some profit in his life."

Amanda and Sergei weren't a business to be done. Petal wasn't a profit in his life.

"Okay, so if I read your state of mind, I guess I have to, since you don't share your concerns with your partner, I made a couple errors of judgment, like anybody might happen to do, and isn't that part of the whole deal when I'm no more nor less than human? A San Francisco citizen who came up the hard way, night law, catching scraps, doing my best? Can't you give me an answer stead of just prowling around with that..." He inclined his head toward the shining blade, not wanting to excite anybody. "... thinking of taking a life before my time? Making me nervous so I stepped on my favorite designer sunglasses from the Calvin Klein Collection – now I'm very nervous?"

His foot scraped over the broken plastic and glass, emphasizing the point.

No answer from Kasdan. Kasdan's continuing no answer of the morning. Ferd sighed, still bearing the burden of discussion.

"Okay, in my own way, try to remember I care for you, Dan. A lot. You're the person I chose among all others to care for. Do I deserve punishment for that, chastisement, is that right?

Kasdan said nothing, but followed as Ferd opened and shut his mouth, moving sideways a little, back and forth, glass crumbling under his foot. "You aren't talking to me anymore, Cowboy?"

Kasdan said nothing.

"Did I maybe hear you think one of those unfriendly words like 'sleaze.'"

It was hurting Ferd's feelings that Kasdan seemed to have no conversation in his present personality.

"Okay, maybe you want..." He restarted: "... let me ask you a question relative to Amanda, okay?"

"Amanda," said Kasdan.

It was a relief that his friend finally spoke, helping Ferd continue their discussion in gentlemanly fashion.

"Are you doing her any good like this? How about Sergei? What's the help here?"

And Petal, Kasdan thought.

"Anybody else I forget to mention?"

"No," said Kasdan.

"Wow. The suff-inks pronounces." Ferd emitted a dramatic sigh of relief. "The man can talk. The killer speaks."

But another space of silence fell between them. Here in Ferd's dwelling and in Ferd's entire world, silence was a troubling commodity. It distressed him, it said too much. He did his best to wait out the sphinx. Finally he whispered, "Okay then, okay. I have it coming to me. Okay. Go ahead."

"It's not just *happening* to you!"

"It's not?" Kasdan's sudden shout puzzled Ferd.

"I'm doing it. *I* am doing this – "

"Why?"

"I want to. It's necessary."

Ferd disapproved of a failure of both logic and appreciation. The broken sunglasses crunching underfoot, the ignoring of a generous Ronson's table lighter gesture, no metal chunk heaved, no jet of flame to the face. And the unreasonable abandonment of an offered profit center. "So I must have it coming to me. Or is this some kind of special offer?"

Kasdan said nothing. Now that non-response was becoming a habit, Ferd understood him well enough. He too did what he did just because he wanted to.

"Okay, go ahead, partner," Ferd said. He tried to help by adding: "Cowboy." He smiled into Kasdan's eyes. He was ready to move things along. He approved of Dan's procedure. A relieved boy was smiling at his best playmate. A holiday had come; he was looking at the surprises life had brought him. There was an odd greenish glow in his eyes, shiny and reflective, like the petroleum product under Kasdan's Honda when he parked overnight. Ferd had met Dan's eyes before, but not as directly, was that it, was that why they seemed to shine with a rainbow glow? His designer sunglasses were crunching like snow under the tread of Kasdan's shoes.

"Get on with it, Dan."

"Are you in a hurry?"

"I said get on with it, go ahead, isn't that clear enough? I'm talked out. I'm otherwise occupied. I can read your mind."

"Not so good at that, Ferd."

Ferd approved of the sarcasm; he fully appreciated it; all he needed in return was for Dan to appreciate him. "Use it..." He didn't want to say the knife. "... Since that's what you're doing. You didn't ask my advice, did you? A gun makes too much noise, doesn't it? That what you thought? So a..." He inclined his head, he ducked, swallowed. "... I hope it's sharp – is more satisfying in the long run." He moved closer, his palms turned outward. Kasdan smelled eager fresh sweat.

"Hey, pal, don't you feel great, so full of life? There's blood in your eye but it doesn't sting, I guess that's the excitement there, the capillaries burn out – you feel so young, don't you, with those glowing eyes? Why don't I hear you saying thank you?" Ferd's breathing was irregular, considering whether to take a breath, thinking it over, taking it, then taking another. "Go ahead," he said. "Do your business. I'm ready."

He fell. His knees scrambled among the broken sunglasses. He was still gabbing.

"I'm ready. I make you only a skinny one-sixty, so you have to use whatever you got, go ahead, get to it."

Kasdan moved away from the noise, but held the knife low, pointing upwards.

"You're so serious all the time, you need a sense of direction. Let me help. I'll make you do it, Dan. One-sixty at your age, so next you either plump up or shrivel down, that's old age, that's what lies ahead."

Kasdan shifted away, braced against the wall. The man on his knees was causing the man with the weapon to cringe.

"You can't stop now. It's easy. Don't resist, pal." Ferd ducked a little. Sandy hair fell over his forehead. He looked up again. "Cowboy? Even if you're across the border to senior, you're my... hey, should we say amigo? How about that?"

He reached up and took hold of the blade. He stared at his hand and the thickness seeping between his fingers. "Did I ever tell you when I was a kid I could recite Lincoln's entire Gettysburg address, plus his zip code?" Ferd's hand tightened, heedless. The blade was swaddled in Ferd's fingers. He moved until they touched Kasdan's fist, wrapped around the handle. "I'm fine, but I need your help with this, Cowboy. I can't all by myself, so do me, do me, Cowboy."

Struggling there, the curtains falling over them, Kasdan's own finger was cut by the serrated edge. His hand was touching another slippery hand; his arm was spattered with blood. Ferd's wrist was twisting the blade down, down, reaching into himself. This strength, where did it come from? And then suddenly the twisting stopped, the strength was gone, a softness came to Ferd along with the spurting, pooling fluids.

"I'll be dead soon. Then you can stop worrying."

Kasdan stared. Ferd's hand opened. Kasdan pulled his own hand away. He released his fist around the handle of the knife, but it didn't fall. The blade lay deep inside. Viscousness was swelling onto Ferd's arm, thick spots accumulating and dropping. Ferd said: "Hey, finish what you start..."

"We'll get you to the Emergency Room," Kasdan whispered.

"... It's okay, please finish, can't you?" Ferd pulled the blade out and let the knife slide to the floor. Metal clacked against wood; blood was gushing, running fast. "So our good deal is over, Cowboy?" The leaky sound of his sigh filled the room. "Hey, non es problema."

Kasdan kneeled to press his sleeve against the hand with its limp fingers hanging, nearly severed. He tried to spread his palm on Ferd's belly. Ferd shook, fell, gushes of blood and something whitish, wriggling and ropy, pumping out of him, and he was saying, "I have to do everything, don't I? But it's okay, you're my amigo..."

"I'll call an ambulance!"

"... keep the book, keep the deck of hundreds..."

"I'm driving you to the hospital!"

"No, no, we can stop cutting now. I'm dead."

He was and they did. He winked at Kasdan. He closed his eyes. A voice said: "So make your own plans now and thank you."

CPSIA information can be obtained at www.ICGtesting.com
Printed in the USA
LVOW04s2118081015

457571LV00013B/241/P

9 780988 412279